DOMINO:

What I do is luck.

I don't mean to say my power is luck.

I mean – I do luck.

In a fight, my enemies' guns will jam. All of them, one right after another. Or they'll misaim and hit each other. I've taken shelter from a tornado in a house, had it collapse on me, and then, like Buster Keaton, stepped out unscathed from under an open window frame. I've been blown through a plate-glass window without suffering a cut. I've been twenty feet away from a frag grenade when it detonated, and been missed by all the shrapnel.

The problem is that my luck has a sense of humor – and it can get awfully mean spirited. Some days, it doesn't even feel like it's on my side...

BY THE SAME AUTHOR

Quietus
Terminus

MARVEL HEROINES

DOMINO: STRAYS

TRISTAN PALMGREN

ACONYTE

FOR MARVEL PUBLISHING

VP Production & Special Projects: Jeff Youngquist
Assistant Editor, Special Projects: Caitlin O'Connell
Manager, Licensed Publishing: Jeremy West
VP, Licensed Publishing: Sven Larsen
SVP Print, Sales & Marketing: David Gabriel
Editor in Chief: C B Cebulski

Special Thanks to Jordan D White

MARVEL

© 2020 MARVEL

First published by Aconyte Books in 2020

ISBN 978 1 83908 050 0

Ebook ISBN 978 1 83908 051 7

This novel is entirely a work of fiction. Names, characters, places, and incidents are the products of the author's imagination or are used fictitiously. Any resemblance to actual events, locales, organizations or persons, living or dead, is entirely coincidental.

Sales of this book without a front cover may be unauthorized. If this book is coverless, it may have been reported to the publisher as "unsold and destroyed" and neither the author nor the publisher may have received payment for it.

Cover art by Joey Hi-Fi

Distributed in North America by Simon & Schuster Inc, New York, USA
Printed in the United States of America
9 8 7 6 5 4 3 2 1

ACONYTE BOOKS

An imprint of Asmodee Entertainment Ltd

Mercury House, Shipstones Business Centre
North Gate, Nottingham NG7 7FN, UK

aconytebooks.com // twitter.com/aconytebooks

For the kids who ate the first marshmallow.

"Every day of my childhood, I was told I was a mistake. An aberration. A mutant.

I was tortured and branded. And told my gift was a sin against God.

And I believed it. Until one day, I recognized the emotion in the doctors' eyes.

It was fear.

And that changed everything. And I stopped being afraid.

And started to realize that the world could bend my way.

And that my enemies were just dice for me to roll.

And best of all?

The dice were loaded."

GAIL SIMONE, DOMINO #5 (2018)

"Fortune makes a fool of those she favors too much."

HORACE

PROLOGUE

Funny, the kinds of things you remember.

Not "ha ha" funny, or post-irony ironic funny, or Ray-Liotta-and-Joe-Pesci-in-*Goodfellas* funny, or anything so godawful literary as a metaphor.

I guess you kinda had to be there.

What I remembered most was the smell: blood and ash. Two things that don't usually go together. If a body's burning, then it's the cooked-meat smell that really worms into your nostrils and gets to you. It even gets to me. I've hit the age where I've stopped pretending that it doesn't. You have to do a lot of hateful things to get through in this world, especially in my career, and so you put on your wading boots and get through it. And try not to think about it again.

These days, it's not the smell that bothers me as much as what it's covering up. The absence underneath. The things I'd rather remember instead.

Like her face.

Somewhere along the way, I stopped remembering her face.

I've flipped through magazines and Instagram feeds,

thought I saw her, and nearly jumped out of my skin.

Of course, it wasn't her. The women in the pictures were too young; they weren't quite intense enough. And they were having too much fun, doing things like clubbing or taking pictures of their food. Time-wasting nonsense. Even before I found out more about her, I knew she wouldn't have bothered with that.

But I thought these random flashes of her had kickstarted my memory. That I could finally remember what Mom, what Beatrice, looked like.

I saved those pictures. Only when I went back to look at them, all the pictures looked different. They weren't as I remembered them. The diamond-hard eyes I'd thought I'd seen were gone. I was left with a phone full of pictures of strangers.

Now, when I try to think of Beatrice, these people get tugged along in the undertow of memory too. And it all gets even more jumbled.

"Funny" thing is, jumbled and chaotic is my element. I'm at my best balanced on a razor, listing into the breeze, and letting chance and fortune pick what happens next. Where there's no railings, no instructions, and I don't have time to feel awful about it.

But the time finds you anyway. And that's where I start to lose focus. In my profession, you can't ever lose focus. Lose focus, and you're either dead, or worse – useless. Close enough to dead that the margins are imperceptible.

Maybe it'll be easier if I start with what I know. Start tracing the outlines, and fill in the center later. I can tell you a few things.

I could tell you what her hair was like: dark like mine but neater, thinner, and with a gray streak. What she wore: military fatigues, cut out of regulation, with the nametag torn out. But her face – the only thing I remember now is the impression of it. Those diamond eyes. The eyes of a fanatic.

She was a killer. And there was lots of rage. Oh, yeah. Lots of rage.

That part, at least, felt right. I could believe I was related to that.

Let's take it from the top.

My name is Neena Thurman. But, like most of us these days, I have more than one name. Call me Domino.

ONE
CHICAGO, NOW

One of the things nobody ever tells you about the badass, super-exciting mercenary lifestyle is what a grind it is between jobs.

Oh, there's glamour. Not going to lie about that. You start off street-poor like I did – with no education but with plenty of ability – and there's no more glamorous way to go. Mercenaries are short-lived, but the idea is to live enough for ten people in a handful of years. My friends and I turned it into a competition: after the check from a high-paying job clears, we go out and see who can spend their earnings the fastest. Bonus points to whoever spends it all clubbing. Extra bonus points if it's at the same club, in one night.

Some of my best memories came out of those nights. The parts I can remember, anyway. (Brings a tear to my eye, imagining what I can't.)

If you're the kind of person who dwells on the long term, who can't sleep if you don't know what you're doing next week, this isn't the profession for you. You know, there's a psych experiment in which some scolds in lab coats take a preschool-age kid, sit them down in front of a marshmallow, and tell them that if they don't eat the marshmallow for five minutes, they can have two marshmallows. The kids who wait are supposed to have better self-control, foresight, outcomes in life, et cetera.

If you're the kind of person who would've waited for the second marshmallow, this isn't the job for you.

To do what I do, always take the first marshmallow. *Don't* trust anyone who promises you anything.

Don't count on having any kind of future.

The present's the fun part, anyway. It's the only part that's real.

And then there's the rest of it. The hardest part – well, there's a lot of hard parts, but the hardest part that doesn't involve something like, say, trawling through sewer water with open wounds – is finding someone 1) trustworthy enough to pay what they say they'll pay, 2) with a job worth your skills, 3) with the credit rating to handle that advance and extra expenses, and 4) not a total scathead.

That fourth part is the most common deal-killer. Surprise, surprise. So it's the one I pay most attention to when I meet my clients, or their agents, or talk to them on an identity-masking VOIP service, whatever. The job interview is two-way. You'd be surprised how many people won't tell you what it is they want you to do, or will just outright lie about it, until they have a chance to look in your eyes. Sometimes they need to make sure I'm sharp enough to handle the kind of job they're desperate enough to hire someone like me to do. Or they just want to meet me for the sake of meeting me.[1]

I've got an advantage in first meetings. There's a brand around my eye that most people assume is a scar. They focus on that, rather than on me sizing them up. I don't mind the misconception. Makes me look tough.

I mean… tougher.

So it was that I came to meet Rebecca Munoz, in an apartment I lied was my home, on an ice-slick Chicago winter evening. She knocked on the door just after working hours. The line of headlights outside the windows had been thick for hours, and would be for hours more. I was honestly surprised Munoz had made the meeting on time, traffic as it was.

She was one of those planning-ahead types.

I came prepared to refuse her. She had sent me a long story about her adult-aged kids cutting off contact with her, refusing to see her. They had gotten involved with some kind of church that had, she said, encouraged them to do this. Not the kind of thing I usually deal with, and for several very good reasons. But I would give just about anyone a chance. *One* chance.

She looked unsteady, uncertain when she came in – like most people did when they saw my belt holster slung over the coffee table, collectors' piece pistols artfully placed in plain view. But then it was like she just stopped seeing them. And her raised eyebrow said just how unimpressed she was.[2]

Her most striking feature was the lines under her eyes. She looked like she hadn't gotten sleep in days. Or had spent

---

[1] I've got more of a reputation than I care to have.

[2] Hey, not everybody appreciates beauty. I take great care of the Kimber Eclipse Custom II.

weeks catching, at most, one or two hours a night. Her black hair dripped. She'd gotten some snow on it, and the building was so cold that the snow was just now melting.

She sat on the chair opposite my sofa. The first thing she said was to outline how she wanted to pay me, and through which banks. Not the kind of thing she would've done if she hadn't already been sure she wanted to hire me. She didn't even look at the brand on my eye.

People think they can stare at it without me noticing, but I can always tell.

When she started counting money out on the table, I held up a hand. "I just said I would *meet* you. You're acting like I've already signed on the dotted line."

"I wasn't aware you people put anything down in writing."

There's that old, familiar feeling: my hackles rising. *You people* could mean a bunch of different things. Could mean *mercs*. Could mean *muties*.

She asked, "What's the point of putting anything in a contract if no judge will enforce it?"

"It was a *metaphor*." I ground my teeth. "That email you sent, about your kids? It was thousands of words long." Cute picture, though. Hispanic fraternal twins standing side-by-side at high school graduation. The brother was shorter, sister was taller, and both were freckled. But the picture came with metadata that said it was years old. Those twins were in their twenties now. "I'm going to be honest. I stopped reading halfway. If you have a job for me, you can tell me without the sob story."

Sometimes the best way to sound out new clients is to pick a fight and see what happens. And what she might've just said made picking that fight a pleasure.

"I didn't think it was all that complicated," she said. "I just want to hire somebody to find out what happened to them."

"Do you?" I asked. "If I find out they're exactly where they said? What then?"

She didn't have an answer, or didn't want to give it. She met my stare just as hard as I was giving it. Again, to her credit, without looking at the brand.

"Would you really let that be the end of the story you want to tell yourself?" I asked.

"You think I'm here to tell myself a story?" Also to her credit, she didn't hide her contempt.

"That's what most of my clients want. Certainly most clients with family problems. They try to hire me because they see the kind of story they're in and they don't like it. They want to go back a few chapters. Undo someone else's character development. Or just keep from turning those last pages. But it's never that easy."

Not many people can change the genre of the story they're in. I've met a few who can. I couldn't turn this woman's story from a tragedy into something else. And I didn't really think I wanted to. Not for any kind of money. And I'll do a lot for money.

Rebecca Munoz was still in her winter coat. She pulled her hands back into her sleeves. I, in my combat-ready slimwear, was forced to pretend I didn't feel the cold. The headlights made iridescent waves on the frost inside the window.

My friends, Diamondback and Outlaw – back when we were still operating by ourselves, before we even got our riverboat, the *Painted Lady* – rented this place for just this kind of meeting. Sure, it's not as cheap as just getting a hotel wherever. But I don't trust hotels for sensitive work. Besides, you never know when things will blow up, get hairy, or turn you into a wanted woman. It pays to have your hidey-holes set in advance. Places like this, where your friends know where to find you but the law doesn't, are worth every chunk of change that takes away from our clubbing.

Before you accuse me of planning ahead, this place was Diamondback's idea. I don't hate planners. Sometimes I even need them. I just don't like to do it myself.

Rachel – Diamondback's given name, though you can damn well go on calling her Diamondback until she says otherwise – may have come up with the idea, but I didn't let her execute it. Rachel has a flair for the elaborate and the expensive. Letting her pick our places would've shaved tens of thousands off our Girls' Night Out budget. I turned the operation over to Inez, our Outlaw. I may have overcompensated.

In the end, Inez isn't any more practical than the rest of us costumed mercs. She's got her aesthetic, same as Rachel and me. She goes for low-down, dirty, and practical. So practical that, if I didn't have my boots on, the floorboards would have given me splinters. And so practical that the most functional furniture is the bar. The liquor cabinets are stocked and the taps work.

Inez is from Texas. When she was out looking at the property, she didn't see things like cold weather prep the same way as the rest of us. Cold is alien to her.[3] I made a

---

[3] You can tell from her outfit.

mental note to find an excuse to send her down here, force her to spend a night.

I'd come here direct from my San Francisco apartment. Every time I start to feel like San Francisco is an unlivable hellhole, I return to Chicago to remind myself what real unlivable hellholes are like.

(Hey – I grew up a Chicagoan. I'm allowed to insult my city. To whatever extent it is still my city.)

"All I want," she said, "is my children."

I kicked my feet up on the coffee table and reclined.

"Yeah. And your kids don't want you to have them."

"They only say what they've been told to."

"Your kids are adults."

Her jaw shifted. She was visibly grinding her teeth. But her voice remained calm. "You don't believe adults can make poor decisions?"

"*Believe* me, I freakin' know."

"You're making one right now."

"Is that a threat?" I asked.

"No. Just telling you you're making a poor decision."

I'd done my research before this meeting. Rebecca Munoz wasn't super-powered, wasn't a mutant, or anything like that. Doesn't mean she couldn't be hiding something, but everything I'd found led me to believe that, if that *was* a threat, she was severely overconfident. She was just an ordinary person. Playing in my superpowered world.

I swung my legs off the table. Leaned forward. "Have you ever considered that you might have driven them away?"

I threw it out there to provoke the rage and the waterworks. It was coming, sooner or later, I thought. Might as well get it over with. This apartment was full of things she could throw at me, but I trusted my luck to dodge them.

But I didn't get any of that. All she gave me was flint and steel. The steel was in her expression, the tightness of her cheekbones and jaw. And the flint was in her eyes.

"They're going to hurt people if they don't leave where they are," she said.

Unexpected answer. But still in the bounds of the genre.

"If they're the kind of kids who are set to hurt people, they'll manage it no matter where they are," I said.

"They're *not* those kinds of kids."

There was more venom in her voice than there had been in the past several minutes of back-and-forth sniping. I met her glare.

Rebecca Munoz was a mother of fraternal twins, Rose and Joseph. Up until the past year, they'd lived with her. They'd moved out together, giving their lives over to some church. The kids were old enough to make their own decisions about that.

Bottom line is this: I've got no respect for people who try to impose what *they* want on the people they say they love. Honestly, that covers about ninety percent who try to hire me for "family issues." I should just have a form rejection for anyone who comes to me with a job like that.

Look, my aversion to long-term planning is one thing. But if I skip my due diligence on the people who walk through my doors, I end up helping some jackhole stalker track down his victim. Or, as it could be in this case, an abusive parent finding their adult children who'd finally managed to get away.

This would not be the first time I've dealt with that. The

last jerk who tried that on me, a real piece of work of a father, found himself dangling from the Golden Gate Bridge by one foot. And I'm not going to tell you what I do to corporate types who try to hire me as a strikebreaker.[4]

"You've heard of Dallas Bader Pearson," she said.

Not a question. A statement. I hate when people do that, especially when they're wrong. I had no idea who Dallas Bader Pearson was. "If you're using all three names, he must be some kind of serial killer. That's the rules, right?"

"He's worse. And if you don't know, you must not live here."

I spread my arms in mock surrender. "I really don't know."

"He's all kinds of involved in city politics."

"Who isn't?"

"He had his own radio show, broadcast on what used to be one of the best news stations in the city."

"Good for him." I didn't hide the boredom creeping into my voice.

"He and ten thousand of his followers are going to embark on a spiritual revolution that will turn the world into Paradise."

I blinked. "OK, that was less expected."

"He's a liar and a psychopath, but he's very good at convincing people he's not. He can't possibly believe that, but his followers do."

I scratched my chin, interested despite myself. "He can't have ten thousand followers, or even I would've heard of him."

"No, but the number's important to him. He's into numerology, prophecies of the apocalypse."

The more I heard about this, the less I liked it. And I didn't

---

[4] Been a while since the last one of those. Maybe the object lesson I made of the last lady had been enough.

think that was possible. "OK, so he's a nutcase. So what?"

"Look, Ms Domino–"

"Just Domino."

She shot me an arch look, just to let me know how childish she found this whole thing. She and I might as well have not lived in the same world. "Have you ever dealt with fanatics?"

Have I ever dealt with fanatics. I answered her look with a withering one of my own. "That's just about all I deal with. Fanatics and the people they hire."

"Have you ever wanted to save someone from that – but they wouldn't let you?"

That gave me pause. "Yeah. Of course."

"Who?"

A sudden, involuntary swell of anger turned to bile in my throat. For just a second, I tasted algae-covered Florida swamp waters. I pushed the memory down. "I'm not here to bare my soul to you. We're discussing a business relationship."

"No, we're not."

"You don't think so, you came to the wrong place. Door's over there–"

"If it were *just business,* I should have cut my losses long ago. These are my children."

"It's *just business* to me."

She smiled curtly. "Then, if that's all, I'm prepared to pay your asking price."

A neat little rhetorical trap. All of my objections, so far, had been over the nature of the job, not her ability to pay. I could see she'd brought enough cash for the opening bid. She had it splayed out on the coffee table in front of me.

But this wasn't a debate class and I wasn't a judge. I didn't have to be fair, and I didn't have to navigate my way through word puzzles. If I didn't want to do something, I didn't do it.

"No," I said.

"No? But I've done everything you asked–"

"I've met with crown princes and corporate oligarchs who were less presumptuous than you, lady."

For the first time since she'd come in, she looked shaken. "I don't have any other options besides you."

"That's not my concern." And I doubted that was true.

She didn't say anything to that. I sighed, and stood. Rebecca flinched like I was about to physically throw her out, but I walked past her and toward the frost-limed window.

I just didn't want to see her any more. And I didn't want *her* to see how angry she'd made me, especially because I couldn't explain the reason why.

"Do you really think I'd be able to change their minds?" I asked.

She said, "So long as they're in there, I'm not sure there's much point in talking about things like 'changing their minds.'"

"So you want me to abduct them."

"You don't have to take them to me if that's your problem. I want you to take them into the outside world. Show them that they can live outside Dallas Bader Pearson's church."

"No," I said. "I'm not a chaperon, a tour guide, and I'm definitely not a motivational speaker."

"I can tell."

"If you don't like my attitude, you can leave."

She was silent after that. I heard her coat ruffling, a footstep. When I turned around, she was already on her way out the door.

TWO

Conference call. That evening. By encrypted video app. Me and my besties, going over our options for our next jobs. I needed a break, but somehow seeing my friends didn't boost my mood. I was still in the freezing-cold Chicago apartment, while, from what I could tell from the hazy background of their video, they were living it up on a rooftop bar back in San Francisco. They were scouting for new employers, too, but – *somehow* – they'd contrived to do it in a more hospitable place than me.

Rachel was in one of her many violet evening dresses with slit thighs (better combat mobility), looking effortlessly glamorous. Inez had the cowboy hat she took everywhere, no matter how many times it threatened to blow off in the rooftop winds.

Rebecca Munoz hadn't been the only meeting I'd had that day. None of the other job prospects looked any brighter. I still hadn't gotten over that swell of anger and bad memories. I told Inez and Rachel about my meetings, and I wasn't sparing in describing what Rebecca Munoz and I had said to each other.

"Dontcha think you were a little hard on the gal?" Inez asked.

Rachel chimed in, "Poor thing sounds like she just wasn't ready to step into our world."

"Then she shouldn't have come to us in the first place," I said.

I was being hard on her, and they knew it. Usually, they supported me in that. But – unlike usual – it bothered me that I was being a hardass. They sensed that too.

I couldn't stop feeling pissed, for reasons I had trouble putting my finger on.

"It wasn't our kind of job, and she should've known it," I said. "And the way she acted – like she kept assuming I knew things, like who this Pearson creep is–"

"Hold up there," Inez said. "Pearson? As in Dallas Bader Pearson?"

Perfect. I'm the Chicagoan, and the *Texan* is the one who'd heard of Pearson. "How'd you know?"

"Not many other big-name Pearsons in Chicago. You've heard of any others?"

"Surprised you've heard of one. No offense. It's not your area."

"Yeah, but I pay attention to the world around me."

Rachel asked, "Darling, who hasn't heard of Dallas Bader Pearson?"

"Are you two screwing with me right now?"

"Do you see my face right now?" Rachel asked. "It's my very-not-screwing-with-you face." She was, I admit, managing a reasonable poker face.

Inez said, "What Rache means to say is that we're always

screwing with you – but we still know the name."

"You two aren't from my city, and you know more about it than I do."

"*Your* city? Last time we all talked 'bout Chicago, you didn't act like it was yours."

Yeah. But it was.

"Come on," Rachel said. "I follow the news."

I fixed her in my gaze. After a few seconds, her very-not-screwing-with-you face cracked.

"OK," Rachel said. "All right. I follow people on Twitter who follow the news. But that's how most people do it."

"So what do people on Twitter who follow the news say about Dallas Bader Pearson?"

"There was a big scandal a year or two ago. He was forced to resign from some civic position, city council or the like. It started with a sexual harassment allegation."

"Started?"

"There was more than one," Rachel said.

"It came in a box of a dozen," Inez added, scowling.

The anger was back again. I didn't know why this was affecting me. I dealt with monsters and criminals as a regular part of my working day. But I was on edge, and this was pushing me over.

"And then after that, allegations of abuses at his church, financial crimes, all kinds of bizarre stories," Rachel said. "He was asking retired couples, dementia patients, to sign over all their properties to his church. Things like that."

"So a real swell guy." I dug my nails into my palm.

"A couple of his surrogates have Twitter accounts, and posted some really bizarre defenses of him. That's what really made it blow up there," Rachel said, with a faraway look as if half-remembering all this. "People making fun of them. It was in everybody's trending topics."

I turned to Inez. "Is that how you heard about this, too? Twitter?"

"I don't have anything to do with anything called Twitter."

"So how'd you hear about it?"

"Rache."

I actually snorted. "Great. Perfect."

"Honestly, I'm surprised nobody's hired us to assassinate him already," Rachel said.

"I don't think Rebecca Munoz was looking to get anybody killed." Probably. The thought must have crossed her mind, but she hadn't mentioned it.

I wondered why not. If she knew enough to find me, she must've known what I was capable of. Maybe she just wasn't that kind of person.

But it was almost always naive to think that.

"And what a shame that is." Rachel flapped a hand through the air as if brushing away a fly. "Honestly, a man like that – I'd be tempted to take the work *pro bono*. It would do the world a favor."

"We're not in this to settle someone's family squabble," I reminded her. "That doesn't pay. Not in the end." And it didn't matter how many bills Rebecca smacked on the table.

Reputation is important for us mercs. You start messing in domestic disputes, get known for it, and soon enough that's all anyone comes to you for. And you get bankrupt and miserable.

"I know. You know how many expensive habits I have to

support. Still..." Rachel let the thought linger, "...after that business with the Creation Constellation, I've started to build up a little heroism complex. Money isn't the only thing that feels good." And now we were working with old-fashioned heroines, too. The three of us used to work alone. But, in the incident Rachel had alluded to, three more women had joined our team... including Black Widow, a real Avenger.

"There's revenge, too," Inez said, with a grin that, back when Inez and Rachel and I first met, would have made Rachel back away fast.

Rachel said, "Yes, well – that was the unspoken part of that sentence, but you go right ahead and say it." A tolerant smile. "Also, I would have gone with 'vengeance.'"

"Rebecca Munoz wasn't trying to hire me for anything like that. It was all about her kids." I unclenched my hand. My palm stung from my nails. "And they're adults, and they can make their own choices. For all we know, they're on Twitter making fools of themselves like all of Pearson's disciples. And there's nothing we can do to change that."

"That's a little defeatist, don't you think?" Rachel asked.

"She's right, Rache," Inez said.

Rachel looked like she couldn't decide whether to seem offended or startled. "I thought you were on my side! Aren't we gearing up to argue Neena out of her decision to refuse the job?"

"We sure ain't," Inez said. "What do you think we're gonna do? Point a gun at those kids and *scare* the cult out of them? Those types don't work like that."

"Well, no..." Rachel hesitated. "Damn. But it would be nice to do something."

"We're not the right kind of team for this one," I said. "Not our skillset. Not for what the client wants." A tired kind of numbness was seeping through my muscles. I couldn't stop thinking about the word Rachel had used. *Defeatist*. It felt like a defeat, all right.

That wasn't something I experienced all that often, and it wasn't helping with my anger issues.

"All right," I said. "So we're decided."

My posse had expanded recently, but Inez, Rachel, and I have always been the core. They've been with me since we knew we were forming a group.

We all had histories we don't talk too much about. We all didn't stand up in times and in places where we really should have. The three of us, coming together – well, it was maybe a chance to start putting some of those wrongs right again. Rachel had it right. We were all starting to develop a heroism complex.

But we were still mercs. We still needed money. And things had gotten more complicated lately. Like I said, the three of us weren't alone any more. Atlas Bear, a Wakandan exile with precog abilities, and White Fox, a South Korean superagent, had joined the team around the same time Black Widow had.

Don't get me wrong: I liked our new partners. Liked them a lot. But.

But.

They all had their other loyalties. Atlas Bear to Wakanda, no matter that she'd been exiled. White Fox to South Korea. Black Widow to the Avengers, and God knew who else. I was still working out how I felt about them, let alone how to manage them.

Inez and Rachel, though – I knew how I felt about them. More importantly, I knew how *they* felt.

I don't know when I realized I would take Rebecca Munoz's offer. It was probably right in the middle of when I was telling Rachel no, and Inez was giving her some very good reasons why we shouldn't.

Neither of them seemed surprised when I called them up later that night, and told them I wanted to take the job. The rooftop party was still going in the background.

I don't know how long I'd been laying there in that freezing-cold apartment bed, trying to get to sleep, just staring at the frosting apartment windows. I didn't want to know what either of my watches said.

I dialed the contact number Rebecca Munoz had left me. She sounded like she was still up too.

"You've got my starting price set," I said. "But that doesn't count expenses. I've done some checking around, and your credit rating isn't great."

Even though this was just a regular phone call, I could *feel* the acid in her eyes.

"I'm a single mother in Chicago," she said. "Of course it's not."

"You'll still be on the hook for expenses. And I can't promise that, once I get your kids out, they'll want to *stay* out. Understand?"

"Understood," she said. "And agreed."

I couldn't bring myself to say I was hired. That felt too final.

I still wanted to find out more about these twins, whether they really *wanted* to leave. Or could even be talked into it.

So I just hung up the phone. That was finality enough for now.

I lay back on my bed and wondered how the hell I'd found myself like this. I didn't used to trap myself into so many emotional decisions. It's an understatement to say that a job like mine is best done cool-headed. If you want to get anywhere, you had better be like ice.

Ever since I'd had to kill my mother, I'd found myself bothered by things that had never bothered me before.

THREE
THE EVERGLADES, SIX YEARS AGO

You expected me to maybe tell this story in order?

That's not how I operate. Chaos and luck never take things in order. There is no order. Order is a narrative, a story people tell themselves afterward. It's something people impose on events.[5]

When you flip a coin, don't expect it to come up heads just because the last was tails. Not even when you can manipulate luck. Luck has always been generous to me, but luck has no memory, no narrative, no order. Even at its best, most generous, that's just not what it *is*.

So that wasn't the start of this story. But it was where I started to figure it out.

And nothing else I tell you is going to make as much sense without it.

---

5 Same thing with the footnotes. My thoughts don't lead neatly from one to the next. They branch like forks of lightning.

You're going to have to trust me.[6]

All my life, I'd been haunted by a face.

Someone I couldn't place. Someone who, every time I thought of her, a weight settled on my back. Like a lead blanket. Smothering, but, in some strange sense, comforting. If there was a fire sweeping my way, or the roof was collapsing, I could toss it over myself and feel at least a little safer.

All of this was even stranger because I had no idea who she was. All I knew was the face, and how I felt when I thought about it.

I'd had a busy life. I'm not a super hero, but I've been super hero-adjacent. You probably know the names. Cable brought me into the merc life, taught me what I needed to know to get my start. I did some training with Professor X, but didn't want to stay part of that organization, or any organization. And I've been on a lot of teams, even led some of them. X-Force, Six Pack – teams you'd know if you followed the right kind of news.

But, in this part of the story, I was working for myself. Inez and Rachel weren't a part of my life yet. I was on my own for not the first, but certainly the longest, time in my life.

It was only after I'd gotten my feet under me as an independent operator that I felt like I was finally ready to chase that face down. Find that feeling. Make some kind of connection with it.

See, one thing I didn't talk about – and tried not to think about – was that big chunks of my past were missing. My

---

[6] You should probably never trust me.

memory was punched full of holes. That much trauma will do that to a person. But trauma wasn't the only thing that was back there. There was also that face. The sense of comfort that rode along with it.

I wasn't a natural introvert. I'd learned how to be, over long and callous years out alone in the world. But it chafed. A big part of me wanted that sense of comfort, of connection. The longer I worked alone, the more I wanted to feel it again.

That was what brought me to one of the most miserable places I've been in my life. The Florida Everglades in summer.

The Everglades – where it rains every twenty minutes, the air is so humid it feels like you're always under a waterfall anyway, and you sweat your body weight every day. Just imagine a bath where, every time you step in, you step out filthier.

I was sweating buckets now, and I wasn't even going through the marsh the hard way. My contact Jonathan and I had rented a motorboat and cruised along the coast at an easy pace. Even with the breeze, my skin felt like I could peel it right off.

I had no clear idea what I was looking for. I was just looking. Counting on my luck to find it for me.

Every mutant's unusual, but what I can do is more unusual than most. Unusual enough to make you question the nature of reality, or whether a God exists and just whose side She's on. Real head-spinning stuff. I've had lab coats who, after they've met me and seen what I could do, wandered away muttering that they must be in a simulation – that a real universe could not *possibly* act like this.

See, what I do is luck.

I don't mean to say my power is luck.

I mean – I *do* luck.

I can't just let it happen. I have to be active, have to be doing something. When I am, things go well for me. It happens in ways that seem like coincidence. But the coincidences keep stacking up.

In a fight, my enemies' guns will jam. All of them, one right after another. Or they'll misaim and hit each other. I've taken shelter from a tornado in a house, had it collapse on me, and then, like Buster Keaton, stepped out unscathed from under an open window frame. I've been blown through a plate-glass window without suffering a cut. I've been twenty feet away from a frag grenade when it detonated, and been missed by all the shrapnel.

But there are some limits. It has to be a life-and-death situation, or at least I have to think it is. Or just as much high drama and emotion. Means no getting rich at roulette tables. I love my job, but, hell, even I wouldn't be a merc if making money were that easy. I could get beat up just as much getting thrown out of every casino in Vegas, and in half the time, too.

I can't fake the adrenaline or the high emotions that make my luck kick in. That means I've got to keep myself on the edge.

The other problem is that my luck has a sense of humor – and it can get awfully meanspirited. Some days, it doesn't even feel like it's on my side. That window I told you I got blasted through? I survived when anyone else should've been cut to ribbons, but, when I landed, I twisted both ankles in exactly the same place. Could hardly walk for a week. And that frag grenade? It didn't so much miss *me* as hit the thousand year-old book I'd been hired to steal back from some museum burglars.

I'm not gonna lie – my luck is comforting. The time it was stolen from me was a nightmare that made my recurring losing-my-dog-in-downtown-San-Francisco nightmare seem cheerful and carefree.

But I can't think of my luck as a friend. I can't let myself think I can count on it.

Because *thinking* isn't *acting*, and if I'm not acting, I lose it.

It also isn't looking out for anyone other than me.

This was a mission where I didn't feel comfortable bringing anyone else along with me. This was *my* concern, my fixation. No one else's. And yet, somehow, one of my contacts had convinced me to let him tag along anyway.

He sat in the back of my boat. His name was Jonathan Shepherd, and he was somewhere between an old friend and an employer. An extremely dangerous combination for either of our well-beings. We'd worked together on enough jobs, and made enough money together, that I had gotten a little too comfortable around him. Called him by his first name. And even let him call me "Neena" sometimes.

I'd learned things about him I never should have learned about any employer – like that, as frail and self-serious as he looked, he was a surprisingly good lay. I'd promised myself at the time I wouldn't regret that, but I made all kinds of promises to myself that I couldn't keep. Without that sentimental bond, he probably wouldn't have been able to talk me into doing what he had.

After what happened next, it would be a long time – not until I started working with Inez and Rachel – that I would let anyone else call me "Neena" rather than "Domino."

If I hadn't brought him in on this, I wouldn't have found out anywhere near as much about that face I was chasing. But his presence still seemed like an intrusion. When he found out where our trail of breadcrumbs was leading, he insisted on seeing things through. He wouldn't give me the last little crumb I needed to finish the trail until I vowed to take him along.

What a jerk, right?

But being a jerk is what you need in this business, because he got what he was looking for – a trip to the Everglades, tagging along with me – and he still wouldn't say why. It was as irritating as all the bug bites I was collecting out here. Jonathan reclined in the back of our motorboat, his arms and walking cane propped up against the side, watching the marshy shoreline with a perpetual frown.

"There." Abruptly, he pointed to a patch of coastline that looked no different than any other.

I gave him an appropriately withering look – for about the twentieth time that day – but he didn't even glance my way. "That's rough terrain," I said. "You sure you're going to be all right with your…?" I nodded at his cane.

"Just go," he said, his voice tight. He'd been sitting in the back of the boat for half an hour. His bad leg must really have been starting to hurt.[7]

I mentally rehearsed one of the thousand questions I was

---

[7] I have no idea what had happened to his leg and, in this business especially, it's impolite to ask. Must have been a hell of a fight.

going to ask him once we were ashore and he couldn't pretend to be distracted any more, and aimed the boat toward a little marshy inlet. We could follow the waterway for a bit, but eventually we were going to have to get out and slog through the marsh.

Jonathan grimaced and levered himself backward. The back of the boat was loaded with armaments. He started picking through the weapons we'd brought, and selected a light pistol. Jonathan had refused to say what we might be facing, except that it would be a good idea to be ready.

It was luck – real luck, not my power – that saved my life here. And a little bit of stupidity.

They could've caught me completely off guard. If I'm not paying attention, my luck isn't working for me. That's the way I'm going to die someday – someone's going to sneak up on me from behind and put a bullet in my head, or a semi's going to plow into my motorcycle from my blind spot. My luck can't defend me against what I can't see. That's fine. When it comes, I'd rather not see it coming, you know?

They must have been hiding in the marsh, wading waist deep. If they'd just opened fire from cover, that would have been it. Lights out.

Instead, they tried to get clever. "Identify yourself!" a voice called.

It wasn't a genuine attempt to get me to surrender. They just wanted to distract me, get me to slow down. Make for an easier shot.

I turned and, just quickly enough, saw them. A blur of motion. A human-shaped figure, all in dark gray camouflage netting.

When the missile shot toward my boat like a dart from a blowgun, I had just enough time to realize what was happening. Enough to react. To jump.

There was no time to stop for Jonathan.

I hardly felt the scum of algae and mosquito eggs as I plunged through into the cloudy water underneath. Then the shockwave struck. Indistinguishable from a freight train. If I'd hit the water at a shallower angle, I would've gone skipping across it like a stone. As it was, the blast just knocked me down so hard that I felt like a swatted fly. The water might as well have been a brick wall.

But the shockwave didn't crush my ribs like an aluminum can. Nor did any piece of the shrapnel do much more than nick me.

Lucky me.

My lungs burned. I hadn't had time to take a breath before the impact. I'd been shoved under so hard that I didn't know which way was up. The salty water was cloudy enough that, when I opened my eyes to look around (ouch), I couldn't tell what direction the light was coming from.

I swam into a patch of marsh reeds whose stalks helped me reestablish up and down. When I broke through the surface, it still felt like the world had tilted sideways. My head spun. I spat out the water I'd inhaled, as quietly as possible, and tried to get my bearings.

I'd emerged among the reeds, half-hidden, but not hidden enough. If whoever had shot at me was looking, they could have found me, easy. But they weren't looking.

The shrapnel from the blast hadn't killed me like it should have. Instead of a sliced-up neck, I had ended up with almost symmetrical cuts on my arms. The salt water stung them viciously. The skin around them was already red. I brushed a film of algae off one, and grimaced. My medical kit had been in the boat.

With Jonathan.

My heart froze. There was no way he could have survived that missile hit. He just couldn't have moved fast enough.

I tried to focus on the immediate. On myself, on my injuries. I was going to have to find some cleaner water, and ideally disinfectant, soon. My luck may step in to save my life, but it didn't give one whit if I was in pain. I learned *that* well enough while I was still very young.

Every time I look into a mirror and see the brand on my eye is a reminder of that.

I spat out more foul-tasting water. Made a little fountain out of it. I couldn't tell how much noise I was making. My ears were still ringing. Fortunately, I doubted my attacker could hear me either. He'd fired from short range.

A floret of smoke still hovered over the shoulder-mounted launcher he'd fired and discarded.[8] Another hung over the remains of the motorboat. The shooter had taken cover in a circular frond of grass on a little hillock. A neat little hunter's blind with command of the area. The inlet I'd driven down made the most natural approach into drier land, and this had been a reasonable place to guard. Something I would have paid attention to if I'd expected this much opposition. Which I hadn't.

Not so soon, anyway.

---

[8] Super-heavy artillery for guard duty. He'd been waiting in ambush. Someone must have tipped him off that we'd be coming – but I had no idea who.

The site I'd been heading towards was miles inland yet. As far as I knew, this part of the coast was a nature conservatory. Officially, it was.

My assailant was wading into the marsh, toward the wreckage of my boat. He wore heavy gray-and-brown camo. He'd ditched the one-shot shoulder-mounted launcher, which let me get a better look at it. An AT4 shoulder-mounted rocket launcher, a mainstay of the US armed forces. Interesting, that. Could mean nothing. Could mean a hell of a lot.

See, I didn't have any idea who I'd come out here chasing.

Jonathan hadn't told me anything. And now he'd never be able to.

That idiot. That stubborn, earwax-for-brains moron. It was easier to be enraged right now than distraught.

Mr Overkill was saying something I couldn't hear over the ringing. He held his hand to his ear. Earpiece. He was speaking a lot louder than he needed to. Like me, he'd been partially deafened by the blast.

He wasn't looking around. He hadn't seen me escape the blast. And while he held his rifle – an M4 carbine – at the ready, his posture was that of a man who only expected something grisly, not something dangerous.

I sank deeper into cover, leaving just my nose above water, and waited.

The front half of the motorboat had been blown clean away, but the rest was, surprisingly, still in one piece. He grabbed the boat's remains, pulled it closer to him.

Much as I would've loved creeping up on him, introducing myself, and then showing his nose to the back of his skull, there were more productive ways to spend my energy. Like trying to eavesdrop.

I had paid very, very dearly to get this far. And so had someone else. Jonathan hadn't been the first to die.

FOUR

Being caught off guard had been the theme of this whole operation. Someone who knew me, knew my luck's limitations, had taken aim right for my weak point.

Only their aim had been just a little bit off, because they ended up hitting a lot of other people instead.

I wouldn't call them innocents, but they deserved better than what they got. The first to buy it had been one of the hackers I'd hired. He had been expensive. I was loath to spend so much money on anything that wasn't fun or weapons hardware[9], but had figured that, if I didn't chase down this memory *now*, I would never be able to.

For all my life – and the past few months in particular – I'd been thinking about a face I didn't recognize. And a face that seemed more and more familiar. Every time I looked into the mirror, I saw a little more of it. An extra few lines, under my eyes, here or there. Sharper cheekbones. If I'd grown my hair out a little more, I could've been a dead ringer. The older I

---

9 Or fun weapons hardware.

got, the easier it was to see.

It didn't take much imagination to figure that the face I was seeing, the one I couldn't forget, was related to me.

Given how long I'd had the face in my imagination – an older sister, maybe. Or a parent.

I can still feel the goosebumps I got when this occurred to me. I hadn't grown up knowing any kind of family.

I'd grown up in a cage, surrounded by lab coats who were as cruel to me as I fantasized about being to them. There had been other kids too. So far as I knew, none of them were family. None of them looked anything like me. There were all different kinds of skin colors, but I was the only one so pale. None had been so old as the face I remembered.

The other kids were taken away one by one. After each of them was taken, the rest of us never saw them again. Eventually, I was the only one left.

Nobody ever told me what happened to those kids, but they didn't need to. I knew.

Those kids would never have a chance to grow as old as that face I remembered.

The idea of a blood relation struck me with the force of a lightning bolt. The face would not leave me alone. Deep down, I knew I wouldn't leave it alone, either. I knew I was going to have to tackle it eventually. But I knew I couldn't do it alone.

It's hard to have friends in this business. At least friends that you keep. I've been on plenty of *teams*. I have people that, push comes to fisticuffs comes to blazing firefight, I know I can count on. Cable, Deadpool. Lots of people who will even do something so personal as, for example, travel halfway across the world to attend your birthday party. But people who are part of my life, day-in, day-out? People I could *feel* close to? That was a little different.

A big part of the problem there was me. Honest assessment. I know that, after a while, I tend to push people away. Actually, that's an understatement. I get abrasive as diamond-coated sandpaper. Just the way I was raised. As I grew up, I trained myself not to get close to anyone because, as soon as I did, they got taken away from me.[10]

That's one of the reasons Rachel and Inez have been such treasures. We get each other. We tolerate each other. They put up with my darker moods and idiosyncrasies, and I do the equivalent for them. Most importantly, no matter how much time we've spent together, we never get tired of each other. I'm learning how to have friends.[11]

But, back then, I didn't have them.

(Bear in mind the only reason I'm spilling my guts like this is because I know you're not in a position to tell anyone I know about it.)

The closest thing I had was Jonathan. Hard to think of him as a friend, in retrospect, but any oasis in the desert. And I had, y'know, slept with him. I was still in the promising-myself-I-wouldn't-regret-that phase of the relationship.

He used me, and I used him. We both knew that. I knew he was stealing data from me, had placed bugs and eavesdroppers in my PC, but, at the time, that just seemed normal to me. Part of how human beings related to each other. We didn't do

---

10 And this happened outside the cage I was raised in, too.

11 I don't think I'll ever fully *get it*. But some days I get closer than others.

each other favors, like real friends would. We did exchanges.

He was also one of the sharpest, most well-connected employers I'd worked with, and the only person I felt safe coming to with my half-remembered face. I sketched it out for him. He agreed to run it through some facial recognition databases if I did a job for him. Which I did. Only got shot at six times.

So then he'd found, in some cobwebbed old database he refused to divulge, a scan of an old driver's license. And there it was – a terrible, pixelated, photocopy-artifacted photo of *that face*. At least I thought it was. The state that issued it, Florida, had no official records for it. It wasn't much to go on, but the paucity of the data said something by itself. It meant someone had gone to lengths to erase it. This suggested heavy government involvement. Or at least someone with high-level access to those levers of power.

I hired a hacker I'd worked with before to do more digging. We'd met so he could hand over the fruits of his labor in person – the most secure kind of data transfer, as any hacker knows.

It still wasn't secure enough. We were intercepted by big, serious boys playing big, serious games. A sniper had been stationed nearby, waiting for us. And in a public place, too. We'd met in the streets of downtown Denver, and there had been passersby all around us. The sniper had been atop an old, three-story-tall bookstore, with people coming in and out every minute.

The first bullet drilled straight through the back of the hacker's head.

I could have just as easily taken that bullet. I'd been lucky.

That's one of the hateful things about my luck, though – just because it's on my side, doesn't mean it's on anybody else's. If my luck causes someone else's aim to wander, that bullet still gets fired. And it can just as easily end up going into someone else's brain.

When it was just me I had to worry about, the sniper was easy to duck. Easier than it would have been if, say, the whole weight of the US military had been behind this. If that had been the case, they could have sent in the troops, stormed the square.[12]

But by the time I'd identified where the shot had come from – the spray of blood exiting my hacker's head had drawn a clear trajectory – police sirens were screeching all across the city, and the rooftop was empty. All I remembered seeing was an all-black uniform, and a matching face mask.

The method of assassination said a great deal about the means of my attackers. They were incredibly well funded, enough to have military-grade armaments, but they may not have had as much manpower as they did money. That sniper had had no backup. A coordinated team, shooting at the same time, would have gotten the job done.

I made the mistake of telling Jonathan what had happened. His face hadn't given away anything, but I could tell he'd gotten intensely interested. Just by looking into this one person, this one face, we'd done something to bring the wrath of some well-prepared killers down on us.

I had no idea why. I was the one who'd started this. I should have walked away. This was stupid; there was no

---

12 Which made the US military weapons I'd later spot in the Everglades all the more eye-catching.

profit in it, no real work.

But that's not how I operated. Not once somebody had already shot at me.

I'd found the dead hacker's research on his body. He'd dug up an old flight record. The name on the old driver's license had been an alias, but it was an alias that the hacker had traced to another alias, and then to another. And one of those aliases had, at some point, registered a helicopter flight plan with a secret layer of a secret layer of the US government. The kind of secrecy that meant, at some point, you'd stopped being affiliated with the USA at all. If there was no oversight, no Congressional or agency approval, not even any funding, the only things to differentiate you from an under-the-radar PMC or other paramilitary force were the uniforms and an itch to salute a flag. In other words, aesthetics and vanity.

I'd dealt with organizations so secret that not even all of their members knew they existed. Some conspiracies had the same goals, same methods, but didn't know their counterparts existed.

Don't ever think you know what's going on in some layers of the US, or any nation's, government. *The X-Files* wasn't imaginative *enough*.

The helicopter's flight plan had her leaving somewhere deep in the Florida Everglades. Several miles inland, on land earmarked for conservation. Satellite photos showed nothing there.

Jonathan told me he knew of a facility not far away. Top secret, classified, layers upon layers of all that nonsense. But he wouldn't tell me where it was, how he knew about it, or why he was interested in it. Not unless I took him along.

    I had known, at the time, that it was a mistake. But because I'm an idiot, that hadn't stopped me.

FIVE

Back to the swamp – to the stinking salt water, the fearless mosquitoes, the slop covering me, and the stinging cuts on my arms.

That was everything that, to that point, I knew. Given how malleable a person's memory is and how much I'm reshaping things in trying to remember it, maybe even a little more than I knew.

The most definite things I remember are the blur of confusion and shock, melding into rage. The least these jerks could have done was tell me why. I'm always ready for a good villain's exposition. I'll even take notes.

But, no. The only way anyone had communicated with me so far was in attempts on my life.

Revenge would have been very sweet. But I made myself hold off. I had to find out more.

So I sank down to my nose in the marsh and, as the ringing in my ears faded from an acute pain to just a background one, I eavesdropped. Lots of back chatter with a voice the guard addressed as "base." A triumphant note in the guard's voice, balanced with tension. Caution from "base." The guard approached the remains of my boat, carbine in hand.

I'd gotten lucky in another way. Real, unfiltered luck this time. The guard had only seen one figure. Me. Because of his bad leg, Jonathan had been reclining in the back of the boat. The sun had been high overhead, the sparkling reflections off the ocean behind us blinding. He wouldn't have been able to see my features through the glare.

I heard a low whistle. From my angle, peering through the marsh reeds, I could just see his shoulders tense.

"Yeah. Only one."

I caught a glimpse of the wreckage of the boat. Half of the backside had been blown off, and what was left of the craft tilted precipitously into the water. The only reason it hadn't sunk more was because we'd already almost nestled ashore. The bottom of the boat rested flush against the ground. All the weapons and ammunition we'd carried had been wasted by the rocket attack. And so had Jonathan.

His arm, what was left of it, dangled over the side of the boat. Most of the rest of his body was visible through the charred gash in the boat's side. He was half-immersed in the brackish salt water. As the boat sunk, the water was bubbling up all around him, consuming him. At the angle at which he lay, his head, if he still had one, would have been wholly immersed.

I'd promised myself I wouldn't grieve for Jonathan, not until I had the time – but, as you've already seen, I wasn't good at keeping promises to myself.

There was a reason why, after all this, it took a long time for me to trust myself to get close to someone again. I still have nightmares about how I felt then, looking into the wreckage of that boat and seeing Jonathan. Imagining it happening to Rachel, or Inez, or, hell, my little dog Pip.

Even at the time, I knew what I'd seen had affected me, but I thought I'd still be able to brush it off. I still thought I could get out unscarred.

I didn't know that this was just the first blow.

I'll say one good thing about myself: it did not take long for grief to crystallize into rage. First at Jonathan, the idiot. And then at this guard, and whoever it was he represented. Twice now, they had tried to kill me. Twice they had missed, and gotten people close to me instead. And for what? Because I'd started chasing a half-remembered face, on a whim?

These guys were professionals. Best cybersecurity measures either I or the hacker I'd hired had seen in a long time. If they were that well guarded in electronic space, they'd no doubt have better out here. More than cameras, more than armed guards. Surveillance the likes of which it would be a mistake to try to predict. (Even I hadn't expected them to have security, certainly not of the shoot-first type, this far out. Goes to show that, in this business, no matter how paranoid you are, you're not paranoid *enough*.)

The soldier who'd killed Jonathan uttered a vicious curse. It didn't seem to be at the state of the body. No, from the ease with which he prodded Jonathan's body with his booted foot, this man seemed inured to gore. "No," he said to his headset, spitting it like it was poison. I stifled my breathing, trying to overhear as much as I could.

He pulled something out of his ear in disgust, waited. Probably getting lectured. After a moment, he plugged it back in.

"Heavily armed. Coming to stir up trouble, at the very least. No sign of… no, sir."

We'd stumbled into some kind of sting operation. I wondered if the person this guard expected to see down there had been me. I got a chill down my back. Hard not to feel like people kept walking across my grave.

"Yes, sir. I'll bring him in for ID."

I risked pulling back a pair of reeds to get a better view. The soldier was dressed in all black, just like the sniper in Denver.

After sharing a few more words with whoever was on the other side of the radio, my assailant hoisted himself out of water and disappeared into a patch of trees. I was just getting ready to follow when I heard the rumble of a motor. A beat-up gray pickup truck pulled into view. Conspicuously out of place among the expensive weapons hardware he'd just used against me, but still well camouflaged for the area. It was rusted out, weighed down by age. Had someone passing by discovered it, they probably would have figured it was just an abandoned vehicle.

Sure enough, when my ears cleared enough that I could pay attention to the motor, it *purred*. Not at all what a mistreated old clunker of a truck should sound like. The skin was just that: a covering.

He loaded Jonathan's body onto the truck, dumping it unceremoniously into the bed. While he was doing that, I was already swimming across the inlet. I pulled myself up onto drier land behind a patch of trees that had bent inward at a forty-five degree angle, like some hurricane or other had just about ripped them off their roots. They looked how I felt. The pain of the shockwave's body-blow was just catching up with me as the adrenaline of the attack faded. My cuts' stinging had turned into a scream.

One cure for that was more adrenaline. As the truck pulled onto a slender dirt road threading through the marsh's dry spots, I darted after it. I kept my head low, keeping out of his mirrors. I lunged for the truck bed's door and pulled myself onto it.

The next time the truck slowed, I unlatched from the door and swung myself underneath. Another thing the truck had going for it: good suspension. Other than getting the skin scraped off my back a couple times, the ride was almost comfortable.

The truck and its driver *had* been far from home base. Waiting for us, possibly, or maybe they just had a very wide security net. We stopped briefly outside a gate and guardhouse for an inspection. The truck was passed right through without anyone checking underneath. Love it when an improvised plan comes together.

What little of the compound I could see from my angle was illuminating. A cluster of tiny gray-green buildings, colored to blend in with the marsh. Had those been all that they seemed to be, they couldn't have held much. But the buildings were small enough, and spaced far enough from each other, to hint at a significant underground presence.

Camouflaged or not, the buildings *still* should have shown up on satellite photography. But I'd checked more than one source, and nada. That meant one of two things. First option: cooperation from all the databases I'd checked through, both public and private, from commercial search engines to NASA. That would have meant a lot of people, and a lot of money. Second: it could have meant that someone had, after the databases had been put together, hacked into them and smoothed over the ground. Stitched together other pieces of landscape, or digitally altered the buildings out of existence.

Given what I'd seen so far, my money was on the second option. This operation was well funded, expertly crafted, but their operating principle seemed to be *the fewer people involved, the better*. Maybe if my hired hacker had stayed alive, seen the maps, he would have been able to spot the artifacts, the copied landscapes, that would have given it away.

I had just missed it. Negligence.

All very interesting, but I couldn't do anything about it now aside from feel more and more uneasy. The truck stopped outside one of the smaller buildings. The driver hopped out. He was met by three men and a gurney. They dumped the body onto the gurney and took it toward the building. There was a ramp around that building's back entrance, apparently for just this kind of thing.

The truck started up, kept going. I waited until it had rounded a corner before detaching, rolling to the side.

There were no guards posted on the exterior of any of the buildings. I did note plenty of cameras, though. I had no choice but to hide in the ditch until sunset.

Night wasn't too far away, but it was still excruciating. I ever mention how much I hate mosquitoes?

Still – don't do anything you hate without squeezing some bit of worth from it, even if you have to do it like a rolled-up tube of toothpaste. I did learn something from the wait. There was nobody around. I heard a distant rumble of another truck, a pair of muffled voices – maybe from behind one of the doors – but that was it. Even if somebody had taken a search plane directly overhead, looked down at the right time, they wouldn't have seen much more than a cluster of buildings like shacks and some beat-up trucks. At best, unremarkable grinding poverty for rural Florida. At worst, a drug-smuggling operation. Both more innocent than what was actually going on here.

Coils of thick black greasy smoke churned into the sky from the building I'd seen the three men enter. The chimney was maybe overlarge, but otherwise looked just like you might expect on a rural cabin. But the smoke didn't seem like wood smoke. Didn't smell like it, either.

I never saw any of the men who'd entered the building exit it. Either they were all still there, or my guess about this complex having a massive underground presence was dead-on.

One of the many downsides of spending so much time alone is that my imagination won't let me get too lonely. It conjures faces, voices, to keep me company. Sometimes friends. Sometimes enemies.

I couldn't get Jonathan out of my head. I felt him, lying there beside me.

"You weren't able to save a single weapon?" he asked.

Most of our arms had been on the boat. I'd carried my personal weapons on me, a Desert Eagle and a Beretta 92FS... but they hadn't survived water immersion. I'd ditched them before leaving the marsh.

He asked, "How many ways could you have done this better?"

It was a fair question. I hadn't been ready at all. Twice

now, I'd been caught off guard by opposition I hadn't seen any reason to expect. Certainly, after the first assassination attempt, I felt like I'd been on high alert. But that hadn't been high enough.

After the hacker died, I should have been more aware. I'd stepped on somebody's toes, somehow. I should have felt it.

"Do better," he told me. It was a demand. A job he was giving me.

Even all the time we'd spent together – even after I'd gone to bed with him, never mind that it had just been once – I felt like I barely knew him. But I still saw him. Heard him. Felt him.

Pathetic, huh?

Well, that's what happens to you when you're alone for so long. You get pathetic.

I'm better these days, but I have Inez and Rachel to thank for that. Back then? Different matter. That was the whole reason I'd come out here to begin with – seeking that kind of connection, a feeling of family, that I'd only ever been able to invent for myself.

Or remembered feeling with that face.

After too many hours of listening to Jonathan, the sun touched the treetops. Time to move. With sunset to the west and most of the base to the east, the cameras – infrared or otherwise – would have a hard time balancing against the glare.

I couldn't avoid all the cameras, though, so I didn't bother to try. Just had to hope no one was watching live. If they pulled up the footage after the fact and found me…

Well, it wouldn't matter by then.

I wasn't planning on keeping meek and silent for long. I wanted answers. And, more than that, right now I wanted blood.

I'm pretty good about riding my rage, keeping it in check until I have an opportunity to inflict it on somebody. But I was having trouble now. It was something about this place. It was more than the mosquito bites, more than the itchiness of the swamp sludge drying on my skin and hair, more than the never-fading pain from the cuts. Something about this place had reached deep inside of me, found a deep chord of anger, and *twanged*. There are a million different shades of hate, and I hadn't felt this one in a long time. But it was familiar. I could have placed it, if I'd wanted.

I sped down the ramp the men had taken the gurney. Quietly, I popped the door open and ducked through – and right into a smell of blood, ammonia cleaner, ash, and heat thick as a brick wall.

It took a moment for the rest of my senses to catch up with my nose. The room was rectangular, much longer than it was wide. The walls were filthy, ash-stained cement. The ducts of some kind of complex ventilation system ran overhead, no doubt linked to the disguised chimney. And, at the far side of the room, on the other side of a row of cabinets, was an enormous, industrialized metal box with all the aesthetic appeal of a water heater. It stood three times as tall as I was, and it was thrumming like an engine. I could feel the vibrations in the cement floor, through my boots.

All the heat in the room emanated from it. It was an incinerator. Sized for bodies.

It took my eyes a second to adjust to the bright fluorescents on the other side of the door. Fortunately, the incinerator technician wasn't all that observant. He was facing away, checking something on his machine. I had plenty of time to hide among the cabinets and empty gurneys on my side of the room.

The technician was singing something to himself. Poorly. Some kind of crooning folk song. It told me a couple of things. He didn't expect any of his companions to stumble upon him and embarrass him. And he was comfortable with what he was doing. He'd done this before.

The incinerator wasn't large enough to burn more than one corpse at a time, but the fact that it was even here spoke volumes. Nobody got units like this to dispose of documents. These were for bodies, and only bodies.

And this facility produced enough of them that they expected to get a lot of use out of it.

The technician was alone. More evidence that, whoever these people were, they were short-staffed. Just about every body disposal I'd ever witnessed[13] hadn't been a solo operation. At the very least, you needed someone to listen to the jokes you told. People who work with corpses are real freaking comedians.

There was no sign of Jonathan. The coiled black smoke had started maybe an hour after I'd seen them take him in. There wouldn't be much left of him now.

All the pent-up rage I'd bottled since the first time I'd been shot at – since I'd watched the hacker's forehead explode – came rushing back up on me.

---

13 Need to do a surprising amount of that in this business.

One of my weaknesses is that, between the moment when somebody recognizes what's about to happen to them and when the violence really begins, I like to wait a bit. Let it sink in. Give them a second to think about all of the decisions they'd made that had led us both to this point.

I cleared my throat. "Hello," I said.

The technician made a show of it. He opened with a double-take. His shock turned to recognition, to terror, to acceptance. A real one-man play.

Given my choice of violences, I prefer firearms. The *pop* and kickback are all I need from life sometimes. But feeling someone's teeth crack loose against my knuckles is a close second.

By the time I released the technician's collar, let him slump to the floor, my anger had only darkened. Usually the first burst of violence helped. It didn't get rid of the rage, but crystallized it, helped me focus. Not this time. My head was still a fog of hate.

I didn't, even then, have any inkling of what I'd actually found. I wonder if I could have recognized it if I'd let myself – what I could have pieced together if I'd stopped and thought about it for a moment.

But it wouldn't have done me any good to figure it out then. It would've just made the rage worse.

SIX
SOMEWHERE, FIFTEEN YEARS AGO

I told you hate has a million textures. One of them and I went a long way back. It was the first thing I remember feeling.

Memory is a funny enough thing even when it hasn't been tampered with, and my memories of childhood definitely have been. It's not something I talk about all that often. But my first memories come a lot later than most people's. The earliest I can remember is seven, maybe eight years old. And only then in bits and pieces. Maybe that's for the best, considering the kinds of things I *can* remember.

But it still makes me anxious. Those memories were stolen from me. Someone went in my head, ripped them out.

I have real intimacy issues. And someone getting that intimate with my head makes me sick thinking about it. Which is one of the reasons why I try not to.

I grew up in a cage, remember. Being studied, prodded, poked, and finally tormented and tortured. Even considering involuntary repression, I don't remember as much of it as I should.

Damnedest thing is, I don't remember what I did to get *out* of there, either.

There are still days when what I remember is too much.

I grew up in a facility called Project Armageddon. Things just got cheerier from the name.

I remember my room – which I now properly think of as *my cell*. It was joined to a common room with a bunch of other cells, all belonging to other kids. All my age. Several times per day, we would be let out – sometimes to get exercise, but most often just to the common room, where we would meet, play, or listen to one of the lab coats pretend to be a teacher.

At the start of it, my cell was filled with things. Puzzles. Blocks. Colorful books and reading tools. Nothing that said too much about the outside world, but the lab coats hadn't wanted us to grow up unstimulated. Sometimes there were even toys. I remember being given a doll. Not knowing what else to do with it, I turned it into a play-weapon against the other kids. It swung well, especially gripped by the feet. Satisfying.

As we grew older, I needed more than play-weapons.

The lab coats did not like it when we got along together too well. They turned classes into competitions with rewards and punishments – real painful punishments – attached. Everything was a zero-sum game. When there could only be winners and losers, and losers got their cell run through with random electric currents for so many nights in a row that even an adult would have broken down from sleep deprivation, you did everything you could to be a winner. "Playtime" became the worst part of the day. That was when the lab coats left all us kids alone in the common room and pretended not to supervise. I tried to stay to myself, or, at best, to avoid the rapidly forming gangs who targeted the rest. Only in-fighting among the gangs gave the rest of us any respite.

I'd like to say I held my own, but I was a kid. I wasn't as vicious as I could have, should have, been. I was still learning to harden. And I would have a long time to go on learning it.

I hope the lab coats got their day's entertainment in, watching us turn on each other. I'm not sure if things were getting worse for them in the outside world, or if they had planned this all along, but they started getting meaner. They took away the things they'd left us in our cells, until, eventually, we only had plain gray walls, a bed, a sink, and a toilet.

We knew we were being manipulated. The lab coats didn't bother to hide it. But knowing it didn't make a difference, not when the punishments were so severe.

Then the tests. At first, they were every other week. Then every week. Then every other day.

They took me to an office, where they sat me down in front of a contraption. A flashlight had been mounted on a stand and aimed at a sheet of paper with a slit cut through it. The light shone through the slit and onto a copper plate.

They started by just having me stare at it. That was fine. That wasn't getting shocked, sleep deprived, or beaten up. But, eventually, they asked me to change the silhouette the light made when it fell through the slit. I reached for the sheet of paper, and they smacked my hand away. Apparently I was supposed to change it without touching anything.

This is one of the places where my memory, mercifully, gets foggy. I think the shocks and the sleep deprivation were affecting my ability to *make* memories. I'm sure our food was drugged. But it still seemed like there was more to it than that.

There were other tests. Sometimes they rolled a handful of dice in front of me and gave me a little – at first – shock when the dice came up anything but all sixes. Or they shuffled a deck of cards, made me draw one, and shocked me every time it wasn't a joker. They never told me what they wanted, or why.[14] I think my not knowing was crucial to their tests.

I compared notes with some of the other kids I was still on speaking terms with. The tests were all different. I was the only one who got the screen and light, or the dice and cards. Some kids were being asked to lift impossible weights. Others were asked, over and over again, what object the lab coats had set behind an opaque partition, or to guess what was on the lab coats' minds. Or to put out a little fire by looking at it.

Some word from the outside world filtered down to us. Mostly through eavesdropping on the lab coats, or the echo of a radio bouncing down the corridors. And that word was that not everybody had been born equal. I knew that; believe me, I *knew* I was at the bottom rung. But some people were born even more different than others. Cursed, it seemed like, from the way the outside world was treating them.

It did not take long for it to dawn on us that we were among the cursed.

Mutants, they called us, but I heard plenty of other words. Muties. Abominations. Freaks. Dangers. Little terrors.

---

14 It would be a long time before I manifested, or understood, what I was doing to luck.

When we were old enough to have figured that out, things changed. The only time the lab coats guarded their tongues around us – the only time they were nice to us – was when they were about to take us for more tests, or do something more horrible. I don't know what they wanted from us, but they weren't getting it.

That was when some of the kids started disappearing.

It was almost a relief at first. The earliest to be taken had been two of the worst bullies among us. Although I had gotten one of the two to permanently leave me alone with a wellaimed nut-kick, I still hated them. And while I was a little uneasy, looking into their empty cells, the hate still outweighed it. One of the millions of flavors of hate I was still acquainting myself with.

But then more of us kept disappearing. Kids I was indifferent to; kids I liked. The lab coats never said where they went. After a certain time, we were afraid to ask. The lab coats seemed to find excuses to shock us more when we did. They gave us plenty else to focus on. The competitions never got easier, and the strange tests became more frequent.

A dozen of us disappeared in one day. There were only five of us left.

We were still let out into the common room every day, but we stayed away from each other. We knew what was coming. I think the lab coats were maybe hoping we would finish each other off, but we had wised up to their tricks by then. We weren't participating any more. In our own individual ways, we braced ourselves for the end.

Eventually, I was the only one left.

I only remember a few things after that point. My memory

has great big holes in it, like dough stretched too far.

Close to the end, before the last of the other kids were taken away, I figured out that the lab coats were more interested in me than any of the others, but also that I frustrated them more. They were looking for something, and I was *close* to giving them what they wanted. But not quite there. They kept playing card tricks. Dice tricks. Punishing me when things didn't turn out the way they wanted.

They graduated from physical torture to emotional extortion. At one point, they gave me a kitten, told me I had to take care of it. I knew what they were doing. They only ever gave you things to take them away.

They thought that they might coerce me into showing them *whatever* they wanted to see if they threatened something important to me. Knowing didn't keep me from falling right into their trap. Even back then, I thought I was hard, but I wasn't hard enough.[15] I fell for the cat.

I made grand plans to smuggle my cat to safety through air vents too small to fit me. But they struck sooner than I had expected, before I could arrange any of that. Two of the lab coats took me to an office. They held my cat in front of a stun gun, and told me that, unless I showed them what they wanted, they were going to use the gun on my cat.

The stun gun would just hurt a person. It would *kill* a small animal. They thought they could force some kind of demonstration from me. Turns out they were onto something.

Getting me emotionally invested in something, feeling so strongly about something that my own life might as well have

---

[15] Not like now, of course… just ask my puppy.

been in danger, was one way to get my luck to manifest.

As one of them moved the stun gun in, the other chose just the wrong[16] instant to sneeze. His head swung down, toward the prongs.

The electric arc leapt right into his eye.

I had no idea what was happening, what I had just done, or even whether I had done anything. The only thing I knew was that the lab coats blamed me for what had happened. That was when they gave me my brand. A permanent mark, over my eye, so that every time I looked into my cell's mirror I would remember the pain I'd experienced when they'd given it to me.

I don't remember what happened to the kitten. One of the gaps in my memory swallowed it.

All I know is that, when I got out of there, she was gone.

The longest, biggest hole in my memory ripped open after the incident with the cat. That was the last I remembered of the lab coats or the Project Armageddon facility.

The next thing I could remember, I was out in the world.

For a long while, that was all I thought I needed to know. This is not a time I wanted to think much about. I don't remember feeling like anything was missing. First thing I can remember for sure is standing outside the Church of the Sacred Heart in downtown Chicago on an icy December night. My lips were chapped and bleeding. My fingers and toes were so cold that I dreaded warming them up almost as much as I did staying out there. At least now they were numb.

---

16 And the right.

The pain of warming them up would have been a terrible, deep-down kind of hurt, like making a hundred little needles out of my bones.

Funny thing is, one of the things I can remember most clearly is the feeling that I hadn't just gotten there. I knew *exactly* what warming my hands up after being that numb would feel like. I had been out in the world for days, for weeks, maybe for months. The open sky was no longer overwhelming. Snow was no longer otherworldly and enchanting, just mundane and deadly.

I can't remember what happened in any of that time. Repressed trauma, maybe. *Maybe*. It didn't bother me because I felt like my memory was intact, and I didn't want it anyway.

I wished I knew how I got out of there. I wanted to know if I had hurt any of the lab coats on my way out. And I wanted to know where the place was, so that one day I could come back and hurt them again.

It was all gone, like a month-old dream.

Standing outside the Church of the Sacred Heart might as well have been an image from one of those dreams. It was a fragment of memory without a beginning or an end.

I don't remember meeting Father Rudolpho Boschelli. Just like the outside world itself, the first time I remembered him, it was as if he had been in my life for a long time.

He said he remembered meeting me. I never wanted to ask him about it, but he told me the story, several times. Usually as a reminder of how far we came afterward.

He said I looked at him like I already knew him. Like I'd seen his type a hundred times before.

Like there was no point in him saying anything because I'd already heard it. Like we were soldiers on opposite sides of the front lines. Like we were generals – well, he had a different metaphor every time.

The point is, I made an impression. Enough that, even months after I'd settled into the Church of the Sacred Heart's underfunded orphanage and our relationship had evolved in a different – if not necessarily better – direction, he kept returning to that story.

I had to take him at his word.

It seemed so normal – not having all that memory of things I really didn't want to remember. None of it felt strange. All of the kids at the Church of the Sacred Heart had parts of our lives we didn't want to talk about. Only natural to assume that the rest of them couldn't fully remember it either.

It was only much later, when I had the presence of mind to *want* to think of that part of my life, that I realized how odd that was.

Well – *realize* is the wrong word, because I already knew it. It was just the first time I let myself think it.

But by then any trace of my path back "home" had vanished. All I was left with was the brand over my eye, and several of the million shades of rage.

SEVEN
CHICAGO, NOW

The day after I told Rebecca Munoz I'd accepted her job, I called Inez and Rachel in to help me study and infiltrate Dallas Bader Pearson's compound.

Always nice to have good friends to watch your back, cover for your weaknesses – like being caught off guard. Or spending so much time in your own head that you start bouncing off the inside of your skull. But I worry, as always, that my luck will do something to get them hurt. Divert a bullet meant for me into one of them. Or a knife, or a laser, or a freaking vampire merman, or anything else my luck has helped me escape in the past.

Inez and Rachel can more than hold their own in a tight spot. They know the risks and still say they wouldn't dream of leaving. My luck, almost as if it knows how important they are to me, has left them alone. So far.

One of the hazards of working as a merc is a certain paucity of... shall we say "subtle" resources. Shoon'kwa – Atlas Bear to you – our exiled Wakandan teenager,[17] had joined my posse not too long ago and brought her hypertech airship with her. But that was more than this mission called for. The problem with bringing in the big guns on a small-scale mission is that the big guns tend to draw lots more attention. There were plenty of groups – heroic, villainous, and otherwise – who, if they saw a Wakandan ship zeroing in on Chicago, might think we were gunning for them. Last damn thing I wanted was a firefight erupting over the skies of Chicago before we ever got to our destination.

That meant commercial travel. And that meant, already, one of my posse had problems. I spoke with Shoon'kwa over secured video. She was in San Francisco too, in some hotel room somewhere. Inez was reclined in a seat behind Shoon'kwa, her hat over her eyes. I was surprised Shoon'kwa had joined the others. She's not the partying type. But we all need company sometimes. It's been a long time since she's been home.

It was just about dawn there, but she didn't look tired. She doesn't sleep much. Precognitive abilities, especially precognitive abilities that will only show different ways the world could end, will do that to a teenager.

"Why, in the name of… of anything at all," she asked, "would I trust my life to one of those aluminum and plastic tubes?"

I would have sworn Inez was asleep, but she lifted her hat, and said, "She's got a point, peaches. I've just gotten used to not traveling in those flying fart cans." Most kinds of air travel

---

17 She's a tremendous little bundle of anger and violence – why I love her so much.

pale once you've flown Wakandan.

"Because," I said, "I said so, and I'm the boss."

Shoon'kwa glowered. I'm not sure I've ever seen her happy. Satisfied, yes. But that's different from being happy. She's got an awful lot of weight on her shoulders. Not just precognition, but also the whole exiled-from-her-nation thing…

Trying a different tack, I said, "I don't want the quarry to see us and you don't exactly fly quiet."

"I've never had to fly quiet," she said.

"I'm not the quiet type, either, but we do whatever the job needs, and this job needs me to make sure that no one gets too curious about us."

Shoon'kwa leaned back in her seat, folded her arms. Like Black Widow and White Fox, she was new to the team, and we were still feeling out what was and what wasn't worth fighting over. I still didn't trust her, and she didn't trust me. All standard rough edges when you're putting together a team. Been there before.

"I think," she said, deliberately, "my craft requires maintenance after all those holes we blew in it in Buenos Aires. We would all be better served if I worked on it."

She thought she was fooling me. She had no intention of staying behind. I could see the flicker of the lie in her eyes. I could have called her out but, like I said, I was still feeling out what was worth a fight.

"Fine," I said. "Inez. Get Rache and anybody else who wants to come along. But fly commercial. Come quiet. Clear?"

"Clear as high noon in Tombstone," Inez said.

That gave me half a day on my own to get started. Plenty of time.

A good part of my job is learning fast, adapting on the fly. When Rebecca Munoz hired me, I'd been away from Chicago for so long that I'd never heard of Dallas Bader Pearson.

Support your local libraries, kids. They're more helpful than you think. *Especially* in the smartphone age. Dallas Bader Pearson and his type are all SEO experts, and do all their best lying over the Internet and on social media. So I got myself to the Harold Washington Library. Got into their newspaper archives. Got cracking.

Dallas Bader Pearson had gotten himself into the city council, put onto all kinds of task forces, from mundane water and utility groups to Chicago's very own human rights commission. The most vital thing in the world to Pearson seemed to be that people thought of him as important. He billed himself as a religious leader, which was fine enough so long as nobody started looking too much into what kind of religion that meant. The secret to success in local politics is to just not shut up – not once, not ever – and Pearson was very good at that. He did a very good job of playing the victim, the unjustly persecuted innocent. He said it was a federal government plot to repress him and the downtrodden folks he was so privileged to represent. Even the people who weren't buying what he was selling tended to give in eventually, if only to get him to shut up, and to move on to more important business.

As to what his Church of the Spiritual Revolution stood for and believed in – he used to do a good job of keeping that vague. As far as people on the outside knew, he was an outsider activist, a priest who devoted his ministry to social advocacy, fighting racism and poverty, and whose religion was an important driver of his politics. Inside, the millenarianism started: the numerology, the prophecies, the anti-government paranoia, the belief in an imminent cleansing apocalypse, a nuclear war. Outside his compound, his most widely known belief was that he believed that someday he'd have ten thousand followers, and that only those ten thousand would come with him to Paradise.

I wasn't able to find much specific about the rest. If he kept it vague and nebulous on the outside, it was probably a different kind of vague and nebulous on the inside. The important thing to people like Pearson is power. Not power as in government power, or power as in military people, but power over people.

He wanted people wrapped around his little finger. It was a psychological need, a fixation. It didn't matter how he got them that way so long as he did. The words were just a means to that end. He could have even sincerely believed what he said, but, if he'd found he would have gotten more followers by disavowing it entirely, he would have.

Over the past two years or so, it all started to go downhill for Pearson.

He wasn't on the city council any more. He'd lost his voters, and just about everyone outside his group who'd been willing to put up with him. It started with a support group of former church members. People who'd gotten suckered into his movement, seen the crazier, abusive things happening in its deeper levels, and got out. They'd been joined by the concerned family members of people still trapped inside. They raised a big stink about what was happening in his church, and, like Pearson, they never quit.

That had gone on for years. It never got out of hand for Pearson until a couple local publications, and then the *Chicago Tribune*, got wind of them (and got over Pearson's preemptive threats to sue them for libel). Believe it or not, people still read newspapers in this day and age. The *Tribune* exposé made a big difference.

Pearson did his best when everybody in Chicago knew his name, but didn't think too much about how he'd earned it. Now people knew all about the apocalyptic millenarianism that, until then, he'd saved for his most devout followers.

A couple of years ago, Pearson might have had a shot at snatching a party nomination for mayor. There was talk that, after one of Illinois's senators resigned in disgrace, Pearson was on the governor's short list of candidates for a replacement appointment.[18]

Now no one admitted to knowing him, let alone voting for him.

It started with a pair of sexual harassment allegations at city hall, quickly hushed up.[19] But the stir roused the attention of some independent journalists, one of whom managed to get in touch with two former members of Pearson's inner circle. The exposé that resulted was thorough, well documented, and devastating. And prompted journalists from all over the country to pile in like monkeys into a barrel. Soon, Dallas Bader Pearson couldn't set foot outside his compound without being mobbed by journalists. So eventually he just didn't leave.

---

18 Funny how all the anti-federal-government rhetoric in the world disappears as soon as someone offers you a position of power in it.

19 You know how many people say they'll listen to victims and then immediately don't.

The stories that came out were salacious.

During meetings of his inner circle, he would single someone out – almost didn't matter who – for public humiliation. He would force everyone else to come up with something they hated about that person, riled them up to screaming and shouting, sometimes violence. He called it "emotional clarification." Next week, the person he'd targeted would be right back with all the others, screaming and shouting at the next victim. It was a way to pull apart any alliances that might be forming in his inner circle, and draw every member closer to him. And a way to uncover more of their emotional vulnerabilities.

He sold himself as more than a preacher, more than a guru, more than a prophet. His followers were supposed to have no life outside of him. He targeted vulnerable people. People beaten down by poverty, abusive families, physical or mental illness, or just plain lost in life. He had agents planted throughout his congregation. Whenever someone new came, those agents would welcome them, pretend to be their friends, find out why they'd come. When the mark met Pearson himself, Pearson miraculously knew what they wanted, and had some words on how to get it. They all led to getting more involved with his church.

He put his followers to work. "Community projects" like proselytizing, gardening in the compound, cooking and cleaning, caring for the elderly retired folks shut up in the church's dormitories, watching children kept separate from their families… and eventually becoming agents like the ones who'd manipulated them into joining. They were put on starvation rations, told that any more was decadent and materialistic. Some members only got three hours of sleep for days at a time. Anything to keep them strung out and weary, too dead-eyed to resist.

He encouraged his members to bring their families to his church, especially if those families included children or the elderly – people not really in a position to say no. He had a special knack for the elderly. He took them right out of retirement homes. The more dependent, the better. What he didn't tell people was that, once inside, families were swiftly separated. Pearson called it "communal living." It was blackmail. If one of Pearson's followers decided to leave, it was nigh-impossible to do it any way but alone. Some of the people interviewed in the exposé and the articles that followed had left behind parents. Siblings. Children.

Why did he do it? Dallas Bader Pearson wasn't a masked super villain. He (probably) didn't have a grand project or end goal. If I had to bet on anything, it was a combination of psychopathy and raw emotional neediness. Pearson was a greedy, craving creature. He accepted money, but it wasn't money he was most concerned with. It was attention. Getting a reaction. Earning adoration. Everything in his life was structured around these things, like a junkie's. He would destroy his followers' lives to get it.

Now, *some* of the exposé and all of the articles that came out afterwards must have been sensationalized nonsense. Things that get a lot of media attention usually are.

I didn't care what was true and what wasn't. What was important was the degree to which the Munoz twins, Rose and Joseph, were going to resist being pulled out of there.

And if they were under as much control as Pearson sought

to exert over them, the answer was going to be "with every possible means."

Even if they no longer believed in his religion – and I doubted anyone in Pearson's inner circle really believed – they knew that, by the standards of the outside world, they were dead. And they probably thought, sometimes correctly, they'd burned all their bridges with their family. For Pearson's closest associates, the only way to keep going was to stay in.

It might have just been easier to just drag Rose and Joseph Munoz out of the compound in a sack, and dump them on Rebecca's doorstep. Let them sort it all out. But they would be right back at Pearson's compound the next day.

Doing that would have fulfilled the letter of the job, but not the spirit. I'm a professional. I don't shirk.[20]

No matter how many times I tried to focus on the Munoz twins, my thoughts kept circling around to Pearson. It wasn't that I expected to pit myself against Pearson himself. That wasn't what I'd been hired to do. It wasn't what was best for the Munoz twins. I was never going to help them by doing something so simple as killing him.

One of the reasons I hadn't wanted to take this job was because I'd always known it wouldn't be anything so neat and tidy as a shootout or a fist fight.

Though I would be lying if I told you I wasn't thinking about coming back, after the Munoz twins were out, and killing Pearson anyway. I probably wouldn't have had to spend much time fishing, either. Surely *someone* in this city

---

[20] OK, OK, but I swear I had good excuses for the times I did. Like my employers backstabbing me. But Rebecca Munoz wasn't one of those employers.

must have wanted Dallas Bader Pearson assassinated. All I had to do was let them find me.

That was how I finally got comfortable with this job. I started thinking of it as a dry run. Target acquisition. The next time I came back, I was going to kill Dallas Bader Pearson. And that was going to feel as good as the rest of this job felt miserable.

Rage, as always, is a hell of a motivator.

Interesting thing about Pearson's political career: though he ran as a religious man, he rarely centered his religion. To the outside world, he took care to appear, at his most extreme, like a preacher whose sermons were more about social justice than anything to do with faith. Nothing about his "spiritual revolution." That was for the insiders.

It said a few things about him. He was smart enough to know how his hokum sounded like hokum to anyone who hadn't already bought in. He didn't believe a word of what he was saying.[21] He was one of those self-important showboats who had whole walls full of photographs he'd taken with celebrities. He knew what was most important to him – gratifying his own ego.

He must have justified it to his followers by saying that the more outsiders he won over, the more easily he could convert others when the time came. And they believed him because they'd believed things that were far harder to swallow. Easier to believe than to leave.

One of the big mistakes people make with a movement like this is thinking that it can be defeated by rational argument.

---

21 At least he hadn't when he'd still been on the city council.

By poking at its flaws and internal inconsistencies. But nobody gives half a pigeon's crap about logic and consistency. It's all about emotional attachment, about *belonging*. Guys like Dallas Bader Pearson understand that intimately. They're the kind who say they'll debate anyone, and they will. But they won't even try to argue reasonably. That's why they'll win.

People don't respond to reason. They respond to what men like Dallas Bader Pearson are selling.

A long time ago, I would have insisted, to you and to myself, that I was better than that. Beyond brainwashing. That I never would let myself fall so far into anyone's power. But that's self-deception. Just another kind of weakness.

One of the ways that manipulative dipsticks like Dallas Bader Pearson trap you is by convincing you that you really *are* infallible – that you couldn't have fallen for a conman. After all, if you had fallen so far in hock to a conman, given so much of your life to him already, that would make you some kind of loser. If you don't admit it, you're not a loser, right? It's Exploiting Insecurities 101. Conmen study this stuff as humorlessly as accountants study tax law.

I'm not gonna lie. Not in these pages. I'm plenty insecure, a lot of the time. First, best step to being stronger is to recognize that.

And I'm strong as hell – which means facing down all those kinds of insecurities. Constantly. With a dead eye.

And a dead aim.

EIGHT

I was still putting together my psychological profile by the time Inez and Rachel arrived. They came with White Fox and Black Widow.

They arrived via airplane and then rideshare, and looked none too happy about it. Four people crammed into the back seat of a tiny Camry all the way from the airport to the Harold Washington Library. This right after they'd just gotten used to traveling Wakandan style.

Well, I came here flying commercial too, so they could all deal with it. I was still irked with Inez over the state of that apartment. Inez had dressed just as light as usual, but, to my incredible chagrin, didn't even shiver as she stepped out of the rideshare. Like me, Inez is a mutant. Her gifts include super-strength and super-endurance. There are times when I wonder if super-cold-resilience is part of the package.

Rachel, more sensibly, was dressed in a lavish violet coat. The fur trim hung nearly to the ground. Even after all the time we've spent together, I'm still seeing her in things I never have before. I have no idea where Rachel keeps all these clothes.

While this outfit did a good job of cutting a shapely figure, it left enough space to conceal the diamond-shaped grenades she always carried with her. Rachel contributed more to the team than just her social graces. She was our explosives and incendiaries expert.

Black Widow and White Fox are newer to the posse – new enough that I still think of them by their assumed names, rather than their given ones – but we've already been through a handful of hells together. And, honestly, I knew more about Black Widow than I'd care to admit. One of the key members of the Avengers? Who *wouldn't* be a little in awe? I still have a couple action figures of her sitting on my shelf.[22] She's one of the few people I hang around with who I know has seen more action than me.[23]

White Fox has only shared a little bit of her history with me, but I knew she was in the running too. She was the last of the kumiho: a nine-tailed fox demon straight out of Korean mythology. They used to take the form of beautiful women to seduce men and devour their hearts. Now she uses that form to blend in. Just looking into her eyes, though, you could see something beyond human in her. She had an inner glow, like moonlight, underneath her eyes. Don't make the mistake of thinking White Fox is beyond human concerns. She will – gracefully, luminously – grind you to paste if you threaten the people and the causes she cares about.

Shoon'kwa, as she had threatened, had stayed behind.

---

[22] They got the hair right… if not the eyes. A dab of black paint does not make an eye.

[23] Though Deadpool's still the title-holder.

Allegedly to finish patching up the holes some of Rachel's explosives had punched in her craft during our last big operation. We'd been working with Tony Stark on that one, and he'd said he'd cover repairs. Still, if it had been *my* giant hypertech airship, I wouldn't have been satisfied unless I'd patched it up myself. So she had an excuse. But an excuse was all it was.

Black Widow said, "If having us take the long way has been some kind of power play, I'm going to be even more disappointed."

"Didn't you used to be a spy?" I asked. "You traveled undercover all the time?"

"When I had to." The message was plain: she didn't think this job was worth her doing anything.

"You didn't have to come along. It'd be nice to have help on this, but I don't need it."

"Call it professional curiosity." A smirk. Still gauging me as a leader. Judging what I'd sign them up for.

"It's hardly that we're against doing the right thing," White Fox said. "But… religious movements, an already half-beaten cult, a pair of adult siblings who've made their own decisions… doesn't it seem a little small fry, after what we've already done together?"

"Then think of it as a nice vacation from saving the world," I said. "For people with our talents, a *small fry* job should be easy, right?"

Funny how often small fry jobs could turn into big, thorny problems. They all knew it. Just because a job didn't call for guns blazing all the time, that didn't mean it was easy. What we'd been asked to do could become a big, messy, emotional horrorshow and they knew it.

"You really are determined to do this, aren't you?" Rachel asked.

"It *is* quite a change from the last time we chatted, peaches," Inez said.

"Yeah. Well. I have my buttons. Consider them pressed."

I haven't been telling you my stories about my battle in the Everglades, and my childhood, for no reason. As I'd been reading about Dallas Bader Pearson, my imagination had jumped back to them, too. Little flashbacks peppered every article. All those memories were knotting together, becoming one big tangle of trauma.

The stories about families bringing their children into Pearson's cult were the first thing that had done it to me. If you want to get on my bad side faster than you can blink, show me a kid in a cage. Next thing had been Pearson's megalomania. His sense of destiny. The ease with which he twisted other people around him, made every effort to appear selfless while doing it. I'd known more than a few monsters like that. One really stuck out in my memory.

Somewhere along the line, it had become important to me. It all left me unsteady on my feet, and it took all of my effort to hide that. The longer this argument went on, the more they'd see it.

So I didn't let it continue. I turned and led them into the library. Decision made. Debate over.

I'd spread my research materials across a table. Splayed-open magazines, newspapers, city planning maps and permits, and – the focus of my past hour – an old *Tribune* "Life & Style" article on Pearson's home in Forest Glen. Complete with an aerial glamour shot of the whole complex.

The article predated Pearson's fall from grace. Still, it was plain that some of Pearson's lifestyle choices had struck the writer as odd. She twisted herself in knots to avoid referring to his movement as a cult. He didn't have a compound, he had a "home open to adherents of his church." His followers weren't creepy zealots, they were "enthusiastic and faultlessly full of praise for the man who'd given them so much."

Whatever. The real prize was the detailed aerial shot of his compound. Pearson, like most cult gurus, was paranoid. But he'd been enamored with fame and praise. His own headline in the "Life & Style" section must have really stoked his ego. So he'd made no objection when the aerial photographer had gotten close in for a detailed shot.

The Church of the Spiritual Revolution had taken over an old, failed boarding school. The school had been a place where families, and sometimes courts, could send "troubled" children in need of a "structured environment." The patina of caring had been so thin they might as well not have bothered. It had been a jail. The story-and-a-half-tall fencing ringing the campus didn't make any pretensions. The top of the fence was bent inward... to prevent anyone from climbing *out*. Parents or judges sent kids they couldn't be bothered dealing with in any other way here.

If I'd been a little less lucky, I could have ended up in a place like this rather than with Father Boschelli.

When the shell game of the school's financial plans caught up with them at last, the whole project folded in a month.[24] Horrible as the boarding school had been, it, like a lot of

---

24 Don't fret about the school's founders – they escaped with hundreds of thousands of dollars of public money.

abominations, had provided jobs to the local community. So the locals hadn't been inclined to ask too many questions when Pearson had bought the whole place up and moved in with all his followers. Such a large church moving in must have seemed like a godsend. A *good investment* in the local economy.

All gone sour now. Pearson hadn't been interested in providing jobs to anyone beyond his loyal followers. Anyone from the outside community who joined his flock quickly had their wealth drained from them, and shortly after cut off ties with friends and family. And then the sexual harassment allegations and the exposé had brought the media vultures swooping down.

The article's writer had been told that about three hundred people were living in the compound, but that information was months out of date. After Pearson had been exiled from city government, he'd called as many of his followers to his compound as were able to come. The boarding school had been like a little college campus: six buildings, including live-in housing for students and faculty, classrooms, a good-sized church with a bell tower, and a single rec building. The dorms were still in use as dorms, and the church for Pearson's sermons. I couldn't find any details on how the other buildings were being used.

What I knew from the investigations that followed the exposé was that the compound was all but sealed up. The fences had been reinforced, and barbed wire added to the top. Guards stood behind the gates, monitored the paths between the buildings, or watched the fences. Mail was supposedly still getting in and out, but I had no doubt that any letters that left the compound had been heavily edited and censored – if not written to script. So far as any article I'd read knew, there was no cellphone access inside the compound. Pearson's followers gave up their worldly possessions when they went inside.

There were definitely more than three hundred people living inside now.

I could sneak past guards, past cameras, past all kinds of electronic surveillance equipment. What I couldn't sneak past was lots of eyeballs. Especially lots of people who knew each other well, and would certainly recognize someone who wasn't acting the way they were supposed to. That would be our first, and maybe our biggest, obstacle. I *couldn't* underestimate it. I'd had an easier time sneaking into paramilitary bases with shoot-on-sight policies than I expected I would have in this place. It didn't matter that the people we were up against weren't trained soldiers or professional killers. This was still going to strain our abilities.

I said, "We'll need a safe way in and a safer, quieter way out. Latter's going to be a lot harder than the former." I nodded to Black Widow. "If you're still of the opinion this is beneath us, you can have that job. You and White Fox are going to help us get in and out, and be on standby if anything goes sour."

If Black Widow still wanted to pick a fight, she didn't choose this moment. I just got some curt nods. Inez watched me for an overlong moment.

I said, "Just because this place isn't a paramilitary base, or a secret government lab, or a freaking alien superfortress – or anything else you've all dealt with – doesn't mean it's going to be a cakewalk. Especially since our goal is to get in without causing much of a fuss, so we don't traumatize or hurt the two people we're there to pull out. And *especially* since we've got to get those people *out* – again without causing a fuss."

I almost would have sworn Rachel pouted. "I suppose you won't have much use for an explosives expert, then," she said.

"Now, now," I soothed. "I didn't say that at all."

NINE
THE EVERGLADES, SIX YEARS AGO

In this business, always come prepared for explosions. I'd brought plenty of grenades, explosives, and incendiaries with me to the Everglades, but they'd all drowned with Jonathan and the boat. I was going to have to improvise.

The incinerator technician had been unarmed, but this room had everything I needed to make some nice fireworks.

The tricky thing about anger issues is that they'll tell you they know what you can do to resolve them. They'll whisper answers into the back of your head, real insidious-like. Their answers don't resolve anything. They're just more fuel. Keep pouring them on, and the fires in your head just get hotter.

In the base under the Everglades, my anger issues had told me that removing the front teeth of the incinerator technician who'd cremated Jonathan would make me feel better. And it had. For a second.

I'd done some quick scouting after knocking out that

technician. Just outside the door, a brightly lit, metal-walled corridor sloped farther down under the earth. As I'd expected, this crematorium was linked to all of the other buildings through underground tunnels. What I *hadn't* expected was how deep this complex went. Someone had put some serious money into digging up this place. The corridor had branched in directions that didn't correspond with any of the buildings on the surface, implying an even deeper structure below.

Whoever these people were, though, this place hadn't been designed to be pleasant to live in. Down one branch of the corridor, offices and living quarters were jammed in together, hardly larger than a walk-in closet. The offices all had transparent walls, so that anyone walking down the corridors would be able to see inside. I was a little surprised the living quarters allowed their occupants any privacy whatsoever.

Another sign the crematorium saw heavy use: there were two empty gurneys just past the door. No padding, no pillow, not even a shroud to hide a corpse. Just straps to keep their cargo from falling out.

I had two entry options: stealthy and subtle, or noisy and chaotic. Stealth had gotten me this far. But I'd already seen some security cameras peering in my direction. Heard voices, idle chatter, from down the hall. There were half a dozen people around, maybe more. If I went on, I was going to be spotted. The tighter quarters wouldn't leave me many places to hide. I didn't think I could count on stealth to get me much farther.

And that – the raging anger issues taking up more and more space in the back of my head told me – would be just fine.

I did all my best work in chaos. I had been on my back feet long enough.

I didn't have long to sort through what was in the room and tally my resources, so I did it as quickly as possible. First thing was the flammables. This room was stocked with all different kinds of cleaning fluids, rags, about a dozen different kinds of aerosols, and hand sanitizer. All innocuous items that, in the hands of someone who knew what they were doing, could do a lot of damage.

I rooted around underneath the incinerator, into the trays where all the ashes were supposed to drop. In the trays, I found teeth, bits and pieces of metal from Jonathan's mechanical watch, shards of charred bone – all the gruesome little bits that a funeral crematory will pick out of Grandpa's ashes before handing it over. I didn't even know why I'd looked. Confirmation, maybe. I hurled the tray against the wall. The dark, greasy ash blended in with the years of filth baked into the walls.

I sized up the incinerator technician's clothes. Unfortunately, I couldn't have made a good disguise out of them. He was just too big. The sleeves would have dangled below my wrists, inhibiting my combat prowess. A stolen uniform wouldn't have kept me hidden except at long range, anyway. These goons' outfitters were the smart kind – no face masks.[25] With the brand over my eye, I'd stand out like a zebra in a horse race. Whatever my plan was, it couldn't include disguises. Just distractions. But there were plenty of

---

[25] Sure, masks help them dehumanize and disassociate, if you're going to order them to commit atrocities. But it makes infiltration *actually* as easy as it looks in the movies.

distractions to be had.

One thing aspiring super criminals always underestimate about underground lairs is how difficult they are to wire safely. Super criminals don't budget much for electricians and regular inspections. Judging by the buildup encrusting the crematorium's walls and ceiling, this place had been built decades ago. I doubted the wiring had been updated since.

I didn't have to search hard to find electrical junction boxes. One was in the crematorium itself, handling the incinerator's power demands. Another sat in the hallway outside. The bundles of wires inside were tangled, tightly bound, and covered in dust from years of neglect. And connected to the security cameras and fire suppression systems.

I knotted a rope of cleaning rags together, dangled one end into the incinerator, and slammed the door shut around it. The other end I sprayed with antiseptic hand sanitizer – alcohol-based – and tied it around a bundle of aerosol cans.

I considered my friend, the incinerator technician, and seriously debated leaving him. The anger had only gotten hotter. There was no way this man had not committed atrocities. But, no matter how I justified it to myself, I couldn't make myself do it. It wasn't fair. I didn't know *for sure* what was going on here. And I might want a hostage later. I dragged him into the hallway and deposited him inside a utility closet.

Then I returned to the crematorium and started the incinerator.

It was hardly the perfect crime. Any half-assed investigation would find the source and cause of the explosion in three heartbeats. But I would be long gone by then.

I backed against the wall. A hollow *poompf* popped my ears.

The heat sucked my breath away. The facility did not skimp on fire safety. The instant I saw the orange-gold reflection of fire shimmer across the walls, the alarms went off. Overhead sprinklers kicked in. But a spray of water was no match for the conflagration I'd unleashed.

Fire licked up the walls and against the crematorium's junction box. I ducked into the hallway, just as a spray of sparks erupted from the box. The lights flickered, and the spray of water attenuated. But both returned to full strength a second later.

A cherry-red fire extinguisher sat behind protective glass. I ripped the extinguisher from its case. Careful to hold it with a pair of rags I'd wrapped around my hand, I smashed its butt into the second junction box. Again, and again, until something gave, and sparks spat out against my arm.

That was too much for the electrical system. The overhead lights died. The alarms dwindled to a whine, and then to nothing. The spray of water dwindled to drips.

A second shockwave of heat popped my ears. The next batch of aerosols had gone off, showering sparks and metal debris across the crematorium. The fire inside the crematorium was the only source of light in the hallway. I slammed the crematorium door shut just as I heard the first shouts of alarm from deeper down the hallway.

I paused for a few seconds, listening for whichever direction seemed to carry the most voices. Then I hurled the fire extinguisher hard down the hall in the opposite direction. It *clanged* off into the dark, where no one would find it.

Then I turned towards the voice. Started running.

Afterimages darted in front of my eyes. Retinal shadows

of fire and sparks. I charged through them, trying to trace my memory of what the hallway had looked like, but mostly just following the voices.

The voices got close. I flattened myself against one wall. Several pairs of heavy, booted feet juddered the floor as they ran in front of me. A blur of motion swirled the shadows.

I waited until about half of them had passed, and then stuck my foot out. My ankle found someone's shin. I hooked around it, yanked back.

A cry of alarm split the darkness. A heartbeat later, I felt a heavy impact through the soles of my boots. Another voice shouted, and then a second heavy impact shook the floor.

The hallway briefly lit fiery orange as one of the first responders opened the crematorium door and yelped. Looking behind me, I saw a figure jump back, beaten away by the heat. Someone else was dashing toward the case where the fire extinguisher had been. I heard another yell of dismay when they found it gone. They started shouting at each other.

They still didn't know I was among them.

Moments like this were what I lived for. I think I was grinning. It was hard to be sure; my attention was split in a hundred different directions.

I saw reflections of a wan light spill down the corridor ahead. Somewhere deeper, the lights were still working. Silhouettes shifted across the walls. More guards, running this way. Again, I shifted to the side.

I waited until one of them was so close that I could see the pale outline of his face. Then I stepped out in front of him and smashed my fist into his jaw so hard his feet left the ground.

He slammed into the next guard, and they both fell to the

ground with a shout. I heard boots squeak on the floor just behind me. Then a voice; someone starting to yell something.

I whirled, letting my elbow lead the way. It made contact with something soft – it felt like someone's throat – and the yell cut off in a choke. I jerked my arm upwards, into his chin, silencing him.

My memory insisted one of the gurneys was nearby. I grabbed around, felt its sharp steel corner. I shoved the gurney hard toward the open crematorium door. The gurney was heavy enough to punch like a torpedo, and the frame was at the right height to catch a person in the small of their back. Half a second later, someone cried out, crashed to the ground.

There were two, maybe three guards left. Their silhouettes were framed by the fire in the crematorium's doorway. They were in abject disarray, shouting for each other and for their fallen comrades. I doubted they knew someone had attacked the others. They were still hunting for the missing fire extinguisher, or trying and failing to cover their eyes from the stinging, acrid smoke.

I could have stayed, finished them off. But I'd done what I needed to. This segment of the complex was lost to chaos and terror, and was down somewhere between half and two-thirds of the nearby guards. But those guards wouldn't be alone. The longer I stayed, the more people would show up.

I took off running. The hall branched several times, but lights only shone down one of them. I followed the lights.

All the security cameras I passed were off. The corridors ahead were bare. Everyone who'd been near had come running to the fire. Distantly, footsteps pounded after me.

A third empty gurney sat by one of the walls. I tried not

to think too hard about what a place like this would need all these gurneys for. Instead, I seized it by its handles and shoved it down another hallway, in the direction I wasn't planning on taking, and took off down the other. I heard another shout, and then a pair of heavy footsteps chasing the noise the gurney had made as it crashed into an office.

On days like the one Rebecca Munoz hired me, it was hard to like my job. In moments like this, it was hard not to *love* it.

The corridor terminated in a round, heavy door like a bank vault. A titanium locking bar jutted through the floor and ceiling just ahead of it. An alphanumeric keypad was mounted in the wall. Numbers one through ten, all the letters, plus a few symbols. Millions of potential combinations.

And now I heard more footsteps, a couple corners away, heading my way.

Good thing I was me. The footsteps even helped convince me my life was in danger, keep that adrenaline going. Activate my talent.

Knowing I would probably only have one shot at this, and acting like I knew exactly what I was doing, I typed a combination.

The locking bar *ka-chunked* as it lifted. The vault door clicked and nudged open.

The vault door was heavy enough that it took an extra few seconds for me to push it open and squeeze inside. But I managed to get to the other side, and get the vault door closed, just before the footsteps rounded the last corner. I felt the locking bar *ka-chunk* again.

I breathed out and reclined against the door.

I found myself facing a hallway narrower than the last. The

steel walls were heavier-duty, and there were far more doors here. Most of those were open.

Power in this section had gone uninterrupted. There were security cameras here too, engaged in idle back-and-forth sweeps. No one had taken control of one to focus on me. Yet. If someone was managing the security systems, likely all their attention was focused on the fire. But still it was only a matter of time.

All that joy and exhilaration came skidding off the edge of a cliff. All it had taken was finding what I'd come here looking for.

The adrenaline let me forget the unaccountable rage prickling the back of my head, and the uncomfortable familiarity of these corridors. If I'd been paying attention, I might even have been able to place it. At the moment, I would have sworn I *was* paying attention. I was looking up and down the halls, into the offices – watching for movement, listening for voices. I should have been looking inside myself, too. At what this place was doing to me. The fury dredging up from nowhere. The need to *hurt* people.

I couldn't explain it. But my failure was that I wasn't even trying. I was just letting the emotions wash over me, with no other critical thought given them.

It wasn't that no other place had ever had this effect on me. It was that one place *had*.

I'd been here before. Not this complex exactly, but a place just like it.

I peered into the open doorways that I passed. They all had a single hard bed, a toilet, a sink, a mirror, and no other fixtures. It did not take much imagination to see that these had been cells. They were larger than a standard prison cell, and seemed only fit to house a single person – but, still, a cell.

I thought again, though I did not want to, of the empty gurneys. The crematorium.

One of the doors, in the middle of the corridor, was still closed. This one just had a deadbolt lock. No elaborate keypad and vault combination. Openable from the outside. I clicked it loose.

The door did not swing inward easily. There was carpet on the other side. The bottom of the door scraped against it.

What I saw on the other side took my breath away.

This was different from the others. It was trying very hard not to *look* like a cell. There was plush, vibrant purple carpeting. A bed with a mattress, several pillows, and – impossibly – a homemade quilt, stitched out of fabric patterned with stars and moon shapes. The sides were worn and threadbare, and the stitching visibly irregular, even at a distance. It was well-used and loved.

The light that spilled over my feet was golden, warmer than the lights I'd seen anywhere else here. Some kind of filter made the lights seem more natural. The walls were morning yellow. A very impressionistic painting of a garden window covered one of them. A bookshelf occupied another wall. It was filled with slender, colorful, hardcover children's books. A fat wooden chest, a stereotypical toy chest, sat against the base of the bed. All kinds of games – board games, dice and puzzle and math and counting games – were scattered messily across the floor.

And, in the center of it all, a slender boy in orange coveralls.

I've always been bad at judging children's ages. It comes

from not having much of a childhood of your own. But this boy couldn't have been more than six, seven years old. He was so thin, it was hard to tell. He had a very fine sheaf of copper hair over a head that seemed too big for him.

He was looking over his shoulder at me. When he saw my face, he started. He scrambled against the back wall – the one with the bad painting of the garden window.

In spite of everything, I suddenly felt guilty. "Hey, hey, hey, hold on," I said, hands raised, palms flat. "Not here to hurt you."

He planted himself flat against the wall, and hugged his knees tight against his chest. His eyes darted to the space between the door frame and my legs, and back again. He was debating running past me.

I could have caught him if he did. But I wondered if he was considering running from me – or running from his cell.

"What the hell is going on here?" I asked, and immediately, absurdly, regretted swearing.

He gave me a good, close look. Like I told you, I could tell when people are looking at the mark over my eye. And this kid was staring right at it.

"You're not Mom," he said.

"Hey, look at you – all observant and everything. Good for you. Can you answer my question?"

I've never been good with kids. Best way to make me feel awkward is to introduce me to a child. If only there'd been some way to let him know that I was almost as scared of him as he was of me.

Somewhere distantly, another alarm was going off. It echoed, muffled, through the vault door. A stress headache thudded behind my temples. Getting out of here was going to be trickier than getting back in. I figured I could still do it. But the window was closing.

"Leave me alone," he said. For such a young kid, his eyes and his voice were like steel.

"I can't do that." The back of my head had been working through everything else I'd seen. The empty cells, the empty gurneys. The crematorium. I was immediately, and instinctively, afraid for this kid. "I can get you out of here, but first can you tell me what this place is?"

"They told me someone like you might come around. Told me what to say. Stay away." His voice raised an octave. "Please."

"Kid – do you *want* to stay here?"

He blinked, as if he needed a moment to process that question. I took that as a no.

"Then come on. We've got to get moving. I'll tell you who I am after you answer my question." I took a step into his cell, reached for his arm.

He said, very carefully: "Fortune makes a fool."

A shock, cold as ice, ran through the center of my back. It was as though someone had jammed an icicle deep into my spine.

I spun, certain that I'd been shot. But the corridor behind me was empty. And when I tried to turn back to the kid, my legs and back wouldn't quite work. A seeping numbness spread through them. It was like I really *had* been shot, my spine perforated.

I stumbled gracelessly to my knees. The kid whimpered at the sound of the impact.

One of the advanced classes at Professor Xavier's institute

will teach you to recognize the signs of post-hypnotic suggestion.[26] It's not the most practical course. By the time you recognize that you've been carrying subconscious instructions inside you, and that they've just been triggered, it's already too late. The machinery of your mind has already been tripped against you. You can't stop the mechanism once it's in motion.

The world tipped. My vision went gray, and then black. I felt my cheek slam onto the metal floor.

If anything happened after that, my memory robbed me of it.

---

[26] In this lifestyle, it comes up often enough that the tropes have been codified.

TEN
CHICAGO, FIFTEEN YEARS AGO

I've known for a long time that my mind had been tampered with. It was the only way the shroud that had fallen over my memory – the one that blocked out when and how I escaped the facility that raised me – made sense. Repressed trauma wasn't a good enough explanation. I remembered all of my other traumas, and too well. It would have been a relief to forget.

The only way I could have gotten out of that facility and not remembered how was if somebody had the power, ability, and need to make me forget.

For such a big revelation, that dawned on me slowly. And only after I realized that other people remembered more of their childhood than I did.

Far too long, my memory loss seemed unremarkable. The other kids couldn't remember when they were very young: infancy, ages two and three, and so on. It never occurred to me that this normal part of childhood development was not analogous to mine. Normal people forgot most parts of being a toddler. Normal people did *not* forget major events that happened when they were thirteen years old.

I couldn't have asked. I didn't have the right mental vocabulary. By the time I'd figured out how strange it was, I never wanted to think about it again.

And my time at the Church of the Sacred Heart had been almost over, anyway.

There are two options for how I ended up at the Church of the Sacred Heart. One: I must have been brought there deliberately, by someone. Two: I had brought myself there – again, deliberately.

In either case, I hadn't wanted to escape. How do I know? If I'd wanted to escape, I would have.

There was no security, certainly nothing like there had been at the lab coats' facility. Oh, if any of us had disappeared, the police would have been called.[27] But I could have avoided them. Walking around the neighborhood after I arrived, I'd found plenty of places in the outside world where I could hide and survive. There was a sewer access point under the Ashland Avenue bridge that was sheltered enough from the weather. A derelict apartment in the Ukrainian Village with a window openable from the fire escape. Places where I could be alone and manage for myself.

There was just one adult, a volunteer, watching the dorms at night. The doors were not even locked – a fact which, at

---

27 It happened several times.

first, I had not been able to comprehend. It had not occurred to me that, if there were a fire or other crisis, us kids would need to get out. In the lab coats' facility, there had not even been a pretense of anyone looking out for us.

It was the first thing – that I could remember, anyway – that made me feel safe.

I didn't go because I didn't want to go. Simple as that. I may not have had the memories, but I trust that I was still myself in the parts I don't remember.

I don't remember the first time I met Father Boschelli, but I *do* remember the two of us trying to get accustomed to each other. Father Boschelli always wanted us to call him "Father Rudolpho." The other kids did. I didn't want to get that close to him. That just seemed like a good way to get hurt. I didn't have the trust.

I think of him a lot more kindly now than I did at the time. But even now I still think of him as Father Boschelli.

The thing I never appreciated about him at the time is how much energy he had. Look – I have plenty of energy. Can't live this life without it. But if I'd tried to do what Father Boschelli did – manage twenty to thirty kids, and give them all the attention they demanded – I'd have pulled all my hair out inside a week. All the administrative work of managing a neighborhood church fell on him, and then he *also* had to work with us.

Oh, he had help. All kinds of church volunteers, chaperons. A secretary. The cleaning service that took care of our dorms came as a community service, and never charged. But they were in and out. Father Boschelli was the only person who was there every day, no matter whether he was sick or tired or hungry or had a million other things to do. At the end of every day – hell, sometimes by the midpoint – he moved like he'd just gotten up from a nap in the middle of the Dan Ryan Expressway in rush hour. I'd practically *seen* the tire tracks on him. But he never stopped. Some of the other kids got so used to relying on him that they just ignored him.

I don't know when he ever had a day off. Every minute he wasn't with us, he was in the church proper. Even while the other kids were at school, he was cleaning, typing a sermon, managing paperwork, or being hassled by church higher-ups. Or running to school and back to pick up sick or misbehaving kids. If he ever complained about it, I never heard him. He went about his tasks with military efficiency.

He was a large man, with a sizable gray bushy mustache.[28] He looked more like a teddy bear than a teacher or a headmaster – but he could get plenty angry, too. He just knew when to show it. And when discipline called for more tolerance than punishment.

I was so afraid of him those first few weeks that, in retrospect, he must have seen it. He seemed too nice, too tolerant, which set off all my internal alarms.

That, and there was the whole "church" thing. The lab coats had taught us about the major world religions, but that was all. They certainly hadn't invited us to take part in any of them. It all seemed like it came from another planet. My first Sunday in the dorms, while the other girls were filing out for services, I'd asked Father Boschelli, "Are you gonna try to turn me religious?"

---

28 Mustaches were *extremely* new to me and I didn't like them. None of the lab coats had had mustaches.

He let out a long breath, like I had gut-punched him. "No, no," he said. "We don't operate like that. You're old enough to choose your own path."

"Good." I turned away from him. Conversation, as far as I was concerned, over.

He said, to my back, "But you're always welcome at services."

Remember what I'd told you about the marshmallow test? How you can tell someone's suited for merc life if they grab the first marshmallow and eat it? I didn't trust my good fortune, landing in this place. So far as I was concerned, the world would seize it from me at any moment, and throw me right back into my cell – or worse. So I wasn't going to wait for anybody to explain anything, or question too much about how I'd ended up there. I was just going to live in the moment.

The Church of the Sacred Heart was far from a perfect place. But, compared to everything I'd known before and everything I'd expected my life to be, it was an alien planet.

By the standards of most people living in that city, we were packed in tight. To me, it was a palace. There were two dormitories, a dozen and a half beds each. One for boys, one for girls. Dorm life was mostly fine. It was more space than a cell. And even though I'd had my cell "all" to myself, I was accustomed to a lack of privacy. If anything, living so close to other people was *less* invasive than the security camera mounted in the corner of my cell.

Not that it was all peachy. But the whole experience was such a shock to my system that I had trouble separating the unhealthy experiences from the good ones. It was all so new. I don't have many fond memories of the other girls. The adults didn't have enough volunteers to chaperon us at all times. I learned a lot more about how to fight in those dorms.

The first time I punched one of those kids, I didn't hate her. It was just a mechanical fact of life, of defending my interests. One of the girls had told me that I was keeping too much food hoarded away underneath my bed. She'd tried to take it from me. I'd defended my stash. Simple as that.[29]

Even at the Church of the Sacred Heart, there was still a sharp dividing line between us and the adults. A conspiracy of secrets. The complete trust the adults were asking for just wasn't there, not from any of us. The girl I'd punched never told the on-duty nurse where she'd gotten her bloody nose. And none of them told the adults about my food cache.

I moved it out before long anyway. Plenty of better places to hide my hoards.

We didn't spend all our time at the Church of the Sacred Heart. There was also the school. The Church of the Sacred Heart sent their kids to a pair of private Catholic schools, a junior and senior high, just outside the city. I arrived during winter break, when classes were out, but soon enough I was loading onto a bus with the others.

I couldn't even tell the adults how old I was. I didn't know.[30] A pair of special ed teachers spent a lot of time with me, testing me and trying to figure out what grade to put me in – if any. Given my history with adults "testing" me, you could guess how cooperative I was. I didn't tell them anything about the education I'd gotten. I took enough of their tests to

---

[29] It did not take long for the other girls to learn to leave me alone.

[30] They decided later that I was twelve, close to thirteen.

show them that I was smart, that I'd learned *some* things, and then just stopped. I toyed with them.

What the lab coats had taught me was not what the outside world expected me to know. The lab coats had spoken English, but sometimes it still seemed like they came from another world. For example, the only measurements they taught me had been metric. It took some time to wrap my head around these bizarre inches, gallons, and degrees Fahrenheit. And then there was history... The lab coats had taught us only a little of the outside world. But they'd been blunt in their assessments of the great powers, and the oceans of blood they'd spilled to climb to the top.[31] The version of history taught at the Catholic school was a distorted-mirror version of that, wherein the United States was a relentlessly good actor, and all the blood it had shed was washed neatly into abstraction.

Long nights of intermittent electric shocks had taught me how to play along with being lied to. Only now I wasn't sure who had lied to me.

School was just a pause in life before it resumed back at the Church of the Sacred Heart. Besides the dorms, we had the run of several larger rooms. The kitchen was probably the least trafficked, probably because there was the least space. There was still a decently sized table there, though, which made it a good place to hide out, read, or do my homework. Then there was the rec room, with a donated big screen television, a study and reading room for homework, and a classroom that was rarely used for its stated purpose and more often just

---

[31] Interesting, that. Should have been my first clue that the lab coats were not aligned with the US government, as I later assumed.

a second rec room because it had our one PC.

A PC and an internet connection were magical things when you'd never had either before. I learned more about the outside world from that than I ever did at the school. When I figured out how to use it, that was. That took some time. The facility hadn't let us use electronics of any kind. But when I did figure it out, when I got time to myself to use it – that was the first time I ever remember feeling *free*.

It hadn't been out on the streets of Chicago. Or choosing, for myself, to stay at Father Boschelli's church. It had been right there. In that uncomfortable little wooden seat.

I'm not going to say I learned more from the internet of the early aughts than I could have from classes and educators. Only a moron would say something like that.[32] But it was the place where I started to learn about the kinds of things our teachers *didn't* want to tell us. Or things they couldn't. Like what mutants were.

I didn't necessarily know that I was a mutant. The lab coats had called us mutants, but just because the lab coats said something, that didn't mean you should believe them. There were a lot of other fantastical, wonderful, awful people and creatures out there that the world was just learning about. Super heroes and super criminals and super-people-who-just-wanted-to-get-on-with-their-lives. But from what I'd read online, and some things I remembered the lab coats saying, mutant seemed most likely.

I'd tried very hard to forget everything I'd learned about

---

32 YouTube wasn't around then. Fortunately. There were a thousand paranoid cranks inside me waiting to be born if I'd stumbled down the wrong algorithmic wormhole.

myself at the facility. Things like how they'd tested me with dice and card games, or the others for strength, or agility, or weird things. The sewn-up holes in my memory made it easier to pretend I'd forgotten. Compartmentalization, it turned out, was the first, best way I had to deal with that trauma.

This had been the first time I'd felt safe enough to think about that part of myself again. I wasn't quite ready to put into words what I'd experienced yet. But I found enough of them to run a few searches.

Even in those earlier days of the Internet, conversation about mutants was clamped down, hard. Most discussion boards wouldn't allow discussing mutants, under the guise of the issue being "too political." Those that allowed it were, uniformly, specifically anti-mutant groups, and violently eliminationist. Posts by actual mutants were rare, few, and probably frauds – at least on those parts of the internet the church's filters would let me access. It seemed that anywhere mutants revealed themselves, even (especially) on the internet, they'd just made themselves targets. That had been enough to chase them off most of the public-facing parts of the Internet.

I made the mistake of looking at the comments section of the *Chicago Tribune*, and articles from a few local news stations. Never again.

It hadn't always been like that. Before the internet became commonplace in every household, it had been run by academics, libertarians, radical atheists, and other assorted nerds. Most discussion had taken place on a distributed system called Usenet.

Usenet wasn't useful any more. But all the archives were

still there. Perfectly accessible. Decades-old conversations, debates, and arguments, splayed open for study in all their gory details like frogs on a dissection table. And, in those more freethinking days, some mutants had identified themselves publicly. Even, in a few places, been welcomed.

Nobody I read had had experiences exactly like mine. If anybody had suffered through secret labs and "educational" torture, they weren't posting about it on Usenet. But every once in a while, I saw shades of myself. People with no memories of parents because their parents had abandoned them young. People who'd been imprisoned by oppressive governments around the world, spent years of their lives in jail, because of who they were.

I still compartmentalized this in a part of myself I didn't access much. I didn't even want to breathe the word "mutant." I had no idea what I was, or what I could do. Only that I'd been treated a lot like many of those people had been.

Even in the "good old days" of Usenet, posts by mutants couldn't remain for long without someone charging in and demanding that they defend their humanity, debate their right to exist, or whether or not they were threats to the world. The difference between the old internet and the new was just how much oxygen the scumbags and bargain-bin bullies consumed. The more they barged in, turned every discussion into an argument about whether or not mutants *should* exist, the fewer mutants posted. Trawling year-by-year through the archives, I watched it happen in compressed time.

The more I read, the less likely I was to tell Father Boschelli or anyone else where I'd come from or what happened to me. I kept my head down, my eyes on my books, and my imagination from wandering too far. At school, in Social Studies and Current Events, some of the other kids had started talking not about mutants, but about "muties."

ELEVEN

Funny thing about growing up isolated from any kind of culture – well, "funny" thing – is the number of times you screw up and embarrass yourself without having any chance to avoid it whatsoever. No context, no clue. The first few weeks at the Church of the Sacred Heart were especially bad. Everything gave me trouble. From not knowing what the hell a Mr Spock was to having no idea what swearing was.

Oh, I'd *heard* swearing all the time. The Project Armageddon lab coats rarely censored themselves around us. (And when they did, that's when we knew to be on our guard more than ever.) But swearing as a tool? As a weapon? For a kid who'd heard a lot of f-bombs and harder stuff all her life, I was cheerfully innocent.[33]

One time I "borrowed" a comic book from one of the kids at Father Boschelli's, and was reading it in the dark, in

---

[33] Sometimes I think a lot of mercs' and costumed heroes' *creative* swearing goes back to warped childhoods. There was either too much swearing, or not enough. Either way, f-bombs alone don't cut it for us. Got to be inventive, use our metaphors.

the kitchen, right before lights-out. I'd say Father Boschelli sneaked up on me, but it was my fault. I was enraptured. In all my life at Project Armageddon, I'd never seen a comic book.

It was a horror comic, about bloodthirsty pirates, ghosts, revenge, and a cruise ship lost on a blood-red sea. It was more intense than Father Boschelli would've wanted us to have. But Father Boschelli kindly didn't point that out. He just asked me if I was enjoying it.

I didn't answer. The lab coats never asked you anything like that unless they were about to take away whatever it was. Father Boschelli nodded as if I had answered.

Then he did the smart thing, the thing I'd been waiting all my life for adults to do. He did nothing. He waited for *me* to take the initiative, and to talk only if I wanted to.

I *did* have some questions about the comic. And I sure couldn't ask the girl I'd stolen it from. "These lines that are in boxes, not the little circles. Who's speaking them?"

"That's the narrator."

"But who's that?" I asked.

He shrugged.

Unsatisfying. But next question: "Why does the pirate captain use such an old gun when one of the other characters has a revolver?"

"That's a good question. Why do you think the writers have him in a sailing ship when there's better ships available?"

"Hmm." My first brush with *aesthetic* for aesthetic's sake. Nowadays, a lot of the guns in my collection are antiques. Functional, but outclassed. But I keep them because... well, because they're cool.

For all the blood, the comic still censored swearing under a cloud of symbols like the letterer had had a stroke. You know, &%*#!, and the like. "What are they saying?"

He was very straight-faced as he answered, "That's an ampersand. That's a percentage sign. And that's an asterisk."

"I know what a percentage sign is," I said, peevishly.

"Then I'm sure I shouldn't need to tell you anything else about it," Father Boschelli said.

A good point, I'd thought, unsure why I'd needed to ask in the first place.

(I was used to thinking of myself as clever. But I wasn't used to someone being clever right back at me.)

That winter, I clung to that comic book like a lifeline over quicksand. The comic was the third issue of a gods-knows-how-long series, and only twenty-eight pages long, but it was enough. I imagined myself with a big blunderbuss in my hands, like the leering, mighty pirate captain as he and his crew stormed the cruise ship.

Kids in my position tend to latch onto characters that make them feel powerful, even – especially – when they're villains the story wants us to look down on. That big pirate, and his big gun, was the only character who wasn't afraid of anything. And he was the only one who seemed to know what he wanted: money. A fine choice. *My* choice.

The other kids and I had a fraught relationship, if you could call a they-try-to-beat-me-up-and-I-break-their-noses-until-they-all-leave-me-alone relationship "fraught." But, for a glorious golden window after I arrived, there were a few weeks in which those kids didn't know what to make of me. A few of them even tried to be friends.

I liked that. For a while.

First sign that wasn't going to last was how even the nice ones treated me when I screwed up something that, to them, seemed simple. Like when we were running around the common room, trying to play. The common room was the biggest space in the orphanage, excepting only the basketball court out back. Father Boschelli had made a valiant attempt to fill it with things to entertain kids of all ages, best as the church's budget allowed. A largish TV, a video game console from two generations ago, board games with missing pieces, books no one read, that kind of thing. Mostly the other kids just chased each other around the couches, pretending to be their heroes. For a while, I tried that.

It wasn't that I knew or cared who Duke Skywalker or whoever was.[34] I liked it because it was *fun*. Because I'd never had a chance to do anything like that with the kids from Project Armageddon. It felt... normal? And, at that point in my life, normal felt good.

Big difference from now, I know.

I was impressed by how violent their imaginations were. Still weren't a match for mine, but at least they were speaking my language. When one of them – a thirteen year-old boy twice my size and with a face like ground beef, the nicest of all of them – thrust a laser-sword through my belly, I got to pretend to vomit blood. This was when I still wanted friends to the point of ingratiating myself with them (rest in peace, that side of myself, I hardly knew ye), and so I did what seemed like the only fair thing and took the fall. Other kids

---

[34] Nowadays, *try* to find a pop culture reference I don't understand. But back then? I'm sure the lab coats all had TVs and film collections, but they weren't sharing.

had recovered from worse injuries and kept playing, but not me. For once in my life, I wanted to be a team player. I choked and gasped, staggered to my knees, and thought of what my dear pirate captain had yelled when one of the cruise ship's passengers had kicked him in the gut. "Ampersand!"

Play immediately ground to a halt.

When they figured out what I'd said – and I, the fool, told them where I'd gotten it from – the night's game turned from dukes-and-laser-swords to laugh-at-Neena. Even the big, friendly kid didn't stop. And the jokes, the not-so-friendly teasing from everyone else, went on for another week.

It seemed like it should have been a small thing, but it wasn't. It was the first time that, in front of all of them, I'd shown just how different a place I'd come from. And, even in that one small difference, I might as well have been an alien.

And, you know what? It *hurt*. Being laughed at by other kids was a cruelty I'd so far avoided in my short, cruelty-filled life. So if I reacted with less than perfect equanimity, excuse the hell out of me.

It was easy, in fact, to react the same way I reacted to the lab coats' cruelty. Shut down. Turtle up emotionally. And start thinking of them as the enemy.

When the big thirteen year-old asked me if I wanted to play again the next week, I don't think he understood why I jabbed my elbow into his stomach. It marked the last time I played anything with them – at least for fun.

The last thing I'd expected was that I would have an easier time being around the adults, but that turned out to be the case. Adults were more predictable than kids. After the first few times they saw me flinch when they stepped near me,[35] they took things slow and careful around me. Father Boschelli went out of his way to try to include me. Unlike some of the other adults, he didn't give up after the first few times I turned him down.

The first time Father Boschelli took me grocery shopping, I screwed up again. I tried to stuff half the checkout candy in my pockets when he wasn't watching. Security caught me immediately. They must have been watching already, as they'd no doubt learned to watch all of Father Boschelli's children. My luck didn't extend to shoplifting.

The store's staff hauled me to the back office, where some very severe mustachioed men tried their best to scare me, to tell me they could send me to jail, ruin my life. I'd faced down more intimidating men in much scarier offices. Compared to those lab-coat-wearing monsters, a grocery store middle manager was a marshmallow. I spent the whole time I was back with him silent, just imagining eating him up.

I think he caught a glimpse of the murder in my eyes. In the middle of his lecture, he was about to set his hand on my shoulder, but halted. Got real quiet after a while.

Him, I could handle. No, what got to me was Father Boschelli. He'd spent the whole time waiting outside that office. After the assistant manager made a show of "releasing" me, I stepped out and nearly ran right into him. It was the first time I had ever seen him angry.

Furious, in fact. Embittered.

---

[35] I tried very hard not to. At the facility, showing weakness around the lab coats was just an invitation for them to make things worse. But I wasn't in control of myself yet.

Anger was one thing. But him, *bitter?* Though it was just a flash in his eyes, I'd never forget it.

I'd had a vague sense that what I was doing was wrong, that the world couldn't possibly have served me up something so nice as all that colorful candy. But, honestly, I hadn't stopped to think about it. I'd just acted. That's how things worked at Project Armageddon: something nice appeared, and you grabbed onto it as quickly and discreetly as you could. Otherwise it would just be snatched away from you. Collecting, hoarding, and hiding away any little thing I could get was more than an impulse, more than habit. It was instinct.

Might say something about my attitude toward money later in life, yeah? Charge for everything I can, spend it all before it vanishes. Most mercs have motives for what they do that run deeper than they like to think about.

(Aw, look at you. You're like my dog. Getting me to spill my heart out just by not saying anything when I talk to you. You little ampersand.)

Father Boschelli thought I'd done it on purpose. He didn't say a word as we marched out of the grocery store, or on the trip back to the bus stop. And, just like that was the first time he got mad at me, it was the first time I realized how scared I was of him. Scared in a way I never had been of the Project Armageddon lab coats. If he didn't want me around any more, I had nothing. Not even hiding holes for all the other little bits of food I'd stolen and sure as hell wasn't going to tell him about now.

I walked, grinding my teeth and shaking. Something had jostled loose inside me. For a couple of weeks, I'd almost gotten out of the habit of thinking of adults – hell, of thinking of the entire outside world – as an enemy.

I might not have stayed at the Church of the Sacred Heart, might have run away that night, had he not addressed the problem head on.[36]

"Was that how things used to be where you lived?" he asked, after we got off the bus.

I looked at him. There were no stores where I'd lived. But I couldn't have told him that.

He took my silence for an answer. "You're not going to have to live like that again," he said.

"I don't understand what happened," I said.

"Did someone train you to act like that?"

"No," I said, because I hadn't reached the level of self-awareness I'd needed to say that the answer was definitively *yes*.

"You may not get everything you want here," he said, "but you *will* get everything you need. That's going to have to be enough for you."

I made a noncommittal noise to indicate I wasn't really listening.

We were almost back to the orphanage's doors. He stopped. I tried to go forward, but he wouldn't move on until I turned and looked at him. And I wasn't quite at the stage where I was ready to keep going alone.

When he met my eyes, he asked, "Do you want to learn how to live differently?"

It took me a while to register that he meant the question

---

[36] Brave choice, for an adult.

sincerely. He was offering me a choice. It left me flustered.

"Sure? I guess." The most eloquent I could have been at the time.

It was a long time before I went grocery shopping again. In the meantime, he made sure I knew exactly where all of the food and snacks were in the kitchen.[37] And he also invited me, again, to Mass.

Spoiler: I eventually did find religion. I'm not going to talk about it much, but I have my faith. I certainly didn't at the time, though. It was such an alien thing to have in my life. Hope was not something the lab coats had cared to instill in us. Redemption even less so. And *faith* sounded a lot like *trust*, which, well...

Suffice it to say I wasn't ready to trust in anything – let alone things I couldn't see or touch.

All but a handful of the other kids went to services. Father Boschelli never forced anyone to go, as much as some of the other adult volunteers would have liked him to. The rest of us stayed back and watched cartoons.[38] That was fine, for the first few weeks, before the other kids and I got to know each other. Before I'd gotten into too many fights.

Eventually, though, the other kids started quietly avoiding me. They shied away to other rooms, or pretended not to see me. Being alone with them started to get so uncomfortable that it made me itch and squirm. It started to sound easier to spend Sunday mornings doing something that sounded a lot like class – where I could just sit still, or sleep.

---

37 I didn't stop making stashes.

38 We promised the adults we would be working on homework but there was not even a pretense of that once they'd left.

Father Boschelli raised his eyebrow when I told him I would be coming with him and the other kids that Sunday, but he, wisely, never said anything.

TWELVE

The first time at church took some instruction. I had to learn how to sit, how to act. I was a bundle of squirming and twitching back then, and had gotten used to just being able to behave in class. But things were different during Mass. I couldn't reflexively check my sides, or tap my feet on the floor, without getting a bunch of rude looks. Even cracking my knuckles got a nudge from the kid beside me.

So I sat as still as I could. I paid attention to the people around me, and tried to behave as they did. There were still some things they did automatically, like the *Amens,* or standing and sitting back down, that I lagged on. Twice, my voice was the last to echo through the church. After the last time, I just gave up and stayed silent.

I understood ritual. All my life had been ritual. Rootless tasks imbued with a weight of meaning. Some of them had been created for us by the adults: spend so many hours studying per day, perform well on tests. But the most powerful rituals were those I made for myself. Little rituals that, later, I understood were just me trying to control things that were beyond my power. That dark, anxious little place where superstitions are born.

The best performance I'd ever had on one of the lab coats' tests had been, strangely, a morning when I'd been sick, had thrown up right beforehand, and had been out of my mind with a fever. After that, before any big test, I'd refused to eat breakfast and tried to make myself nauseated by thinking of vomit. It never seemed to help, but I never stopped doing it.[39]

On nights when I'd fallen behind the other kids on tests, or the lab coats had found some other reason to punish me and I was slated for unpredictable nightly electric shocks, I would start flinching even when nothing had happened. I would count down under my breath from five and then flinch, as if I could summon the shocks myself. I couldn't, of course. But acting like I could *felt* like it helped, even if it actually didn't. Just having something to do, a little placebo, was more help than it seemed like it should have been. During those few weeks when I'd been allowed to keep the kitten, I'd always start petting her by scratching her head and her ears, rubbing her neck, and then stroking down to her tail.

Sitting at Mass, trying and failing to keep my mind off these things, was the first time I'd thought about that kitten in months. Funny thing. I'd been able to put things like that out of my mind for weeks and months. I'd had plenty of time to myself where I might have been tempted to start thinking about it. Put me in a place where I was supposed to pay attention, and make everything incomprehensible, and my mind started to wander.

---

[39] For months, I did the same thing for tests at the Catholic school.

The fate of that kitten was, like the fate of the other kids from the facility, something I had never wanted to think about.

But I knew what must have happened.

I swallowed, and tried again to force myself to pay attention. Everyone around me was standing and pulling out their hymnals from behind the next pew. Mass was the first time anyone had invited me to sing. I cleared my throat and tested my voice.

I got stares, especially from the other kids. If I hadn't already shown them I was willing to fight, I'm sure they would have been laughing about my voice for weeks afterward.

Nowadays, get me a few drinks and put me in a karaoke bar, and just *try* to keep me from monopolizing the mic. But I still had a lot of growing up to do between then and now. The biggest part of which was learning that other people can give me all the strange looks they want and it doesn't matter an asterisk.

Back then, though, all it did was shut me up and force me to retreat into myself.

Everything about Mass made me itchy and uncomfortable. From the costumes and robes, to the strange silences riddled with coughing and shuffling, to the lump of heat building underneath my own throat. There was also just enough activity that I could not wholly cut myself off from the world. Late in the service, I started actually listening to what Father Boschelli was saying. It did not help.

Back in the facility, the lab coats had us read about world religion. Seen from the ivory tower vantage of textbooks, religion had been so abstract as to be meaningless. Impossible to grasp, or to understand how anyone believed. I had known, in the back of my head, that Father Boschelli and most of the other kids were sincere believers, but we had never talked about it, and it had always seemed faintly ridiculous.

Now I could not ignore it. Father Boschelli was not a dry-voiced preacher. He was not a loud fire-and-brimstone type either.[40] There were swells of warmth, and sincerity, in his voice that kept everyone else (but me) effortlessly silent and attentive.

The idea of an all-powerful supernatural force all around us, looking out for me, was not only alien, but alienating. All my life, one being, and one being alone, had looked out for me: me. Even at the Church of the Sacred Heart, being fed and clothed and sheltered by strangers and volunteers, that seemed no less true than it had been at the lab coats' facility.

Every day at the facility, my life had been in danger. Every day out here, I *felt* like I was in danger. No matter where I was, I was walking along a cliff trail at night, a dark chasm beside every footfall. I certainly had never felt like there was anyone looking out for me.

There didn't seem to be anybody looking out for those mutants I'd read about online. Nobody had been looking out for the other kids at the facility – the kids who'd disappeared, and who I'd hardly let myself think about.

The heat in my throat got worse. Those kids. The ones I'd competed against every day. The ones that, whenever I did better than them on tests, I'd sentenced to nights of random

---

[40] Unlike, say, a Dallas Bader Pearson, Father Boschelli didn't want to control anyone.

electrical shocks. The ones who, though I never wanted to admit this, were almost certainly dead.

Nobody had been looking out for *them*.

Up in front of the altar, Father Boschelli scanned his audience. His voice faltered, briefly, when he reached me. Maybe he'd caught some glimpse of the anger in my eyes.

But I caught a glimpse of his eyes too. I hadn't believed that anybody was looking out for me. I was still at that self-centered age where I'd had trouble looking beyond myself, which didn't help. Gratitude was as alien to me as God. I was so accustomed to thinking of adults as the enemy that I had trouble acknowledging what the adults of the Church of the Sacred Heart did for me. Volunteers, staff, and clergy alike.

They might not have been able to look out for any of the people I mentioned earlier. But they *were* looking out for me. It would take me a long, long time to allow myself to be fully cognizant of that. Sitting there in church, seeing the concern in his eyes, was the first time I'd allowed myself to even start to think it. It felt like letting my guard down.

I'd never, ever been good at that. Nor did I want to be. Letting my guard down had always – *always* – been a mistake.

But the truth was that I'd let too much of my guard down already.

One of the many problems with compartmentalizing your traumas is that you don't think about the things you've hidden away as often as you should. Some things will just slip right by you. Things you should have caught, or at least wondered about, long ago.

Father Boschelli *was* looking out for me. I believed that much. But, thanks to the gaps in my memory, I had no idea how long he'd been doing so.

In all the time I'd been at the Church of the Sacred Heart, it had never occurred to me that Father Boschelli might have been complicit in my missing memories.

Until right then.

THIRTEEN
CHICAGO, NOW

I had found my faith in the days since the Church of the Sacred Heart, long enough ago that the days when I didn't believe felt as ancient as Dracula's teeth. But it had been a long, long time since I'd been to a service. Church services didn't do much for me.

Dallas Bader Pearson's people were all getting ready for a service of their own. I watched their figures flit through the darkness, all headed in the same direction.

Inez and I sat in a vegan food market and café across from their compound. From this far away, and under the sick orange glow of light pollution, the compound looked like even more of a prison than in the daytime. Nothing lit the footpaths between its buildings. All we saw were a few desultory window lights and exhausted-looking silhouettes shuffling between them – all broken up by the bars of the fence that surrounded them.

The reflection of the café's fluorescent lights framed our view. A vegan café hadn't been my first choice of stakeout campsites, but there hadn't been much else open at this hour and on this side of the street. Just this and a chain coffee shop. And I'd much rather spend money at a local business than a chain.

I'd expected Inez to throw a fit. Usually she thrived – positively traded – on her roughneck stereotype. She just sauntered right up to the counter and ordered a black bean quinoa wrap (with tempeh bacon) like she'd been in places like this a hundred times before. Huh. Hidden depths.

My understanding of her couldn't take that much shaking right now. The entire time she ate her wrap, she looked at me, playfully daring me to say something.

I didn't take the bait. Some mysteries better left unsolved, et cetera.

I picked up my headset, slipped it over my hair, and levered the mic into place.

"Rachel, go," I said.

"Finally," Rachel's voice answered.

"Hey," Inez said. "We're not staying for dessert?"

"You and sugar? Right before an operation?"

"Exactly. Me and sugar – right before an operation."

I wasn't being picky about vegan food when I hadn't ordered. Some of the rage and nausea the earlier part of the day had stirred up were still swilling around inside me. I knew it would only get worse inside Pearson's compound. I was doing, I thought, a good job of hiding my anxiety from Inez. The last thing I needed when we finally got in was to be so sick with anger that I felt like throwing up more than I did fighting.

Outside, the skyline turned a brighter, sicklier shade of

orange. Then violet. Half a second later, the first detonation rattled the cafe's windows.

The fluorescent lights' reflection quavered. The barista and cook at work behind the counter flinched.

"Order dessert if you like," I told Inez, gesturing to the counter.

The second detonation, even closer and louder than the first, rattled in my ribs. Inez pursed her lips. She was seriously considering it.

"Only if you split it with me," she countered.

"We'd like that pan of peanut-butter-chocolate bars in your front cooler," I told the startled cook. "The whole thing." The sky outside turned azure. The flash was followed by the sharp report of a third explosion. "We'll be back to pick it up."

I tucked a twenty underneath Inez's plate. Always tip well, kids.

The café's staff had been plenty helpful, too. They'd told us all kinds of things they'd seen at Pearson's compound. We wouldn't have been able to put the final touches on our plan without their help.

Inez and I stepped outside just in time for the next explosion. The sound *popped* in my lungs. A brilliant bright blue-and-violet firework detonated over the suburban skyline. Azure sparks sleeted down upon the roofs of distant houses, vanishing just before they would have touched. The colors made the place look almost pretty.

The cold bit into me, sharp as thorns. I immediately cupped my hands together, blew into them. Inez, of course, didn't look bothered at all.

The next firework was an elaborate one. A crimson sphere

of sparks blasted outward from the center of the detonation, framing a blue diamond. Figured Rachel would find some way to work in her diamond motif. She could be a show-off. Rachel's favorite explosives were the diamond-shaped grenades she always carried with her. But, like any good incendiaries expert, she had more than one trick up her costume's sleeves.

She had taken up a position on a warehouse rooftop five blocks away. The fireworks were close enough to the compound to daze Pearson's people, but far enough away to look like they had nothing to do with them. There should have been a Chicago Bears playoff game finishing up around then, and, though the Bears had been losing the last time I'd checked the radio, I doubted Pearson knew that.

With a show like this, Rachel would bring the police down on her in minutes. But a couple minutes of distraction was all Inez and I would need.

For a few glorious seconds, the next firework's light even overwhelmed the city's light pollution. We could see the shape of the suburban skyline, the low-altitude gray clouds overhead. This wasn't the busiest street, but it still had some foot traffic. People all around us were stopping to stare. The gate guards by Pearson's compound were watching too.

Inez and I kept our eyes down. We would need our night vision. The compound's guards, though, were dazzled. They stared directly at the fireworks.

These weren't hardened paramilitaries. If they'd had any training or experience, they would have known to protect their night vision right away. They were civilians, dressed up by Pearson, pretending to be enforcers. It might seem like that would make this job easier. On the contrary – it made things *much* more difficult. If they spotted us now I felt it was incumbent on me to avoid hurting them. Going full-out on them would have been just as cruel, and unsportsmanlike, as punching a child. They just weren't on our level. Worse, they were most likely just as much Pearson's victims as anyone else inside.

Inez and I strolled along the side of the compound. Heavy black steel fencing separated the compound yard from the street.

"Fox and spider," I said. "You're up."

White Fox had recruited Black Widow into her part of the plan with the prospect of some pleasantly cathartic overacting. I've always suspected that a drama nerd lurks inside every spy's or costumed super hero's heart. A good spy plays a lot of roles.

On cue, a cacophony of car horns split the air, followed by a tremendous metallic *crunch*.

I could not see the collision from here. We'd staged the crash to happen near the compound's main entrance, around the corner from Inez and me. The chilly night carried the sound well. A moment after the crash, we heard a car door slam shut.

White Fox's voice was loud enough to cross the distance. Black Widow's joined her only a few seconds later, doing her best impression of aghast and shocked.[41] Between the two, Black Widow was better at cursing. Lot of words that, when I was younger, I would have covered with ampersands and asterisks.

---

[41] Though I'm afraid that Oscar is going to remain tantalizingly out of Black Widow's reach.

White Fox was trying very hard to sound like an aggrieved American. "Why didn't you watch where you were going, you... you cow!"

"I couldn't see with all those fireworks! You pulled out of that parking spot like someone lit your butt on fire!"

Since the crash blocked the compound's main entryway, Pearson's guards couldn't ignore it. The guards closest to Inez's and my side of the fence started to jog toward the commotion. It was easy to pick out the guards. They, men and women both, were distinguished from Pearson's other followers by their (sometimes-ill-fitting) brown coveralls. A uniform that attempted to not look too threatening, but a uniform nonetheless.

The trick here had always been getting in without arousing Pearson's suspicions. I didn't need to know Pearson personally to know he was paranoid. He'd come to this place, with its prebuilt fencing and prison-like layout, for a reason. If we used conventional diversion tactics, like a power outage, he'd immediately assume the whole thing was about him anyway. His whole compound had turtled up like he expected the hammer of the US government to come down at any moment.

The wages of megalomania were a sense that everything in the world revolved around you. It must have been an exhausting way to live. But it meant we had to step extremely carefully. If he locked down his compound, we were never going to be able to finish our job without hurting somebody.

Inez and I walked as far as a used vinyl record store. It was closed for the night, so we wouldn't be silhouetted by lights behind us. Then we crossed the street. The fence's iron bars looked a lot thicker up close. Climbing over them would take too long, and leave us visible against the skyline. As usual in this business, the best way around an obstacle was through it.

Inez grabbed the bars and pulled. With a harsh *cracking* sound – coinciding with a firework blast – the bars snapped loose just above the ground. Inez bent both bars inward and stepped back, like she was holding a door open for me.

"After you, sugar," she said, all cherubic politeness.

I wouldn't trade my abilities for anything, but sometimes I do really envy super-strength.

I double-checked to make sure none of the guards had noticed. They were still too preoccupied with the car crash, or razzle-dazzled by the fireworks. I hustled through the gap. Inez followed, bending the bars back into place.

The compound's lawns had once been meticulously cared for. There were artfully placed shrubs, several empty cement blocks that – in that newspaper photo – had once supported a flower garden. Even before winter had settled in, the place had gone to seed. I felt the crack of dead tall grass under the snow. Half of the shrubs were poorly trimmed. The other half were dead. Not a good sign. From all accounts, Pearson's church had plenty of money for upkeep. He had probably forbidden his followers from coming out to work on it. That would reduce the amount of time they had to look at the outside world.

The café staff had said the compound had always been buttoned down tight, but that things had gotten worse after the exposé. Dallas Bader Pearson ran his compound like a military camp. Regular guard rotations, watchers up at all hours, and less and less contact with the outside world. Guards were always posted in pairs. When Inez and I had watched, we'd never seen any of the cultists travel about except in pairs. Even going between buildings in their own compound, Pearson's people always had a partner. Traveling in pairs would make it that much harder for dissenters to escape. The guards at the gate were watching inward as much as outward.

Pearson was terrified of people leaving him. And he had enough loyal followers to play along with him. Also not a good sign. Even if Rose and Joseph *wanted* to leave, it looked more and more like we would have our hands full just getting them out of here.

Somewhere in the distance, White Fox and Black Widow were still burying themselves in the part. White Fox shouted, "*Your* car has enough dents and scratches that you can't see it! Look at what you did to mine!"

The car was nothing special, a rental Civic.[42] But somehow Black Widow sounded genuinely aggrieved. "The only thing wrong with my car is that it stopped before it flattened you!"

By habit, I checked and double-checked my sidearms. I had two with me. The first: a silenced Beretta 92FS. I wasn't planning on shooting anybody, but you never knew. I never felt safe without, at the very least, a loaded 9mm. The second was a grappling hook pistol with a three-pronged anchor. One of many tools that's less useful in real life than it is in movies and comic books, but my knack for making lucky shots and strikes balances things in my favor.

Inez carried no weapons, but that didn't mean she was unarmed. I'd seen her punches shatter stone pillars.

---

[42] The insurance would be going on Rebecca Munoz's bill at the end of all this.

We darted through the shadows, past a route I'd seen Pearson's guards walk. I stepped lightly across the snow. I hated to leave footprints, but there were plenty of others all around us, and ours shouldn't have looked remarkable. We made it as far as one of the two wooden storage sheds at the edge of the compound's central, open lot. We hunched against the wall. We were right next door to one of the buildings Pearson was using as a dormitory. A pair of walkers had just left from the main doors, and were coming around the side of the building facing us. We had to wait for them to pass.

"Funny time to ask," Inez said, "but are you sure I'm the right person to come along on this part of the job?"

"'Funny time to ask' is right, lady."

Inez said, "I was hoping we'd be doing a bit more punching than sneaking around." She pulled her hat up, scratched her head. "Thought for sure you'd think I was too bullheaded for this part."

I'd been afraid of her asking just this question, and had been rehearsing lies to answer her. Only now my mind was buzzing too much to remember any of them.

So. The truth. "You absolutely are bullheaded," I said. "That's why you're going to keep me level."

The figures turned the corner. I checked around for more, and stood before Inez could answer.

Infiltration jobs gave me a chance to play with toys in my arsenal that, on most other jobs, went neglected. Several ovoid cameras dangled from my belt. Each of them was black, about the size of a grape. They were shaped like eggs so that, when they landed, the wide-angle cameras on each end wouldn't end up facing straight up or down. They were

Wakandan technology, a gift from Shoon'kwa. They were just trinkets to her. They were also some of the most smartly designed surveillance tech I had ever seen. Multispectral imaging, from infrared to ultraviolet, with built-in facial and threat recognition. When they were no longer needed, they could vaporize themselves with a tiny *pop* and a flash of light.

I threw two around the side of the next building, each in different directions.

"Getting your camera feeds," Rachel's voice said in my ear, a moment later.

Somewhere in the farther distance, I heard police sirens. They were coming after that firework display. "You gonna get yourself somewhere safe?" I asked.

"*Darling.*" I couldn't tell if she was just playing offended, or genuinely was. "I'm already in our van, half a mile away. Like *I* couldn't set timer fuses on a handful of fireworks."

Inez set a hand on my shoulder. "You all right? You've been worrywarting all over."

Rather than answer, I grabbed one of three slender canister-shaped smoke grenades off my belt clip.

Rachel had located her fireworks display very carefully. We were downwind. The smoke was starting to reach the compound. Great big gray clouds of it scudded overhead. An extra cloud or two would not look out of place. Even the smell of smoke would blend in.

With a careful underhand toss, I rolled the smoke grenade against the side of the dormitory building. Waited to hear the hiss. Then I stepped out around the shed, grappling hook pistol raised.

There's little in life quite so satisfying as a grappling hook pistol. From the solid, wrenching *kick* to my wrist, to the clink at the end. They need perfect aim, a perfect eye for the distances involved, and some just plain lucky bouncing to catch on the right obstacle. I had the aim and the eye for distance. As for the rest – I gave the rope a good tug, and the hook caught just right on the lip of the building's roof.

There was no way Inez and I could amble through the center of the compound and not get caught. There were just too many people. Pearson didn't need complex security when he had hundreds of pairs of eyeballs.

So Inez and I were going to take a route nobody trafficked: the rooftops.

I was already halfway up the building's brick wall before the smoke grenade even stopped hissing. Inez was right behind me. I couldn't see her in the smoke, but I felt her weight on the cable.

We made it just in time. As soon as my boot touched the rough surface of the roof, the dormitory's door opened. I looked down. Another pair of cultists had stepped out. These ones were holding hands, and had a six-to-seven year-old child trailing after them.

The kid plainly wanted to stop and stare at the fireworks, but one of the adults yanked her along. Spoilsports.

When he reached our smoke, the adult dragging the kid along muttered something that he shouldn't have said in hearing range of a child. They didn't stop. The kid coughed plaintively as she was pulled through the smoke, but the adults were on a mission. One of them, a woman, said, "Come on! Dad will know if we're late."

One thing you learn sneaking around: people rarely, if ever, look up. Inez and I got clear of the edge of the building as quick as we could, though. Just in case.

"'Dad?'" Inez mouthed.

I shrugged. Cults like Pearson's operated on myths of paternalism, father figures. It was a sign of how far these people had fallen into their own little world that they could call him that without realizing how weird that was.

From up here, we had a clear view of the whole compound. The place was shaped like a bracket. Dormitory buildings on each side. Church and reception hall at the center. And, at the "corners," ancillary buildings that used to hold classrooms. Damned if I knew what they had now. Food storage, maybe. Pearson's people so rarely left their compound that they had to be keeping the necessities of life somewhere.

The café staff had told Inez and me that, more than once, as they were closing up, they'd seen unmarked trucks pull into the compound's central lot. Arms, I was willing to bet. And, while none of the guards I'd seen were packing, I didn't doubt that the gatehouse was loaded with weapons, or that the guards could arm themselves with a minute's notice.

Cults like Pearson's get stars in their eyes when they think of Waco and the Branch Davidians. Nothing would justify their faith and fervor more than an apocalyptic firefight with the US government. In truth, the US government was probably barely aware of their existence.[43] But if Pearson's people believed they were being persecuted and hunted, Pearson would be able to keep them close. Cults like his thrived on a sense of persecution, on having an enemy.

---

43 They always, *always*, catch onto these things too late.

The exposé and sexual harassment allegations would have only made it easier for Pearson to convince his followers that the rest of the world was out to get them.

I was starting to understand why Rebecca Munoz had been so intent on getting her twins out of there. The place was a powder keg.

I carefully rewound the grappling hook pistol[44], and studied the compound. I was surprised that Pearson hadn't turned one of these buildings into his own personal residence. His type usually liked to live large, no matter the conditions his followers lived in. By all accounts, after the exposé, he never left the compound. He had to have quarters somewhere.

In the back of my head, I was already planning an assassination mission.

Rachel's firework show ended with one big, farewell blast. A diamond-shaped burst of sparks showered the sky, lasting as long as the echo rolled around the horizon. Then we were left with curling clouds of acrid smoke and the distant wail of sirens. And a long, hard job ahead.

---

44 Another thing movies won't tell you about grappling hooks is how much painstaking work they are to set up in the first place.

FOURTEEN

All had gone as well as it could have so far. The fireworks had ended just as Inez and I had reached the roof. Now we could sidle right up to the edge without making our silhouettes visible against the sky. On an ordinary job, I would have been pretty damned pleased with myself.

The few groups of pedestrians out below were all headed one way: toward the church. From what we'd heard earlier, I guessed these were stragglers. Only a few lights in the two "classroom" buildings were on. As we watched, more lights in the dormitory went out. The church, though, was lit up. The shadows of four people stood sentry just outside the main doors. The pedestrians formed an orderly queue in front of the guards without being told. Even the kids among them stood still. They were used to being told what to do.

Seven camera orbs left. I selected three spots along the walkways in the courtyard below, and hurled one camera toward each. They disappeared into the night. If I'd judged my throws right, we'd have camera coverage of just about every pedestrian as they went by, assuming they took the most rational route.

"More cameras coming online," Rachel said, in my ear. "Perfect positioning. Lucky throws, dear. All these monitors with different views – starting to feel like I'm seeing the world the way a wasp does."

"Or a spider," Inez muttered. Surveillance and spying always made her itchy. Not her style.

Black Widow must have gotten back in her car and gotten her headset back on. "I hope you all aren't saying you've got anything against spiders."

"Everybody, *shut up*," I snapped.

I was louder than I meant. Fortunately, none of the pedestrians below noticed. I breathed out. Our comms channel fell silent.

All of our cameras and headsets routed to our computer setup in the back of an unmarked gray van. If our tech was working correctly, the monitors should already be bracketing and highlighting faces, algorithmically filling in any missing features. If Joseph and Rose Munoz were out there, Rachel should have already found them. Most likely, they were with most everybody else: in the church.

The compound's buildings were close enough together that, with only a modest leap, Inez and I could turn the rooftops into an alternate footpath to the church. The biggest obstacle would be at the end: a twenty-foot gap and about a story of additional height to reach the church's steeply sloping roof. But that was why I'd rewound the grappling hook.

"Temperature in the dormitory windows is starting to cool," Rachel reported. The Wakandan cameras not only scanned in infrared, but did so with unparalleled precision. "The church is warming up. Lots of body heat in there."

Inez said, "Sheesh. Think about all those people stuffed in there. Breathing. Coughing. Farting. And I'm guessing you want us to go get above it."

I muttered, "I can't help it if warm air rises."

"Sugar, you take me to all the best places."

Usually, I would have been quipping right along with them. I wondered if I was getting humorless as I grew older. My mind had been going to some pretty humorless places lately. Back to my childhood. Back to the Everglades. I thought I'd wrapped those parts of myself up, but they kept coming back to me, like recurring nightmares. It had gotten worse since I'd accepted this job.

It was all part of the same long-running story.

Up here, sheltered from the street lights, it was difficult to see rooftop obstacles like snow guards or vents. Inez and I still made enough speed to clear the first leap easy. And the next. We made good time to the church.

I savored the brief joy of another grappling hook shot. At the top, I once again offered Inez a hand. It was good to feel that she was still there. Her hand felt just as warm as mine did frozen. Together, we clambered up the roof and into the belfry. The window leading from the bell tower into the church proper was unlocked.

We crawled into an attic-sized maintenance space. A dusty PC and a set of switches sat under a small wooden desk. They looked like they hadn't been touched in months.

Inez had been right. The smell up here was... was... well, it couldn't have been mistaken for anything but what it was. Lots of people, living on a poor diet, crammed in a tight space together. Someone had jammed the thermostat up, too, so there was plenty of sweat stink to go along with it. At least it was warmer.

A susurrus of voices filtered up from below. The floorboards underneath us creaked and groaned like arthritic zombies, but the good news was that there was no chance anybody would hear us. Not with that racket. I crept closer to the door and nudged it open.

A wrought iron spiral staircase led downward to the packed floor of the church. The staircase rattled with footsteps and, for a second, my heart jammed into my throat. But nobody was coming up. A handful of people had climbed onto the lower steps for a better view over the rest of the crowd. They were the source of the vibrations.

If a fire marshal had seen what I saw below, they would have had a stroke.

This had been a fairly high-capacity church. But it was nothing compared to what Pearson had done to it. He had overstuffed the church, and then overstuffed it again. There must have been seven hundred people down there. The church hadn't been designed to hold so many. It wasn't a megachurch; it was just a boarding school's old chapel. The walls had pale shadows where some intervening walls – probably for classrooms or an office – must have been. They'd all been knocked down to make more space. If there were any pews left, I saw no sign of them among the crowd. Standing room only.

I honestly had had no idea there were this many people in the compound. None of my articles or other sources had mentioned it. They probably hadn't known. And this wouldn't account for everybody in the compound, not by a long shot.

Add the security guards left at the gate, the sick or infirm in the dormitories, and the place must have held close to a thousand people. The dormitories were probably in no better condition than this church. I didn't want to think about that.

Pearson had wanted all of these people to be able to fit in the church, all the time. Basic safety and sanity hadn't meant much to him. The vegan café's staff had said that they saw Pearson's people heading to the church often, sometimes more than once a day. When Pearson got especially animated, the speakers carrying his voice reached the street. These rallies were, for him, the most important part of his day.

I caught Inez's eye. For the first time, she looked worried.

About half of the crowd were old, sixty and above. The rest were a mix of all ages, including families and at least two larger groups of children escorted by an adult. They didn't dress in uniforms, but their clothes were so much alike that they might as well have. Lots of jeans and slacks, worn T-shirts, jackets that had seen one season too much use. Either poor folks or folk who had recently become poor. And a mix of skin colors, too. More black and brown than white.

I placed a Wakandan camera atop one of the rafters, braced in a corner and facing downward, to give it a clear view of the crowd.

"You've got an eye for dramatic angles, darling," Rachel said. I wasn't sure there was a non-dramatic angle here. "Running facial recognition now."

"Let me know the instant you spot Rose or Joseph." The plan was to find them and then find some way to get them alone, if it was possible to get *anybody* here alone.

"I'm only picking up bits and pieces of faces from this angle.

Algorithmic fill-in will need a moment. Hope you're comfy."

Inez made a face.

It might have gone faster if I'd tossed an orb toward the altar, but Pearson was walking up there now. If anyone was paranoid enough to notice and find a camera, it was him.

Pearson was hard to mistake. He had lost weight since his last newspaper photos, but he was still one of the tallest men in the room. He had the dark hair of a country singer or a homespun Elvis impersonator. Contrary to my expectations, he didn't dress fancy at all. Jeans. Checkered blue-and-white shirt with a dress pocket and a couple of pens. Like a vision of a 1980s dad.

Even from all the way up here, I could tell he had unusual eyes. The skin around them was wrinkled and soft, full of laugh lines. His irises were piercing blue. But the whites were shot through with red. I was surprised he hadn't done something to hide that. There were a couple things that could have explained redness that severe. Sleepless nights. Or drugs. Amphetamines. If I'd had to bet, I knew where my money would have gone.

He held up his hands. The entangled voices faded, but apparently not quickly enough for his liking. He swiftly pointed out people in opposite corners of the back. "You, and you, you pairs. I hope you've got something important enough to share with the rest of us, that you would go on interrupting us this way." An infant's cry broke the proceedings. "Hush those kids up, please. Hush them up. I know they're tired, but we all have work to do. It's important that you hear this."

The people nearest those he'd pointed out hushed the kid up quickly. The child gave a strangled cry as their father pulled back through the crowd, toward the door. Pearson's lips twitched irritably as he watched the man go.

"The outside world sure has been tempting tonight, hasn't it?" he asked. "The enemy just doesn't ever give up. They've taken their campaign right to our doorstep this time. Trying to tempt the weak with images of the material world, and scaring the hell out of the rest of us at the same time."

Figured he'd find a way to work the fireworks into his persecution narrative.[45] I wondered if he believed it. The smart money was on "no," but some people had the strange capacity to tell themselves lies and believe them. He certainly *sounded* aggrieved in a way that I found difficult to write off as acting.

The nearest members of his audience were shaking their heads. Even some people in the back, where I doubted Pearson could see them, were doing it. He paused in a way that seemed to invite feedback. A few people took the cue, raised their voices, shouted their *no*s and *nuh-uh*s.

"I tell you all – I am cursed sick of it. Sick and tired. Of the energy they pursue us with. Of the… the hellish vigor with which they… they're trying to tear us apart. But the good news is that we won't have to put up with them for much longer. We just got another secured letter from our relocation team today. And they have got some good news about what they've been building for us out in Nevada."

Some loose cheers. I tightened my lips. Relocation project. I wondered if Rebecca Munoz had known anything about that – if it had inspired the urgency with which she'd hired

---

45 Even more annoying that, in just this one case, he was *right* to be paranoid.

us. The more isolated Pearson's followers became, the more difficult it would be to reach through to any of them.

Rachel's voice said, "Got about a quarter of the faces scanned. Getting harder now that they're not moving around as much."

Inez said, "Ugh. If you don't need me, I'm gonna get a nip of fresh air." I felt the floorboards shift as she stepped away, toward the window.

Pearson said, "Out there – it's going to be a whole new world. Blue skies from horizon to horizon. No smog. You can look up at night and see the stars. You can take your children out beyond our walls and not be afraid for them. Won't that be something? Aren't you all tired and hungry? For change? I'm telling you here tonight that you're gonna… we're all gonna get change. One way or another. *Change.* I promise you – I will bring you the change. It doesn't matter how tired I am, how worn down, how much our enemies tear me down. I will never stop suffering for you."

Cheers at that. Some ragged, some less so.

"We aren't going to have to be here, surrounded by the enemy and all the material temptations they can throw at us, for one damned day more than we have to. No, sir. No, ma'am. You young folks in the audience, I say *no* to you, too. We are gonna be free of this world." Pearson paused, again cuing a response. He was feeding off the energy of the crowd, an emotional vampire.[46]

From the multiple bottles of water standing by his podium, I was guessing Pearson was ready to ramble for hours. He was

---

46 And I know my vampires. Knew what it felt like to be fed from, even.

hooked on the rush of this. Psychologically dependent on it. "Look at the faces of the folks around you. Young and old, white and black. We're all family here, aren't we? Those of you who could bring your families with you to our promised land know that they'll be eternally grateful to you. But those of you who came alone, who were cut off and forsaken by people still wedded to that damned… that materialist, capitalist world – you have family here."

The crowd stirred, and, as Pearson had requested, looked to the people all around them. Pearson loomed over his podium like a gargoyle, more frowning and severe than maybe he wanted to look – making sure his people were following his instructions.

"Them looking around helped," Rachel's voice said. "Facial recognition locks on twothirds of them now."

"Still nothing?" I had a sinking feeling in my gut. Since we were looking for two people, odds were that we should have found at least Rose or Joseph by now.

"Nada."

Pearson was still going: "Our enemies don't want us to get there. They have… They have marshaled their legions, put everything they have right outside our gates. They don't want the rest of the world to know that we've found a better way to live." He drew himself up. "And, if we have to, we'll show them a better way to die. Because one way or another, we are… are *not* going back out there, not to what we… what you used to be before you all came to me."

The sinking feeling fell deeper.

Pearson pulled a handkerchief out from underneath his podium. He dabbed at his forehead. When he spoke again, his voice had lost some of its fire. "We might have to push it to that some day. Just to show them that we're serious. And because we don't want to be here with them any more. We're going to break free. But they're making it hard on us." His voice cracked. "Very, very hard. I should have given up a long time ago. If I were anyone else, I would have. But people need me."

The main doors pulled quietly open. Most of the people in the audience didn't see it, but I did, and so did Pearson. His eyes darted right to it, even as he continued speaking.

A man and a woman in the security guards' brown coveralls stepped in as quietly as they could. In hushed voices and whispers, they spoke briefly with another man in brown coveralls. After a moment of this, the three of them headed back to the doors.

Pearson said, "I hope you all have good excuses for wanting to leave." His gaze shifted back to the crowd. And even though the nearest people knew that whoever was being pulled out *must* have had that excuse, they glared at the leavers with the rest of the crowd. Pearson continued, "You all know how important this is. We're a united front. We need to present solidarity. I'm tired of being the one force that's keeping us all together. Sick and cursed tired of it. It's more weight than one person should bear. I can't tell you the number of times I've thought to myself, 'Dallas, you just can't go on.' Or started to wish I'd just never been born. But I go on through, because this community... this community is worth it. Much as you people have a funny way of showing your gratitude sometimes. For I do it for you. I do it because I couldn't bear going on while seeing you all suffering out there, in that terrible, twisted... in that world where, without me, without that weight I've placed on myself, you'd be starving right now."

I hadn't heard anything so transparently manipulative since... well, that time I'd visited the Everglades. But Pearson's audience felt differently than I did. I saw a lot of nods and, when he paused for affirmation, heard *yes, sirs* and *uh-huhs*.

Half-consciously, I touched the grip of my Beretta.

At another time in my life, I would've handled this differently. Swung Spider-Man-style from my grappling line, slammed Pearson to the ground, taken him hostage in full view of everyone. And not relented until he or someone else told me where the Munoz twins were. Around when I'd broken into that facility in the Everglades – to pick an example for no particular reason – I would have done that. I hadn't had to think about anyone other than myself in a long time. I hadn't given a damn about the consequences.

Working with a team, *my* team, had changed that. It wasn't that I believed Inez or any of my other hotshots would be in danger if I swung down there. But I couldn't have protected Pearson's people. I wouldn't have done anything but confirm, in their own minds, the persecution narrative Pearson had put them in.

Was this how the world's super heroes felt all the time, being *responsible*? It must have been exhausting. No wonder I'd wanted to be a merc, not a hero.

Rachel's voice said, "We've got to face facts, darling. They're not here."

I said, "We can't just search the compound at random." Pearson obviously wanted as many people to attend these things as possible. The only reason the Munoz twins wouldn't have been here was if they had some other duty keeping them away. It wouldn't have been guard service. The Wakandan cameras would have spotted them by now.

"Now," Pearson said. "Now, now, now… that that is over with, we have some discipline matters to get through before this sermon really gets under way. Don't we?" He paused for emphatic nods from his audience. "We're only going to get through these hard times by being a united front, by showing the enemy that we have *solidarity*, and we've got to work to keep ourselves together."

He turned beside him. For the first time, I noticed a kid standing beside the stage. He was maybe fourteen years old. Short, oily black hair, like he hadn't washed in a while. A jacket that looked like it had belonged to an adult much larger than him. He was not restrained in any way, but he did have two adults standing right next to him, one of whom wore the brown coveralls of Pearson's security staff. My eye twitched. For a moment, I imagined myself back in the lab coats' facility, standing under guard.

The kid spoke before Pearson had a chance to say anything. He didn't have a mic, and I had to strain to listen. "Is this about the letter I sent to my dad?"

Pearson looked him up and down, as if taking his measure. "Yes, son, this is about that letter. Why do you think you're up here?"

"You told me you wouldn't read it. You told me you would just send it."

"Austin. Son. You *know* we have to be careful about how we treat with the outside world. You've been… We've told you that how many times?"

"He's not the outside world. He's my dad–"

"*He is* the outside world." When Pearson spoke again, he was making a visible effort to be calmer. Like everything else he was doing up here, it was all showmanship. "He made the smart choice to send you to us, to try to help you, but now he's trying to take you away again. We can't help you if you're out there. Do you understand that? And nobody's going to be helped if you're spreading lies about all of us in here. That's why we've had to have you in Learning Quarters." Learning Quarters. Another place where the Munoz twins could be.

He paused again, this time to milk another reaction from the crowd. He got it. Real, raw anger. Unrehearsed. Murmurs of disapproval, a shout of dismay.

Pearson repositioned himself, stepping between the boy and the crowd, as if to shield him from them. Suddenly the kid's protector – protecting him from the anger *he'd* stoked.

The kid said something so quietly I could not hear it.

Pearson said, "But they *are* lies." Even now that he was out from behind the podium, Pearson's voice still boomed across the church. I hardly noticed a difference. He had a good lapel mic, and, brief feedback aside, audio people who knew what they were doing. "And, it pains me to say this – you have no idea how much it pains me – you can't trust your dad. Not when he's out there. He left you here. He ran away from us and didn't come back. And now he's cooperating with the enemy. The last thing we need is for lies like in your letter to get out to those... those damned... those rotten journalists. They've done enough damage to us already. Think about how much more they could have done if I *had* sent the letter."

According to the exposé, the cult's defectors reported

doing things like locking people in closets for up to a week, holding them down and pouring water up their noses until they halfdrowned, cutting them off from any family members in the cult (especially effective with children), or just plain beating the hell out of them. My hackles rose.

In a voice just loud enough to be picked up by the mic, the kid said, "I want to talk with him."

"You've been poisoned. It's his fault, really, not yours, but he's gone and left you and he didn't even think to come back for you. Do you really think he cares about you? Do you think that, at the end of the day, you still matter a damn to him? If you did, why isn't he here right now? Why hasn't he come back for you?"

The kid was shivering now, and the crowd had gotten more raucous. Pearson held up a hand, as if to calm them. Then he turned back to the kid. "But it's lucky for you, Austin, that we know just what to do for you. To keep you from hurting us, and hurting yourself."

"More Learning Quarters!" someone shouted.

Another cried, "Just send him to Nevada, on work detail!"

I pulled the Beretta out of its holster. I didn't want to think about what I was doing. Somewhere deep inside me there was still that scared kid who'd come to Father Boschelli, and she wanted to do nothing more than act.

"I'll give you the chance to write another letter to your dad," Pearson said. "We'll see if it's acceptable next week, and I might even send it then. Until then, you're going to have to spend your time in Learning Quarters."

I lined up Pearson's head in the sights, nice and even.

Inez placed her hand on mine.

I hadn't heard her come back inside. I nearly jumped. Good thing I hadn't put my finger in the trigger guard yet.

"Peaches," she said.

I thumbed the safety back on, and returned the pistol to its holster.

Inez asked, "Do you really think that's gonna help?"

I took a deep breath, let it out slow. She was right, and I knew it. This *was* why I'd taken her along.

I didn't have the strength to answer her directly. Easier just to pretend that hadn't happened. Instead, I said, "We need to find out what and where these peoples' 'Learning Quarters' are."

"Don't like the sound of that," Inez muttered.

FIFTEEN

The same pair of adults who'd stood beside the kid, Austin, escorted him out of the church hall. They led him toward the dormitory on the eastern side of the compound.

Inez and I climbed out of the belfry and followed them over the rooftops.

The kid still wasn't restrained, and wouldn't be – not in public, where anyone could see him. But the adults stayed close, ready to grab him. They hardly needed to. The kid just looked down and stayed hunched and small.

We lost them when they stepped into the dorm, but that gave us a good idea where these Learning Quarters were. We studied the building from the next rooftop over. Peering in the windows, we saw blankets spread across floors, bare mattresses, signs that whole families or more were living in spaces meant for (at most) two people.

In the course of day-to-day life, these dorms would be packed. Inez and I would stand no chance of infiltrating them then. Not even in disguise. These people had lived together for months, at a minimum, and knew each other too well. But, judging by all those bottles of water by Pearson's podium and his compulsive resentment of anyone who had the temerity to leave, his sermon would last for hours.

It still didn't mean they were empty. From what we could tell from peeking in the outside windows, the top floors were still occupied. Elderly folk lay quietly in their rooms, or shuffled down hallways to the bathroom. In one window, we saw a teenage caretaker trying to manage twenty infants who absolutely refused to be put down for the night. Their parents had been compelled to attend Pearson's sermon, but the kids themselves must have been too noisy for his tastes.

"What do you think?" Inez asked. "These spitwads likely to keep their jails on the top floor? Where they'd have to pass the most people if they tried to get out?"

"Basement," I said automatically. The facility in which I'd been raised had housed all us kids underground. It was where, if you didn't think someone was as human as you, it felt better to keep them.

When the coast looked as clear as it was going to get, I dangled my grappling rope to the ground. Inez and I slid down it and dropped the last few feet into the snow.

Getting into the basement was easier than getting into the top floors. A vehicle ramp led down to a stubby loading dock and maintenance doorway. The maintenance door had a lock, but it was nothing I couldn't pick, even with frozen fingers. It made a satisfying *click* as it came loose. I pushed the door open into a dark and musty-smelling void. Even with our night-adjusted eyes, there wasn't a lot of light to go on.

We trampled over blankets tossed on the floor. People had

been sleeping on the frozen ground. It looked like Pearson's people had been stockpiling food down here, too. There were only a few full boxes left sitting in the corner. Jars of peanut butter, hard cheese, some crackers. Cheap, shelf-stable food that could be prepared quickly. There were five times more empty, broken-down boxes than full ones. What they had left couldn't have been enough to feed all of the people they'd stuffed in this building, not for long.

We poked our heads out into the adjoining corridor in time to hear distant doors slam. Muted footsteps came from the other side, headed away. I'd have wagered a lot that those were the adults who'd escorted Austin here.

There was more light in this cramped hall, but not much. Half of the overhead fluorescents were dead. The others were flickering or buzzing. The walls were sloppily painted white brick that looked like they hadn't been cleaned since the days this place used to be a school. Reinforced metal doorways lined one side, and only one side, of the hall. I hated to think what this place had been used for when it had been a school, much less what it was used for now. It reminded me, too much, of the cells in which I'd spent my childhood.

Behind some of the doors, we heard muffled voices. I froze when I recognized Pearson's. But it was tinny, like it was coming out of speakers. Painfully loud speakers, given the weight of the door between me and his voice, but still speakers. And there seemed to be more of him, coming from every door down this hallway.

I pulled out another camera orb. Scanned the hallway. Rachel, sharp as ever, figured out what I was looking for immediately. "A good amount of heat in the cracks of most of those doors," her voice said. "It's got to be body heat. Only a few of those rooms are empty."

I hadn't gotten very far when we heard, behind us, the maintenance door we'd used open. Then it slammed shut. Someone had come in the way we had, and they were cursing – muttering something about locks and carelessness. Inez and I glanced at each other. Nothing we could do now. We kept going.

"Stop," Rachel said. "The door you're about to pass has more heat than the others. Might be two people in there."

Sounded like as good a bet as any. I placed my ear against the door. No sound other than Pearson's voice on speakers.

"You feel lucky?" Inez asked, with a grin.

"Always," I said, though I couldn't force a reciprocal smile.

The door was locked and, strangely, harder to pick than the one outside. It took a minute. But whoever was in the maintenance room didn't disturb us, and the lock gave way.

As soon as I cracked the door open, we were assaulted by a blast of Pearson's voice. Inez muttered, "I'd had enough of this crap, and I was only there for a few minutes."

The door was heavier than it looked, and it had looked pretty heavy. Inez planted one hand against it and shoved it open the rest of the way. I nearly fell in.

Rachel had been right. There *were* two people on the other side. Both young, late teens to early twenties. A man, lying down on a thin blanket for bedding. A woman, leaning against the wall, who straightened as we entered. Both with brown skin and long, dark hair.

A flash of recognition trilled through me, nearly as strong as my relief. They had changed since the last photographs I'd seen of them, lost weight and gone haggard, but these were definitely the twins. Joseph and Rose Munoz.

A flatscreen monitor had been bolted onto one of the walls. It showed a big close-up of Pearson's warm and smiling face.[47] That, of course, was where the racket was coming from.

It felt like I'd been holding my breath the entire time we'd been in this compound, and this was the first time I'd been able to let it out. "Rose. Joseph. We're here to get you out. We were–"

Rose didn't have far to go. Two quick strides cleared the closet-sized cell. She drew back her arm, and, faster than I would have credited her for, slammed her fist into my chin.

---

[47] And *he* also looked different. A little younger, and his eyes weren't as red.

SIXTEEN
THE EVERGLADES, SIX YEARS AGO

I came back to myself a little bit at a time. Even air-conditioned, the air here still had enough humidity and Everglades stink to let me know I couldn't have gone far. Whatever the kid's trigger phrase had done to me, it felt like I'd been clocked by the Hulk. Either whatever he'd done had really left my nervous system shot, or, after the guards had come in and found me, they'd roughed me up. It didn't make much of a difference. It hurt as much either way.

An old-fashioned mechanical clock was ticking somewhere. I focused on the sound. It was the center I reassembled my disassociated senses around.

My eyes had been open for a while, but this was the first time I'd consciously registered the office to which I'd been moved.

The office was a jarring contrast to where I'd been last. It had a sparkling clean hardwood floor. I couldn't decide if it was real wood or vinyl, but either way it looked nice. Bookshelves took up a good amount of the walls. Two of them were full of binders, folders, and loose sheets paperclipped together. The binders were labeled with numbers and code names. The last was filled with hardcover books and big, serious-looking textbooks – *A New Manager's Handbook*, *Organization and Hierarchies: A Guide to Office Flow*, and *Sizing People Up in Five Seconds*. The kind of corporate manure that fertilized a thousand boardrooms.

But that was where normality ended. There were shadows on the walls where it looked like someone had hung pictures or, more likely, diplomas. They'd been replaced by a number of religious artifacts. Three crucifixes of varying ornateness. What looked like an image of a saint, a woman carrying her own severed head underneath her arm. Finger bones in a glass case. And, on a far wall just at the corner of my vision, a painting of a seaside… with boiling oceans under a blood-red moon.

Huh.

I was still underground. I don't know why I believed that as firmly as I did, but I knew it was true. Maybe part of me remembered my captors dragging me away, and knew I'd never gone up a level, or been taken outside. The overhead lights were shaded yellow and gold so as to give an impression of daylight. There was even a little fake fern, sitting in a rock garden.

My arms were at my sides. Bound to my sides, as it turned out – very tightly. My hands were numb, to the point that, when I tried to wiggle my fingers, I couldn't tell if they were moving. Someone had strapped me to this chair. The chair's legs were bolted to the ground, so I couldn't rock myself loose either.

The only reason someone would build a chair like this was to do exactly what it was doing now: hold a prisoner. I was not the first person to be shackled here. My blood chilled.

The woman seated at the desk was so still it took me a while to register her. She was on the advanced side of middle-aged. Her bangs hung loosely over her forehead and temples, with a streak of white running down the right side of them.[48] Other white hairs showed here and there.

She was dressed in military-style fatigues but was not wearing them by any dress code I'd ever seen. She'd trimmed her sleeves shorter. Put a slit in her collar to loosen it. And the patch on her breast where a nametag should have gone was not only blank, but showed the frayed stitching from where a nametag had been ripped off. There were matching torn threads on her shoulder, where a sleeve insignia might have gone.

We weren't alone. There was a second chair, positioned just ahead of mine. The only thing I could see from this angle was a tangle of black hair.

It was the kid. The one who'd taken me down with just a couple words.

"I'm sorry we have to meet like this," the woman said.

"I'm sorry too." I didn't have full command of my voice. I sounded slurred, and not as sarcastic as I'd hoped.

As if I hadn't spoken, she said, "We deserved something better than what you tried to do to us, don't you think? We've

---

[48] Like mine. At the time, I'd worn my hair shorter than that, but that was how I'd look later in life – like around the time when I was searching for the Munoz twins.

built so much that I hate to tear any of it down."

I caught the kid craning over the back of his chair to look at me. He darted back to his seat as soon as he saw that I'd noticed. I had to exercise my jaw for a while before I felt capable of speaking again.

"That's right," I said, when I could. "I told all my friends about this place. Big, super-powered one-man armies like Deadpool and Cable. And there's disks with everything I found on their way to about twenty different newspapers now. You're gonna have to tear this whole place down, lady. Secret's out."

She frowned. "You've done no such thing."

"You tell them that when they get here," I said, still slurred. It was less like I was drunk, though, and more like I was just waking up.

"What do you think we were doing with you while you were under hypnotic suggestion? You told one person what you were doing. Jonathan Shepherd. He's ash now."

You know in cartoons, when someone gets clocked really good, and their face turns into a cash register, eyes reading "No Sale"? Yeah. It was like that.

And now that I thought hard about it, I did have a vague memory of sitting in this same chair, answering questions.

"This really is no fair," I said. "Cheating. That's what you're doing."

The woman smiled thinly.

I cast my eyes about the rest of the room. More creepy paintings. There was one of a forest fire sweeping through pines. The moon had turned blood red under the smoke. An angelic figure stood on the horizon, her arms spread wide in a crucifix pose.

It took me a second to recognize the figure. It was the woman sitting in front of me.

"Cute portrait," I said, "Really brings out the gibbering madness." The best way to do this was probably to be blunt. "So. How are you connected to the facility that raised me?"

After everything I'd seen, there was no way this place *wasn't* connected to the one where I'd grown up in a cell. It wasn't exactly the same place. I had enough of the halls and spaces outside my cell committed to memory to know that this was somewhere physically different. But this had to be part of the same project. If I had been in full control of my faculties, I might have been a little more shook up about that.

"I didn't bring you back to the real world for you to ask *me* questions," the woman said. "I've got some for you."

"I thought you just had me under a hypnotic trance. Why didn't you ask me then?"

"You gave us some answers I didn't understand. Let's just say I'd rather hear them from your conscious voice."

There was gentle rapping behind me. A knock. "Come in, please," the woman said, her voice all friendliness and warmth.

One of the facility's guards entered. He was dressed in the same fatigues as the men I'd smashed through when I'd invaded the place. He may have even been one of the ones I'd battered to the ground. That would have explained the dirty look he gave me.

He kneeled before the woman's desk. That move wasn't military at all. Like her, he had torn patches on his uniform where a name badge and shoulder sleeve insignia would have gone. Interesting, that. They still saw themselves as military, but had obviously rebelled from whatever power had put them in those uniforms to begin with.

While they were distracted, I started testing the strength of my bonds – trying to get a sense for how tight they were, for any weak points. I probably wasn't going to be able to break out while they were watching, and while they could activate whatever post-hypnotic suggestion I'd been implanted with. But one thing to know about being a superpowered merc is that, if you want to survive, you never stop trying.

"Pardon the intrusion, Eminence," the guard said. "Acolyte Corporal Hendrickson just passed away from the burns he sustained in the fire. We thought you would want to know."

The woman's face darkened. "Thank you, child. Rise." He did so. "You may leave us."

With another deferential bow, he swept out.

"Not exactly military discipline," I drawled.

"We're not military. If you haven't already figured that out. We're family."

"I've never been big on the whole two-and-a-half-kids-and-a-dog scene, but, to my mind, families don't wear uniforms or bow to each other."

"There aren't many bonds tighter than family. That's why you're sitting here now."

I furrowed my brow. "What's that mean?"

"Most other people in your place would be dead by now." Before I had the chance to pry further, she changed the subject. "I would like to know why you came this way to begin with."

So that was the thing that, when my subconscious had answered her under hypnotic trance, she hadn't understood. "Are you going to kill me after I've told you?"

She blinked several times, and, for a moment, seemed genuinely shocked. "Of course not."

She was lying. Had to be. But something about the way she was treating me didn't feel right. I shifted in my bonds.

"I get it," I said. "You don't want the kid to know. Well, he's going to find out, sooner or later, what you've been doing here, isn't he? Kids are smarter than you think." I raised my voice. "Aren't you?"

The kid craned around the back of the chair. This time, he didn't look away.

"Why is the kid here, anyway?" I asked.

"Lazarus and I are partners in this," the woman said. "Aren't we?"

The kid bent back to look at her and nodded firmly.

"Lazarus, huh?" I asked. "Does that mean you're secretly five hundred years old or something, trapped in a child's body?"

He made a face. "I'm seven."

I caught sight of another painting to my right. This one was of a jail corridor. Not like the one I'd found the kid in – a conventional federal prison, an industrialized birdcage from hell, all bars and right angles. A figure dressed in a flowing red robe was walking down the grated center aisle. Her back was to the viewer, but, from the hair, I was pretty sure it was supposed to be the woman in front of me. Every cell door she'd walked past had rolled open. She was silhouetted in golden colors. The end of the corridor was a hazy, fiery, orange-yellow, as if she was walking willingly into an inferno.

Odd thing about the prison was that it was deserted. No

guards, no prisoners. It wasn't abandoned – the lights were still on – but it was lively as the grave. Had to be, I don't know, symbolic or something.[49]

"Creepy, creepy vibes," I said. "Paint these yourself?"

She said, "A number of years ago. I found myself with some time on my hands. It's a shame I haven't been able to keep up with it lately. Art can be very cathartic. And you're ducking my question."

"Yeah, I'm a little stinker, ain't I?"

"What made you come here?" she asked, suddenly somber. "I would really like to know."

It wasn't just the fact that she was sure to kill me that kept me from taking her seriously. It was that this whole thing sounded ridiculous. Chasing a half-remembered face across half the country. Getting people killed just by trying to fill in gaps in my memory. I'd obviously stumbled onto *something* big, but it just hadn't been worth the price Jonathan had paid. Never mind the price I was about to.

"Lady, whatever you got from me in hypnosis is all you're gonna get. Might as well kill me now. Do it in front of the kid, too. Make sure he knows exactly what kind of person you are." I looked at him. "Do you know about the crematorium, kid?"

The kid blinked several times. His mouth flopped open. I hoped what I was saying was landing.

Once again, the woman seemed shocked. "You don't know who we are, do you?"

"Gosh, if we did introductions, I don't remember them. Because *someone put me under hypnosis.*"

---

[49] People don't hire me to be an art critic.

"Neena," the woman said, slowly. "Lazarus is your brother." Her eyes were full of concern, and I had a hard time telling myself it was all acting. "I would never harm you. I'm your mother."

SEVENTEEN

It took me a minute or two to come to terms with what she was saying. I sat there for a moment, absentmindedly feeling out my bonds, trying to adjust to what she'd said.

She was the reason I'd come here.

Want to know the punchline to the joke my memory had been telling me all this time?

Her face wasn't the one I'd been chasing.

It was close enough that I could see where my memory had gotten the image. There were some similarities, especially around the eyes. But memory is a fickle thing. Age and a hard life had taken more than their fair shares out of her, remolded her like potter's clay. I'd thought of her so often, and for so long, that I had stopped remembering her. I'd remembered the memory, and then the memory of the memory. I'd taken a real face, made an echo of it, and twisted it into an illusion. I'd clung to it like a teddy bear until it had worn out and fallen apart. Trying to convince myself there had been something worthwhile in the place I'd come from.

The best way to think of memory is as a terrible roommate.

It leaves junk on the floor just to trip you up. Dirty dishes piled in the sink. Barges into your room unannounced. And it sure doesn't pay its rent.

More importantly, it's not reliable.

I wished I'd never come here. I'd made myself into some kind of cosmic joke. And, punchline told, the rest of the joke – me – didn't have a reason to be here any more.

"Ah," I said, quietly. Then, "Ampersand."

"You're more shaken than I thought you would be," the woman said. "I'm sorry. I should have taken you to get a medical exam before bringing you here. My mistake. I'll do better next time."

"'Next time,'" I repeated. Much as I'd thought she'd been about to kill me, I liked the sound of that even less. I asked, "You expect me to call you 'Mom'?"

She looked at me like a disappointed schoolmarm.

"My name is Beatrice. You can call me that."

The woman[50] took my silence as an excuse to expound a little more. "Much as I hoped we wouldn't meet again, I've kept tabs on your life. Things have changed a lot since the last time we met. And you're right – terrible things *were* done here. I used to be just as much a prisoner as you."

"Just as much as Lazarus is now?" I prodded. There was no mistaking what I'd seen of Lazarus's living quarters. It was a cell.

"Lazarus is under guard for his own protection," Beatrice said. "And you demonstrated even that might not be enough." She tousled Lazarus's hair. Lazarus, I noted, didn't react. "I

---

50 I could not yet make myself think of her as my mother.

wish I could have protected you the same way. They were close to killing you, you know. When you were younger. You would have been the last of your batch to go."

In spite of everything I was trying to do to keep my cool, I could not keep a shiver from spreading down my back. Nor keep it from showing. "What do you know about my childhood?" I asked, coldly.

She leaned against the front of her desk, folded her arms, and pursed her lips – as if debating how much to tell me.

"You were an experiment," she said. "You and all the other children you grew up with. You were created by a breakaway intelligence agency named Project Armageddon. It was started shortly after the US government learned of the existence of mutants. Their goal was to genetically engineer their own mutants in captivity. Its leaders cut off all government ties a few years after it began, and decided to take things a little closer to their namesake. They thought they could create a 'perfect weapon.' A mutant whose abilities were so potent as to render all future weapons and wars obsolete. Their genetic researchers were sure it could be done. They thought they knew just the power set that could do it, and were sure the X-gene could carry it. With the right engineering."

"Only it didn't work," I said. The tests, the conditioning, and the punishments all flashed through my memory. They kept pushing us harder and harder. Trying to draw something out. "We were disappointments. And when they started figuring that out… the other kids disappeared. Murdered. They thought mutants were too much of a threat to keep around if they couldn't use us."

If I'd been about to be "disappeared," I must have been a

disappointment, too. I had my powers, and they were good ones. Being able to manipulate luck is awesome. I would highly recommend it. But it wasn't what those people had been looking for.

"It was heartless," Beatrice said.

If she was expecting to establish a rapport, she had another think coming. I fixed her in my glare. If anger alone could have shattered my bonds, the chains would be embedded in the drywall right now. I asked, "Where were you in all this?"

"I was one of the original Project Armageddon staff. Data management. I also had the Xgene, though it hadn't manifested in any special abilities. Unlike your lucky self. When Project Armageddon separated from the US government, I wanted to leave. They would have killed me, but my genes were too valuable. They kept me locked away. Their scientists borrowed my genes to implant in one of their test subjects. You, Neena. They gave me a daughter, but they hardly let me see you. One of the guards helped me keep tabs on you, but that was the best I could do. I brought you what I could, just little treats, and tried to help you." That was where my memory of her face had come from.

"I tried to escape, but I couldn't," she said. "I'm not a warrior like you, Neena. So I buried my rage. I let them think that they'd won, that I was willing to work with them. They hardly let me see you, and never let me go to the surface, but, after years of trying, they let me live outside my cell. I had to keep my real self buried. But they let me out often enough that I could make more contacts and converts among the Project Armageddon staff. People who felt like I do."

She nodded toward the closest of the paintings. There was

some significance there that I wasn't grasping yet. And, to be honest, I didn't *want* to grasp it. My patience for this was well past gone. I finished the story: "You found someone who would smuggle me out."

"You tried to fight. You didn't realize what was happening. They couldn't let you make any noise. There were so many guards I hadn't converted to my way of thinking. Project Armageddon had implanted post-hypnotic trigger phrases in all of its test subjects. A way to control you. Edit your memories. My follower used yours to get you to Chicago, point you toward the Church of the Sacred Heart."

My voice was ice and steel. "Yeah. I know all about Father Boschelli's part in this."

That gave Beatrice pause. Rather than reopen that old wound, she said, "They didn't have any proof that I was involved. The guard who'd gotten you out went to the firing squad without breathing my name. But they nearly executed me."

Her voice was passionless. A shade away from being clinical. Of everything wrong about this so far, that seemed the most so – more than the paintings. For a woman who said she was my mother, who'd confessed to risking her life to save mine, she certainly didn't sound like she gave a damn about me.

Lazarus sat still. He was plainly accustomed to sitting through Beatrice's lectures. I wondered how much of this was going over the kid's head. He was a little young to absorb all this, even if he'd heard it before. Then again, so far he'd behaved a lot smarter, and more calmly, than his age indicated.

Growing up in a place like this, he wouldn't have had a choice. I hadn't.

Beatrice said, "All that happened out in the Louisiana Bayou. That's where you grew up. You were the last of their first batch of experiments. After you escaped, they considered that facility compromised, moved us all out here to the Everglades, and set up shop to try again. They weren't going to give up on their 'perfect weapon.'"

"And then you took over," I said.

"And then," Beatrice said, with no small relish, "I took over."

Must have been quite a coup. A bloodbath, I'd have been willing to bet. Projects this secret develop a culture of executions. That would explain why so much of this facility seemed empty.

As if I hadn't said anything, Beatrice said, "It was a bloody fight. But we had grown our numbers in secret. The original Project Armageddon staff were isolated, and they were getting weaker, and older. The men and women on my side weren't in project leadership. They were guards, research assistants, and office staff. They were younger, and they had access to all the facility's arms. We took Project Armageddon over in a night."

Nodding to the religious artifacts on the bookshelf behind her, I said, "You must've spent all your time here preaching and converting. All the people working on Project Armageddon were just as isolated as you were. They couldn't go back to their friends, their families, if they'd ever had any. Super-secret research projects always sound better at the start than they do twenty years in, with nothing to show for them. They would be easy prey."

I'd chosen my words carefully. *Prey* was right. This woman was a predator. I knew the type.[51]

She hadn't missed that. She pursed her lips. "They were looking for a better way," she said. "Better things to do with their lives. I can't tell you how disillusioned they were with the old Project Armageddon. How much pain they were in. They couldn't keep going. I made friends. Helped them see the world the way I did. Everything we could do with it. I taught them that they could do something better. This project had a terrible foundation, but it had the potential to make something that could very much help the world."

I said, "All that time, you knew what had happened to me, kept tabs on me, and never tried to contact me… *Mom*."

Some of the warmth dropped off her face. "I didn't want to. You always were a disappointment, Neena."

I hadn't been ready for that. Maybe it was because I'd never had the experience of being dressed down by a parent[52] that it caught me so off guard. While most of me was searching for a snappy comeback, my mouth sputtered, "Excuse me?"

"How many people have you killed? How much destruction have you caused while you were out hunting for profit? Do you even know?"

"Let me check the balance sheets," I said. "Oh, look. They say I helped save the world a few times, too."[53] I didn't expect

---

51 Years later, I'd find the same thing, manifested slightly differently, in Dallas Bader Pearson. She was more focused on an end goal than he would be, but the same psychopathy and emotional needs drove them. She wouldn't have had these paintings otherwise.

52 Father Boschelli was kind, but I never, not once, thought of him that way.

53 Fact check: true.

her to believe me if I told her how, but some pathetic little part of my ego wouldn't let me go without saying it.

"When I set you free, I knew you'd end up making poor choices. You could hardly help it. It was the way you were raised. The monsters in the old Project Armageddon made you that way." A flicker of pain crossed her face. Agitated, she pushed herself away from the desk, as if to start pacing. "But I'd hoped you'd *learn* from your experiences. That you'd rise above the material world. See that there were better ways." She waved to the crucifixes and then, strangely, to the paintings. "A *mercenary*? You had a lot of potential, Neena. You could have done so much better."

"Ooh, this is gonna turn into a 'why couldn't you be like your cousin, the super hero?' talk, isn't it?"

"You can't joke or snark your way out of this. You're not your friend Deadpool. You're just not cut out for it."

Ouch. I tried not to show that her hit had landed. "Cutting me right to the quick, Ma."

"You killed a man. Lawrence Hendrickson was a friend."

"Funny," I said. "You don't sound all that broken up about it."

"He died trying to keep the fire that you caused from spreading. You didn't even know him. He was just another victim of the chaos you've brought everywhere you've gone."

The name Jonathan Shepherd rose like bile in my throat, but I resisted spitting it at her. She wouldn't have cared. I doubted she cared about Hendrickson. To sociopaths, other people were just platforms to grandstand upon.

I asked, "And what would you have had me do with my life? Sit down and shut up?"

"Even nothing at all would have been better than what you've done. I always thought a measure of a person's quality was the number of people who could trust them. And the number of people they could trust in. You can't trust many people, can you, Neena? Certainly not Jonathan Shepherd."

I *should* have brought him up before she could. I felt the icicle plunge into my chest. I still wasn't over his death.

"After you didn't get our first message to leave us alone, we figured we'd have to be more aggressive," she said. "So we found Mr Shepherd. As soon as one of my people held a gun to his head, he sold you out. No hesitation. We told him we'd leave him alone if he brought you into an ambush, and he didn't pause even for a second."

The icicle drove deeper. "And you killed him anyway," I said.

"He was a dead man the moment he started looking into this. We have to protect ourselves from outside influence."

"You're lying." I didn't really believe that, but I had to say it.

Beatrice didn't answer. After a long moment of meeting my glare, she said, "I suppose it doesn't matter. In several ways, it's good that you came here like you did. You're going to help us advance the project."

"'The project,'" I repeated. My head was still swimming with the implications of everything I'd heard so far. And swimming in general, too. "I've learned to never trust anyone who says phrases like *the project* so portentously. They're always, always losers in overstuffed suits."

"Project Armageddon is going to change the world, Neena. We're going to make it better." She cast her eyes toward the painting to my right, the one of the empty jail wing. "Better than you can imagine."

"Is that what you think these paintings look like? A better world?"

"Project Armageddon was out to make the 'perfect weapon.' They didn't manage it with your generation, but they came a lot closer than they realized. We finished their work."

"Thought you were all upset about me killing people just a moment ago."

She looked at me like I'd just told her I hadn't graduated the fifth grade.

"Neena," she said. "The perfect weapon doesn't kill people."

I gave her the same look she was giving me.

"Think," she said. "*Think*. Past the little things your life has been so far. Of course the perfect weapon doesn't kill people. A perfect weapon wouldn't need to."

"So… what? Some kind mutually-assured-destruction situation?"

She shook her head. "You really do have a limited imagination."

"Let me out of these restraints and we'll test that theory."

"A 'perfect weapon' *changes* your enemy. Makes them so that they were never your enemy to begin with."

Maybe I really was that slow. It took a few moments for the full horror of what she was saying to reach me.

Beatrice said, "However it happened, and however much you took from us when you came, I *am* glad that you're here, Neena. You're going to help us make sure that our weapon is functional."

Beatrice reached out, and set two fingers gently – reverently – on the wrist of the kid sitting ahead of me.

EIGHTEEN

I needed to sit in silence for a minute, work through the implications of this. None of it was good. And, to be honest, I was too emotionally shell-shocked to figure out much more than that.

Beatrice folded her arms. "I can see we're not going to get much more out of you – hypnosis or not. For now. There will be plenty of time to change your mind. This is your new home, Neena. We'll give you a chance to settle in." My stomach clenched in revulsion.

I hated how much of myself I saw in Beatrice. Down to the hairstyle. I was going to have to change that soon, if I ever got out of this.

She reached her hand back across her desk, pressed a button next to an old-fashioned intercom speaker. It buzzed. The door opened, and I heard two sets of footsteps clomp in behind me. Beatrice told me, "You're almost certainly harboring fantasies of breaking free as soon as you're set loose from that chair."

She looked to the kid, who was still hiding from me behind

the back of his chair. "Would you like to make sure that she can't hurt us?"

I couldn't see much of Lazarus from this angle, but from the way Beatrice frowned, I guessed he had shaken his head. "All it's going to take is a few words," she said. "You've even got a post-hypnotic trigger phrase. You don't have to exert yourself if you don't want to."

He let out a breath.

Eventually, he said, "Fortune makes a fool."

The effect was like someone had jammed an electrified fork into my back and wiggled it around my spine. I jerked. The world went hazy, and then doubled as my eyes unfocused. However they'd programmed me as a child to get this kind of reaction out of me, it must have been intense.

But it wasn't as bad as before. Last time, the feeling had been like someone had wired me up to a car battery. This time, the shock was more like a reflex reaction – like when a doctor taps your knee, but across my whole body.

You know those classes at Professor Xavier's institute I mentioned, the ones that taught you how to recognize the signs of post-hypnotic suggestion? The ones that were useless for stopping the command the moment it registered? They weren't so useless afterward. The whole time I'd been sitting in that chair, I'd been repeating the phrase "Fortune makes a fool" in the back of my head over and over again, trying to denature it. That was supposed to work like a vaccine: the more I repeated a defanged version of it to myself, the more my mind was ready to fight it.

The effort paid off. I didn't lose myself to a trance state. My vision swam. When it came back, I was still seated in that chair. Two of Beatrice's guards – acolytes, she'd called them – were undoing the restraints binding my arms to it. They levered me to my feet.

I played along, pretending to be in a pliable daze. It wasn't all that far from the truth. So long as I kept at Professor Xavier's exercises, every time they tried that on me it was going to get easier to fight off.

The acolytes twist-tied my wrists in front of me[54] and marched me out of the office. I couldn't see if Beatrice or Lazarus were following me. I hoped not.

The corridor outside had the same metal walls as those I'd traveled previously, though the lighting was better. The part of the facility I'd sneaked into before must have been one of their less-used wings. This felt like a place where people actually wanted to live.

Though it took me a while to see it, what with lolling my head and pretending I was still in a trance, this place was decorated. Crosses hung on the office doors. Someone had set a table with fake plants at the far end of the corridor. And there were even more paintings. These ones didn't look to have been painted by the same brush as the ones in Beatrice's office, but were unsettling all the same. One painting was of a dark, deserted, and lifeless cityscape, silhouetted by a comet passing far too close overhead. The next, far more amateurish, was of a church congregation with a red-robed Beatrice at the altar, arms spread wide and glowing. The Beatrice wasn't as creepy as the audience. They were on fire. Flames licked through their hair, curling toward the ceiling – but no one

---

54 Amateurs. *Always* bind somebody's arms behind them, if you have to. They must not have had much experience with prisoners. Adult prisoners, anyway.

acted as though anything was wrong. They all sat in rapt attention.

I'd had enough of this.

I moved at a slow, shuffling gait. One of my captors prodded me to move faster. I pretended to stumble. When he grabbed for my shoulder to force me upright, I drove my elbow into his face.

I didn't give his companion – a woman with blonde hair tied back into a bun – time to react. Having luck on your side trains you to act first, measure later. I stomped hard on her foot. In one swift motion, I hooked my shin around her ankle and clubbed my bound hands into her chin.

She crashed into the wall. I whirled in the other direction just in time to see the other guard pull something snub and black out of a holster. It looked like a stun gun. I sidestepped just as he swung it in. I didn't plan for what happened next, but that's part of the joy of luck. The stun gun went wild. It connected with the woman struggling back to her feet, landing right in the small of her back. The impact jolted the other guard's trigger finger. With a spark and a *snap*, she jerked and went down spasming.

I stepped around Mr Stun Gun, hooked my bound arms around his neck and under his chin. Then I slammed his head into the wall.

He flopped atop the twitching woman.

When I turned, I saw the last thing I wanted to: Beatrice and Lazarus, just outside their door. Lazarus's mouth hung open. My captors hadn't gone down quietly, but I'd hoped to be able to at least reach the end of the corridor, out of earshot, before Beatrice had enough warning to come after me.

They were about twenty feet away. I didn't think. I started to run toward them. I had to take Beatrice out, somehow. Maybe hold her hostage. I'd have to make my plans later.[55] When I got there, I would figure out what to do with her.

"You need to use your power," Beatrice told Lazarus. "No training wheels this time."

My bound hands were disrupting my balance. I couldn't sprint. But if I could reach Beatrice faster than she was expecting, I might seize the element of surprise back. She was, at her very youngest, in her fifties, and wasn't very fit. Up close, she'd be no match for me, even if I hadn't had luck on my side.

Lazarus shook his head. He looked like he wanted to shrink back, but Beatrice had her hands on his shoulders. She calmly, but firmly, kept him between me and her.

She said, "Use it or she'll hurt you."

Lazarus opened his mouth.

I didn't hear him speak.

I couldn't have described how I felt.[56] The closest thing I could say was… a great lightness of spirit settled over me. It was the kind of feeling you get when you're drunk at four in the morning, but the night isn't over, and you have good friends to spend it with. The kind of feeling you get when you've been on your feet for three days and finally see a chance to rest. The kind of feeling people get when they say they have a personal relationship with God. The feeling I got when I realized I believed.

---

55 Or to pretend I'd had a plan all along.

56 And *still* can't.

All of these things were contradictions, but they were all true at the same time. My neurons were fizzing, cross-circuiting, shorting out.

Human beings were not meant to feel like this. Something in my head was burning.

It made perfect sense that I would stop running. That, when I reached Lazarus and Beatrice, I would fall to my knees in front of him. I couldn't show them how much it hurt. It did not occur to me.

This wasn't a post-hypnotic trigger. I remembered everything. The beatific, burning, indescribable pain. Beatrice taking Lazarus's hand and forcing him to set it on the top of my head, like a priest bestowing benedictions. Being led back toward the cell block, and then into an empty cell, right next to Lazarus's. And then the burning fading, like red-hot iron gradually cooling to air temperature.

I felt like I had to fight to become myself again.

When I did, I was shaking.

And even when I was myself again, I wasn't *really*. I've been pretty good about constructing emotional barriers between myself and the rest of the world. Survival habit. I needed them – first to survive the lab coats, then in the Church of the Sacred Heart, and as a mercenary. Whatever the kid had done to me had fried my brain. The barriers weren't where they should have been.

I wasn't shaking because I was cold. It wasn't even because I was angry. Anger would have been easier.

It was like withdrawal. Adrenaline pounded through me. I wanted that feeling again.

I was so alone. I should have told Cable, Deadpool, *anybody* where I was going. My emotions clawed at the sides of my skull like a caged animal, desperate to get out. I threw myself at the walls. This cell was so much like the one I'd spent my childhood in, but it seemed so much smaller. I only just – *just* – managed to keep from clawing at the door, scrabbling to get out.[57]

Everything pressed in on me. The overhead lights seemed closer every time I looked. I was still sure we were somewhere far underground. I had no idea how far, or how big this place really was.

I hunched in the corner, pushing my legs against my chest like I had when I was ten. The worst part was that, during the shakes of withdrawal, a good part of me just wanted to feel the burnout again. An unconscious part of me, certainly, but it was there. Separation was a kind of grief.

I tried to focus on thinking about what had just happened to me. Twice now, I'd been taken out with words from that kid. The first time he'd taken me down, it had been more intense than it seemed like a post-hypnotic suggestion should have been. It had felt physical. Like someone had cracked my skull with an ice cream scoop and then cored out my brain. Nothing in any of Professor Xavier's classes had mentioned that.

At the time, I'd let that go. I'd had more important things to worry about. Now that I was here, though, and with nothing left to do but think about it… the strangeness kept accumulating.

Every time it had happened, the kid, and the kid alone, had

---

[57] And then only because I spotted the security camera in the upper corner. I wasn't going to give anyone watching it *that* satisfaction.

done it. Beatrice could have said the code phrase herself. But she had made the kid say it.

Maybe I'd been thinking about this all wrong. Maybe that phrase he'd uttered hadn't been a post-hypnotic remnant of my childhood. The key hadn't been what he'd said, but how he'd said it.

And who had said it.

No one disturbed me for hours. I was exhausted, but I couldn't sleep. Not through all that adrenaline. And, no matter how hard I tried, I couldn't rebuild those emotional barriers. Not for the rest of the night, or what I could only assume was night. I couldn't help it. I even cried. I was shattered, and terrified.

Terrified for myself and, for the first time in a long while, terrified for the world.

NINETEEN
CHICAGO, FOURTEEN YEARS AGO

When I was thirteen, I thought I had all the emotional barriers I needed. I'd spent my whole life building them up. I'd hidden myself away from the lab coats, from the other kids I'd grown up with. Burying any hint of weakness because I knew everyone around me would pounce on it.

I thought I was ready for anything the outside world could throw at me.

Like most thirteen year-olds, my walls weren't as high as I imagined.

After learning my lesson about trying to make friends with the kids at the Church of the Sacred Heart, I didn't even try with anyone at school. I didn't stay in the cafeteria during lunch period. I got the same ham and swiss sandwich and apple every day[58] and brought it to the classroom I would

---

[58] That's the other thing about thirteen year-old me. I was a humorless little twerp. I hadn't really learned how to *live* yet.

have English and homeroom in later. During lunch period, it was empty. Peaceful. Gave me a chance to get started on homework from early-period biology and geography.

Routine was a kind of security. Something I could count on.

Thirteen year-old me and adult me wouldn't really get along. These days, if I catch myself slipping into anything like a routine, I go out of my way to break it. But I still had a lot of growing up to do. I hadn't figured out the security of routine is an illusion. It can be yanked away from you at any time.

During one of those quiet lunch periods, a couple other kids started visiting me. Jason and Luis. Jason was a big, deceptively friendly, red-haired bully who shared first-period biology with me, and Luis was the kind of hanger-on that all bullies seem to effortlessly pick up at that age. I had no idea what they were doing. Roving the halls, maybe. Like me, they hadn't wanted to hang around the cafeteria during lunch period.

Jason pulled himself into the seat next to mine and turned the desk to face me. He ground the desk's legs against the hardwood, making a deliberately loud screeching sound. I winced, and not just from the sound. He was the kind of fourteen year-old who fancied himself a ladies' man, and slathered himself with cologne. Made my eyes water.

"Neena," Jason said. "You're quiet – that means you're smart, right? How are you doing in bio?"

I ignored him.

He said, "Me – I'm kind of struggling. You want to help me out? Maybe study together?"

I could not hide how tense I was.

"Quiet kids are nice kids, right? Help me out."

"You're not getting my homework," I said.

He did a really good job of looking hurt. "I didn't say I wanted that." He and Luis hung around for a while, pretending to chat. Breaking more of my concentration. As he stood to leave, he patted my shoulder, hard enough to make me flinch. He knew I hated being touched. He went out of his way to do it every time he saw me.

One of the problems with routines is that they make it too easy for other people to predict you. Now that he knew where I was, he and Luis came back every day for three days straight. He sat himself in the desk nearest me, and always made that horrendous screeching noise as he turned the chair to face me.

He could've picked someone better to take homework answers from. I was barely making a B-. I knew the material. But the trick with school was that knowing the material was less than half the battle of doing well. I was having trouble focusing. I couldn't adapt to an environment with less immediate rewards and punishments.

My confidence wavered. On tests, I wrote an answer, and second- and third- and fourth-guessed myself out of it, on the basis of thinking I wasn't smart enough to have gotten the right answer on the first try. Multiple-choice tests were especially bad for this. They custom-catered to the paranoia my upbringing had instilled in me. Every right answer felt like the adults were setting me up for a trap. But the worst were essay questions. I couldn't communicate in ways that made sense to anybody else.

And I just plain had a lot on my mind. I couldn't stop poking more and more at the edges of my missing memories.

I was just starting to wake up to the fact that the holes in my head were larger than anyone else's – that missing so many memories wasn't normal. Thinking about that got my mind turned back toward all my traumas, everything my subconscious had been so eager to repress. I hadn't been sleeping well. I'd been spending a lot of nights staring at the dormitory ceiling, listening to the girls around me snore and cough. Exhausted but unable to close my eyes.

I didn't how to make that stop. Or what I could do to make anything better. But the pressure was mounting. A big, molten core of it sat in the center of my chest.

So when Jason kept pushing, the emotional barriers I thought I'd built up crashed down.

One day, he sidled up on the seat beside mine like normal, and then grabbed my bio worksheet and wrenched it sideways. "Gotta double-check my answers," he said. "You don't mind, right? Of course you don't."

I pulled the sheet right back. He frowned, and grabbed for it again. This time, my pen left a big streak down the center of the paper. "Why've you gotta be like that, Neena? Look, you ruined it."

Somewhere behind me, Luis was laughing. Weird, high-pitched laugh on that kid. I still remember exactly what it sounded like.

I grabbed my pen. Tossed it into the air.

Innocuous enough, right?

One of the many things I didn't want to admit to myself was what I could do.[59] How I changed luck. But I wasn't an idiot. I

---

[59] Consistent theme of my childhood, eh? Not wanting to confront what I knew. Or who I was.

knew what the lab coats, with their card and dice games, had been testing. All my life, I'd seen the coincidences pile up. I knew that, when I wanted something to happen bad enough to push myself to get it… things just worked out, and in ways I never could have anticipated.

Admitting all that would have meant considering the idea that I was one of *them*. The mutants. I didn't want to think about what would happen if I did that.

But sometimes I didn't think. I just acted.

I didn't look behind me, so I didn't see what happened. Luis must have been watching the pen as it spiraled upward. He tracked it, eyes wide open. Still open as the pen arced down. It landed, point down, right in one of those eyes.

He shrieked. He'd been sitting atop a desk, and he fell, flailing. His elbow smashed into Jason's nose.

Jason stumbled backward. His foot caught on one of the crossbars underneath the chair. As he fell backward, his ankle twisted. He hollered – until he crashed onto his back, knocking his breath out of him.

Luis ran out of the room, his hand covering his left eye. He bolted straight in the direction of the nurse's office. Jason limped after him, his chest quaking as he tried to gasp for air.

I picked up my pen. Resumed working.

I didn't even have time to finish the worksheet before the adults came for me. I never knew if Jason and Luis had lied about what had happened or if they just hadn't understood, because they told the adults I had jabbed Luis in the eye and then shoved Jason over his desk. My side of the story, that I had just tossed a pen in the air and nothing else, was far less plausible. It didn't matter that I stuck to it. I spent a few hours staring at the wall in the vice principal's office, not even allowed to continue working on my homework, until Father Boschelli came to get me.

I'd like to have told myself that I hadn't meant for it to happen, but that would have been a lie. I *had* meant for it to happen. If not that exact sequence of events, then something very similar.

Maybe that was the reason I didn't even try to convince Father Boschelli what had really happened. It wouldn't have been a lie in fact, but in spirit. And I wasn't ready to lie to him.

Not yet, anyway.

I sat, arms folded over my seatbelt, in the passenger seat of Father Boschelli's beaten-up, decade-old Accord. I stared out the window. We were caught in late-afternoon Chicago traffic, in the rush "hour" that lasted from three to nine every weekday. I had a lot of time to stare. Father Boschelli needed almost as long to figure out what to say.

This was not the first time I'd gotten into a fight, but it *was* the first time I'd been caught. And the worst I'd ever hurt someone.

Father Boschelli said, "I like to think I have a pretty strong stomach, Neena. To work with so many children, I have to. But I was still shocked at what that nurse told me. Did you know that one of those boys could have lost his eye? The nurse said he was lucky to have just a corneal scratch. He's still going to have to wear an eyepatch for a week."

Good. "They deserved it."

"What could they have possibly done to deserve almost losing an eye?"

"They wouldn't leave me alone." Even as I said it, it felt

hollow. My well of anger went deeper than that.

"Is that how you always plan on dealing with your anger? Hurting people?"

Was there any other way?

"You've got to start thinking ahead, Neena. They're suspending you for a week. If it happens again, it could be an expulsion. Or juvie. If that's how you deal with anger as an adult, you're going to spend your life in jail."

That was one consistent theme from adults that I'd never been able to understand. Looking ahead. Planning for the future. I'd always lived one moment strung out into another because I'd had no *choice* but to live that way. I didn't see that changing now.

There was nothing I could count on happening in the future. Not any person. Not anything.[60]

And I was starting to think that I couldn't count on anything in my present.

I had no idea what Father Boschelli would do if he suspected I was a mutant. Or what I would do if it turned out he already knew. I had never been able to stop wondering how involved he'd been in my escape.

"Why do you think God takes things from people?" I asked him.

I'd been thinking of my memory, in particular, but I was also curious to know how he justified misery in general. Like most kids my age, I was self-centered, but I wasn't inured to the suffering around me. A lot of the girls in my wing of the dormitory had terrible stories of their own to tell. Dead

---

[60] Remember that marshmallow test I mentioned? Taking that first marshmallow, not counting on anything else, was going to be my life's philosophy.

parents. Abusive families. Abandonment. Drugs. Senseless tragedy. Most of them had plenty of reasons of their own to learn to live in the moment.

Father Boschelli shifted in his seat, plainly unprepared. "There's no good way to know the answer to that question. But a lot of the time it's not God taking things away from people. It's other people. Like you almost took that young man's sight away from him."

"You're changing the subject from what I asked."

"*Who's* changing the subject?" He didn't sound irritated often, but he did now. "So one of those boys was looking at your homework. He should've kept his eyes on his own paper. And so should you. *Keep your eyes on your own paper.* You'd be surprised by how often that's an answer for religious questions, too, Neena. You can't be responsible for the rest of the world. But you *are* responsible for yourself and what you do."

"It seems like all I ever do is react to what people do to me." And that was what made people upset.

At the next pause in traffic, he glanced at me. He was used to dealing with bratty teenagers, but I was straining his reserves. "Is that how you see yourself? A blank slate, just reacting to the world?"

"Isn't that all most people are?"

"Is that how you *want* to be?"

I blinked. I looked at him, but, responsible driver that he was, his eyes were on traffic. Funny as it might have sounded, that was the first time I'd considered a different answer to that question.

See, the really knotty part about trauma is how much of

yourself gets tied up in it. I'd had no choice but to spend all my energy reacting to it. It had consumed my life. I'd started to think of myself as a reflection of where I'd come from. Worse, an echo. Never free.

Sitting in that car, looking at Father Boschelli, was the first time I'd ever really recognized that in myself.

Of course, that didn't fix anything. Trauma ain't like that. It can't be healed by epiphany.

I didn't often get to spend much time with Father Boschelli alone. On impulse, I almost asked him, then and there, how much he knew about where I'd come from.

But I didn't have the courage. Or the strength.

TWENTY

When we got back, I didn't need to be told I was barred from any activity other than schoolwork. I went straight to the girls' dormitory, to my bed, and stared at the ceiling.

Someone had built us a small basketball court in the lot behind our dorms. Spring had just settled in, maybe to stay. The other kids spent more and more of their time out there. That meant more space inside, all to myself. I had good reason to believe I was a mutant, but I wasn't sure. I couldn't be sure about anything. I had nobody to talk to about this. I certainly didn't want to bring it up with Father Boschelli. Not even because I was suspicious of him, but because he was an adult and he had power over me. Telling him anything would have just made me more vulnerable. I had learned, over and over again, not to make myself vulnerable to anyone – but especially to anyone with power over me.

If it was true, if I was a mutant, that meant nobody wanted me around. It meant I didn't belong here.

School curricula didn't cover mutants. None of the teachers wanted to talk about them, in the same way they didn't want to talk about anything else – like sex, crime, gangs – that scared them. But the news mentioned them. Kids talked about them before and after class, or on the bus. They repeated the things their parents had said. I'd become hypersensitive to any mention of mutants and eavesdropped whenever I could.

Three things were a constant whenever normal people talked about mutants: fear, disgust, and fascination. But the fear was always paramount. People were just plain afraid of mutants. Afraid of their abilities, of their power. Local news lavished attention on a mutant in Wicker Park who, by starting a fire in the palm of her hand, had burnt down an apartment and killed five people. All mutants everywhere became responsible for that. There was talk about mutant sweeps, mutant bans, and camps. On the bus, I heard kids say that their parents thought the president was a secret mutant.

All of Chicago's media, from newspapers to radio to television, were full of lurid tales of mutant violence. Magneto and his Brotherhood of Evil Mutants, fighting Captain America. Ancient immortal mutants conspiring to end the world. Some mutants had visible deformities and defects, but others, like me, could pass. The thought that we mutants could be hiding amongst them, effectively invisible until they chose to strike, only made us seem more insidious.

I'd started to feel just as trapped as I had in the lab coats' facility. The feeling had set in so gradually that I couldn't trace when it had started.

I'd reached the Church of the Sacred Heart in the dead of winter, right before the holidays. It was the middle of April now. I couldn't imagine what it would be like to stay here through the summer.

For the first time in a long while, it occurred to me that I could just get up and go.

Father Boschelli would call the police, get my picture posted everywhere, and have what would feel like (but would certainly not be) half the city looking for me. But I could probably avoid that. Especially with luck on my side. But I didn't know if I could survive anything else. I had nowhere to go. No shelter, no easy way to get food. I wasn't ready to be alone in a world I barely understood.

The night after I'd assaulted Jason and Luis, I didn't think I'd be able to sleep, but I dozed off around six, while the other kids were all having dinner. They shook me awake a little before ten, when they were getting ready for bed. In our close quarters, they couldn't help but jostle my bed frame. None of the other girls said anything to me. They must have heard that I'd gotten suspended. I don't think that surprised any of them. Father Boschelli would never broadcast the reason I'd been suspended, but word would get around.

More staring at the ceiling, letting sleepless miseries compound on each other. I had little to do but think of my future – a subject I'd been avoiding for longer than I'd ever been at the Church of the Sacred Heart. I'd spent enough time here to pick up on things that neither Father Boschelli nor the other adult volunteers wanted to say. Few of the kids who'd come here at my age had bright futures. The ones who didn't stay were shuffled around to different foster homes, to adoptive parents whom they failed to connect with no matter how hard either party tried, or just plain vanished into the bowels of the city. The ones who *did* stay sometimes couldn't pull themselves together enough to graduate high school – and those who graduated went out into the world underprivileged, without family and other fallback resources, and still dealing with all the trauma that had landed them in an orphanage in the first place.

It was tempting to think only in the short term. But, for the first time in a long while, I saw a little farther. A dozen terrible futures dangled in front of my eyes like mobiles. I saw myself in pointless fights worse than the one I'd gotten into with Jason or Luis or anybody else. Or in a jail cell with a stinking mattress and worse toilet. Or rotting in some abandoned factory or foreclosed home somewhere. Or working a miserable succession of odd and menial jobs, always moving on, never staying long enough to let people figure out who and what I was.

The last thought sparked a terrible new one. If I stayed here too long, let my luck run away with me too many times, everybody here would figure me out.

A little after one in the morning, when I was sure all of them were asleep, I crept out of bed... and went back to the classroom that held our one PC. Our overnight chaperon was supposed to come by every now and again, make sure that we were all where we were supposed to be, but I'd learned how to ruffle my covers to make it look like I was still in there.

Those old Usenet posts were right where I remembered last seeing them. I'd read all the ones I could find before, but now I combed through them with a keener eye for detail – anxious to find out what they'd done with their lives. Most of them had been understandably cagey about saying where they lived. These were not X-Men. They didn't have the powers or the temperament to be fighting constantly. They were mostly ordinary people, caught with "bad" genes, who wanted to live quiet lives. They'd gone to places like Usenet looking for people to talk to.

Some people put their powers to work for them. Mutants with enhanced strength, doing menial jobs, keeping their abilities hidden but never really breaking a sweat. Mutants who had a preternatural ability to charm people making a living by panhandling. Mutants with superendurance working extra shifts in busy kitchens, or as elementary school teachers. Or mutants just plain hiding or ignoring what they could do.

But even those people lived in constant fear of being found out. Fear was the one common thread that ran through every Usenet post I ever read. "Normal" people were afraid of mutants. And so mutants were afraid of "normal" people.

Some mutants didn't bother trying to live with the rest of society. One of them used the handle Vagabond. He, or she, or they[61] lived the life of a drifter, but seemed comfortable with it. They traveled through rural western states, from Idaho to Montana to Arizona, picking up odd jobs here and there. But this was more than itinerant labor. See, Vagabond claimed to have been blessed (and cursed) with the ability to control fire. Not only to start fires, but to put them out. During wildfire season, they offered their services to various fire departments. Vagabond would stand side-by-side with a line of firefighters. They would spend their energies keeping

---

[61] They kept switching which pronouns they used, probably to keep themselves anonymous.

a wildfire contained, like a mobile firebreak. The other firefighters could safely extinguish it so long as Vagabond kept their concentration up. Those firefighters, Vagabond said, had a tacit understanding, arrangement, and even appreciation for their talents.

Not all mutants could pass as normal. Vagabond said they looked normal, but that their skin felt red-hot to the touch. Blending in with ordinary folk had never been an option.

They were posting on Usenet in the hopes of contacting a journalist who they could share their story with. It was important to them, they said, that people knew that ordinary mutants were out there trying to do good. And they wanted someone to talk to about the hardships of itinerant life – about the robberies, the beatings, and the privation they'd faced just trying to live.

Other mutants used Usenet for business. One, calling himself Clockwork, was outright advertising for work. He said he was a freelancer, but what he meant was plain enough: a merc. He was a former mechanic with broad experience of a variety of military vehicles: tanks, APCs, armored trucks, and even some convoys. But what really set him apart was his sense of time. He claimed to be able to speed up his personal perceptions, turn the rest of the world into something that seemed, to him, like slow-motion. An obvious asset when working on time-sensitive emergency repairs. Or in a firefight.

Clockwork was not shy. He said he'd killed eighteen, maybe nineteen people (he was not sure if the last one had lived). He'd started out in an LA gang. When his talents had been noticed, he'd shifted to working for a drug cartel, and smuggled cocaine across the border. But when the heat of that lifestyle had gotten to be too much for him, he'd gone overseas to work for poachers, a few seaborne pirates. He claimed to have mellowed out, gotten steadier jobs working for private military contractors. But now, after an undisclosed break with his last employer, he was out looking for work again.

Of all the stories I'd read about mutants, it was Clockwork's that caught me the most. Not because he was a good person. I didn't believe most of the stories he told. He was puffing himself up not just to be more attractive to employers, but mostly to gratify his own ego. He was the type who enjoyed getting into arguments, and had dozens of vulgar and creative insults saved up for anyone who called him out. The thread went on for days and days, into weeks, of back-and-forth sniping with people outraged by him.

No, the thing that struck me the most was how unashamed he was. He was the first mutant I'd seen who hadn't started out writing for an audience of "normal" people. He did not apologize. He did not feel he had to explain himself.

He did want he wanted, and to hell with the rest.

A few other people posted about the X-Men, of a certain school for gifted youngsters. I ignored those. They sounded like a trap, to be honest. Even if they weren't, I wasn't interested in teamwork, or being forced to count on anybody.[62] Running away just to throw myself into someone's "care" seemed like a good way to get hurt more.

---

[62] More than a little ironic, considering the number of teams I'd end up on later on. X-Force, the Six Pack, and now the Hotshots… but I wasn't grown up enough for any of it yet.

The next time I glanced at the clock, it was four-thirty in the morning. Some of the adult volunteers, older people who had trouble sleeping, rose early. If I didn't hurry up, they were going to find me here.

I ventured off Usenet, and started chasing down the names and handles of people I'd read about. It took me a lot less time than I thought it might have. That should have been my first warning sign.

An article in the *Miami Herald* announced that the Coast Guard had halted a drugsmuggling operation and that a US citizen had likely been killed in the action. "Adrian Foxwell, aka Clockwork," was missing at sea and feared dead – and that any information about him should be forwarded to the Coast Guard. The article did not mention anything about his criminal record, or even that he was a mutant. It was the last trace of him I could find anywhere online.

I figured he'd been executed. Dangerous mutant, caught in a firefight. Easiest way for the authorities to take care of him.

I wasn't expecting to find anything on Vagabond, but I did. Too easily.

Vagabond had made the connection they'd hoped for. They had told their story to a tabloid reporter who, in his article, revealed Vagabond's real name: Carla Cuevas. The reporter billed his article as an exposé. Firefighters caught working with dangerous mutants! Fighting fires that those same mutants might have started!

A follow-up revealed that firefighters all over the country had stopped working with Carla, and that she had been imprisoned under suspicion of starting a wildfire in Fresno County, California. I found no records of what had happened to her afterward, nor any evidence that she had ever been a firestarter. Just the thought that she *could* have seemed justification enough.

It was five-fifty in the morning, and I was crushed.

I cleared the browser history, and hustled back to the dormitory just as the first of the alarm clocks started going off.

TWENTY-ONE

I spent the week of my suspension in a sleepless daze. I'd gotten too soft at the Church of the Sacred Heart. In the lab coats' facility, I'd been used to having my sleep disrupted all the time – by electrical shocks, by tests, by just plain terror and anxiety. We never saw natural days or nights, which made it even easier for the lab coats to mess with our sleeping.

At the Church of the Sacred Heart, most days I'd slept better, barely dreaming. It had been like a vacation. The vacation was over.

Having messed up my sleep schedule on the first night of my suspension, I couldn't get back on track. My body was in emergency mode. A low-level trickle of adrenaline seeped through the back of my mind at all times. When I tried to sleep at the same time as the others, my pulse pounded in my ears. I shifted in my bed, increasingly uncomfortable, until I couldn't stand it any more. I threw off my covers, found my shoes, and stalked off somewhere else in the church. Hiding from our chaperon.

Some nights I tried to look up more about mutants. I

didn't have much success. I'd trawled through everything I could find on old Usenet archives. Modern Internet talk about mutants just made me too angry to see straight. If there were secret enclaves of mutant discussion out there, I wasn't Internet-savvy enough to find them.

But, most nights, I couldn't risk using the PC. I heard our chaperon rattling around in the kitchen, or watching television at a low volume. I went to the corner of the orphanage farthest from them, sat in the darkness with my knees bunched to my chest, and waited for the blood in my ears to stop roaring.

When I slept, it was mostly during the day. The other girls had to rouse me for meals. They shook my mattress and stood back as if they'd just pulled the pin from a grenade. Their sour expressions said that they had been ordered to do this.

Father Boschelli was still looking out for me, at least.

He took his turns as a volunteer chaperon along with everyone else. Every Wednesday, he stayed up all night. On the Wednesday after my suspension, he surprised me. I stumbled into the kitchen looking for leftovers. He was already there, eating cereal under the dim glow of the sink lights. Those lights were always on anyway, which is why I'd thought nobody was here. And I hadn't heard him.

His cereal was some horrific sugary meltdown, corn syrup and corn flour mixed with more sugar and cocoa. The kind of breakfast that other kids loved but that made me sick. It was like eating melted ice cream. After I'd gotten out of the facility, I'd loved just about every food I'd found out here, but not that.[63] Certainly not that night, when my pulse was racing

---

[63] Now it's part of my complete breakfast. But it was a taste I had to grow into.

anyway. I think I would have started hallucinating.

I looked at the cereal and then at him, raising my eyebrow.

"Promise not to judge?" he asked.

"I don't make promises I can't keep," I said, gravely.

He snorted. Then used his feet to push out a chair at the other end of the table, and nodded to it.

"You're not going to tell me to get back to bed?" I asked.

"I'm not surprised to see you up. The other girls tell me you haven't been sleeping well."

"I'm surprised they noticed." Or cared.

"They notice. More than you might think. You haven't made it easy for them to do much with you."

Good. I shrugged. "I don't care."

I sat, if only because, at that point, it would have been too awkward not to.

He said, "You care enough to get into fights about it. Were those boys really so bad that you felt you had to?"

I didn't answer. Adults always thought there were simple answers to bullies. They ranged from *just ignore them* to *hit them right back to show them who's boss, and they'll leave you alone.* They didn't realize that sometimes there were no simple answers to schoolyard problems. That sometimes nothing works. That sometimes things were just miserable. And that it would have been insane to expect them to get better. For all his virtues, Father Boschelli was not immune to platitudes.

But he didn't press it. Instead he asked, "This isn't the first time you've fought, is it?"

Maybe he *was* sharper than I gave him credit. I looked at him squarely. "Of course not."

He nodded, unsurprised. I might have gotten up then, but

I had nowhere else to go. If I just left, he'd certainly send me back to the dormitory.

After a silent minute letting his cereal get soggy, he said, "Some of the other girls told me stories. I think they might have been trying to get you in trouble."

"Who?"

"What would you do if I told you?"

I considered. Carefully, I said, "I would thank them for looking out for my welfare. And let them know they didn't have to."

He snorted. "Heaven help you if that's what you think adults sound like."

"It was worth a shot."

"*Was* it? What kind of person do you want to be?"

"What's that supposed to mean?"

"Do you *want* to go around threatening people? Beating them up?"

I didn't understand what *want* had to do with it. It was all self-defense.

But no. I didn't want it. I couldn't help the smallness in my voice when I told him so.

"Neena," he said, "the times when we feel most trapped in life, when we don't see any other choice but the one we're making, are when we're at our worst. Because we always have choices. Even, or especially, when we can't make ourselves see them."

I shrugged. "If you say so."

"I know so. I used to be under… there's no good way to describe it except to say under the power of someone. A woman. I wasn't as young as you, but I was young."

Somehow I kept a straight face. "A woman," I repeated.

"Not like that," he said, hastily. "Think of her as… like a politician. Or a teacher. Or someone high up in the church. Someone you're supposed to be able to trust. She abused that trust." His hand, sitting on the table, curled. It seemed like an unconscious motion. "She had me and a few others leave our friends behind, abandon careers, to follow her. Once we'd gone that far, and found out how bad things could really get, she convinced us that we didn't have any choice but to keep going. That we'd burned all our bridges behind us and were trapped with what we'd done."

The dim lighting and my sleep-deprived mental fog only made this weirder and more dreamlike. I felt like his confessor.

"Did you run away from home or something?" I asked.

"In a manner of speaking. I served in an army."

I could not have lived a life like mine without learning to pay attention to small details, slight twists of phrasing. Father Boschelli hadn't misspoken. Not *the* Army. *An* army.

"What?" I said, feigning surprise. "You?"

"Don't I seem like the type?"

"No." *Yes.* Now that he'd said it, I could see it. There had always been a certain… unflappability to his tolerant attitudes toward us. He seemed like he couldn't have been shaken by anything we could do to him. Like he'd seen a lot worse in his life, and we weren't even close to it.

"Well, believe it. Give me an M4 carbine and I'll disassemble and reassemble right in front of you."

"Blindfolded?"

"No," he said, with a brief smile. "I was never that good. But good enough to get recruited into some agencies that you'll never hear about on the nightly news.[64] She brought me into it. And before I knew it, she'd brought me into a conspiracy inside it. We were going to take over the project... change the world, she said."

I was getting an increasingly bad feeling about this. I stayed silent. Just another little defense mechanism I learned from living with the lab coats: avoid saying anything provocative, look like you're listening, and you might just escape without punishment.

It was the first time in a long while that I'd thought about Father Boschelli in the same way I had the lab coats.

"She was very persuasive," he said, with another little smile. It faded quickly. "Charismatic. For a while, I really did think we were going to change the world. But her... little conspiracy wasn't really about changing the world. It was all about her. She was a narcissist. Do you know what that means, Neena?" Of course I did, but I didn't feel like answering. "Her world revolved around her. She needed to have other people believe in her. She fed off them. And she used a variety of tricks to keep us with her. All of them abusive. Separating us from our families. From all outside contact. Taking all of our savings and pay to 'support the cause.' Keeping us up in 'planning meetings' all night so we didn't have the time or energy to do anything else. Everything she could do to get us in deeper, to keep us feeling like we had no way to get out."

I stayed absolutely still – the surest sign, Inez would tell me later in life, that I was deeply uncomfortable. I'm a squirmer.

---

[64] More likely, though he wouldn't have wanted to admit this and maybe didn't even know it, that he had been recruited because he'd been willing to cut ties to friends and family.

I twitch. When I sit like I'm playing dead, something's wrong.

Father Boschelli didn't say anything else. At last, I couldn't stand the silence. "You felt trapped."

He said, "That was her goal. Getting out was the hardest thing I'd ever done. Because of her, and because of the nature of the project we both worked on, when I got out, I had nothing. No money. No 'official' service record. I couldn't even go to the VA. But it was still the right thing to do. If I'd stayed, I'm sure it would have gotten worse. In fact, I know it has."

"How?" I asked, in spite of myself. "You didn't stay in touch?"

"That's one of the things that makes her persuasive. She's very energetic. Even after I thought I'd severed all my ties with her, dug up all the roads behind me, she still found ways to contact me. It's important to her that she's at the center of everyone else's life."

The bad feeling in the pit of my stomach got worse.

"She keeps finding ways to get me involved," he said. His eyes were on the wall. He couldn't seem to look at me. "Makes offers I can't refuse. Sending me someone to take care of."

Though a lot of this conversation was not landing at the time, I could not miss *that*.

"Separating from her was the hardest thing I'd ever done, but it was still the right thing to do," he said. "It's still something I struggle with every day. But it made me a better person. Making us feel trapped is a weapon that other people use against us, and sometimes it's a weapon we use against ourselves. Are you following me?"

Both more than I wanted to, and less than I needed to.

Terror squeezed my heart. If Father Boschelli knew where I came from, he also might know what I was. Or, worse – was about to piece it together. I couldn't let it show.

He didn't speak again either. Behind him, the sink was dripping, steady as clockwork.

I don't know how many minutes passed before I said, "I think your cereal's ruined." It was just sludge in the bowl.

He ran a hand across his face, through his mustache. If he was waiting for me to say something specific, I couldn't do it. I couldn't absolve him, agree with him, or anything else he wanted.

"Can I go now?" I asked.

"Go to bed, Neena," he said.

Getting out of the kitchen was like taking a weight off my chest. I went back to the dormitory, which meant another sleepless night staring at the ceiling. But that was better than what I'd just been through.

It was not until years later, shaking off the after-effects of brain burnout in a cell buried underneath the Everglades, that I figured out who he must have been talking about.

Her. My mother. The face I'd chased into the Everglades.

The one who, for no reason my memory would allow me to access, had always had power over me.

On my first day back at school, Jason and Luis were waiting for me when I got off the bus.

It was no mystery how they found me. All of us from the Church of the Sacred Heart took the same bus. We had a reputation at the school: the charity cases, the kids who didn't really belong there. All the other students got in through family money, and, though they were too grown-up to say so in words, most of them were proud of it.

The only warning I had when I stepped off the bus was the overpowering smell of Jason's cologne.

Luis's meaty hands shoved me hard into the side of the bus. The roles had reversed. Luis had taken the initiative while Jason hovered behind him. Luis wasn't laughing any more.

"I know what you did," Luis raged. "You did it on purpose. You wanted to knock out my eye? You think I'm going to be scared of you now because you know how to throw a pen?"

Jason said, "Surprised her eye didn't boil and pop when she got that burn over it."

"It's not a burn," I said.

Luis said, "Yeah? Black eye? You get hit around a lot? Bet it could hide a black eye really well."

It could. I'd learned that long before I'd come to the Church of the Sacred Heart.

The other kids from the church were still filing past me. One or two looked, but most just kept going. They didn't want to mess with me, but neither did any of them want to help me. Fruits of my reputation. And, I suppose, of the way I'd treated them.

I could've pushed past, tried to move on. But, even if I got away now, I would just be postponing the inevitable. The only way I was going to get out of this was to give Luis and Jason what they were hoping for. To act afraid. To let them beat me up and go away believing, in some significant way, that they were better than me.

I would have been like all those other mutants who slipped between the waves during the storm, trying to escape notice.

Acting like they really were the dregs of the world everybody thought they were. The extras in somebody else's play.

Luis shoved me again, though my back was already against the bus. Pain spiked through my ribs. "You want to try that a second time? See if you can get lucky again?"

This was a crossroads. I knew it. I didn't have the excuse of the heat of the moment. My head was a lot cooler and clearer than, when I'd rehearsed this moment, I'd expected.

After my suspension, the adults would be keeping a keen eye on me. There were not any around to stop Luis and Jason now, but I knew that if I turned this into a fuss the adults couldn't ignore, I'd get the worst of their wrath.

I knew what I was doing. I wasn't ready, but I knew.

I swung my fist, and cracked it into Luis's jaw.

TWENTY-TWO
CHICAGO, NOW

I've been punched plenty of times, but it always helps to have some warning. Taking a punch well is the opposite of bracing for it: you have to go a little looser, roll with the blow, and you can snap back a second later.

I had no warning. Even if I had, Rose Munoz hit a lot harder than I would've expected.

"Owwwww," I said, holding my nose.[65] "God... damned... asteris–" Even sinking most of my energy into trying to curse, though, I was ready for the next punch.

When I saw her tense, I raised my hand open-palmed, let my luck take over. I caught her fist mid-swing. Her eyes widened at the speed with which I caught her punch, and then the strength with which I held it.

I took a step into the cell, pushing her back. I forced enough space for Inez to step through the door.

Inez could look pretty frightening when she was pissed.

---

[65] Love to sucker punch people. *Love* it. Hate to receive it.

"Missy," Inez said, "you'd better have one good excuse for pulling what you just tried to do to my friend."

"What?" Rose asked.

"I said, you'd better have one good excuse for—"

"I can't hear you."

It was the damned TV. It took up half the wall, showing an all-too-close-up of Dallas Bader Pearson's face, blaring his nonsense. He was saying something about a great spiritual revolution, a statement they would all be remembered for. For all the crowding and apparent poverty around here, Pearson had spared no expense for this television. Especially if all the cells were equipped with one like it.

The screen sat flush with the wooden wall. It had been mounted in such a way as to hide the power and volume controls that must surely have been on the television's side. The carpentry was inexpert, and the corners around the television's edges seemed loose. It didn't look like it would have been too hard to pry underneath and get at the controls. In spite of that, I saw no evidence anyone had tried.

After feeling around the television for any disguised buttons, and cussing, Inez stepped back. Rose saw what she was bracing to do, and grabbed for Inez's arm, but she had no more hope than tissue paper in a tornado. Inez yanked Rose along, so hard that Rose stumbled off her feet.

Inez smashed her fist into the television, effortlessly shattering its screen and crumpling its frame. The speakers stuttered, droned on in broken clips of Pearson's voice until Inez found those and ripped them out too.

The other occupant of the cell, Joseph, was still lying curled in the corner, as if hiding from the television. When

Inez and I came in, he'd turned half-over. Now he bolted to a seated position.

Inez had wrenched Rose's arm so hard I worried she'd dislocated Rose's shoulder. Rose jerked her arm back, holding it close to her chest. Her face was flushed with anger, and now with horror. For a moment, I thought she was about to cry.

"Do you have any idea what you did?" she asked. "How much trouble this means?"

"You want to find out how much trouble you can *really* get in, go on – punch my pal again," Inez said.

"Inez," I warned. *Ampersand*, but my nose still hurt. My voice was an octave more nasal than it had been a minute ago. I was still holding my hand in front of my face, and dropped it.

"Second-rottenest way to repay a rescue I've ever seen," Inez said.[66]

Rose's eyes blazed. "We're not here because we want to be rescued. You're messing everything up. You have *no idea*."

She tried to push through Inez and shove us both back through the door. Inez held Rose off with one hand, but Rose didn't stop trying.

Rose shouted, "Why don't you just leave us alone?" Joseph winced. Rose flinched, as if startled by the volume of her own voice. She dropped to a hoarse whisper. She'd obviously been up for days. "Why do you have to keep ruining the only good thing that's ever happened to me? Why can't you just let us live?"

"Rose," Joseph said, in the same tone of voice in which I'd said *Inez* a moment ago.

---

[66] No, I have no idea what the first one is.

"Father said they'd come, didn't he?" Rose asked him. "They're here, aren't they? Invaders."

Inez and I looked at each other. If Pearson had known we were coming, we were in for more trouble than we'd thought.

"Of course they're not invaders," Joseph said. "Look at them. Do they look like CIA?" Suddenly uncertain in a way that, in any other context, would have been comical, Joseph asked, "You're not CIA, are you?"

I opened my mouth to snap off something sarcastic, about having left my badge in my other leather jacket, but Joseph's tone stopped me. Silly as his question was, there was an edge of real fear to it. He thought there was a real possibility that we were. Somehow, I got the idea I wouldn't be doing any of us any favors if I just laughed him off.

Thankfully Inez picked up on the same thing. "We're about as far from CIA as your sister is from common sense."

Joseph breathed out. Genuinely relieved. "OK," he said. If he was bothered by the insult aimed at his sister, he didn't show it.

"Why on Earth would you think we're CIA agents?" I asked. The CIA wouldn't have any interest in a place like this. FBI, maybe. If they were motivated. But their conspiracy theory couldn't even get its government agencies right.

Again, in any other context, I might have laughed. But I was starting to get the idea that the more I learned about what was actually going on here, the less funny it would get.

"Joseph," Rose hissed. "We can't."

"Rose doesn't think you are, either," Joseph said, as much to Rose as to us. "Or she wouldn't be keeping her voice down."

Rose shot him a dirty look.

"If she really thought you were CIA," Joseph said, forcefully, "she would be screaming for help rather than trying to not draw notice and get us into trouble."

Rose rounded on him. "We already *are* in trouble. Look at what they did." She cast her arm toward the television. "The evaluation officers are going to blame us even if they know we didn't do it."

The only reason I was able to follow Rose's leaps of conspiratorial logic was because I'd heard it before. People who were so thoroughly twisted around one person's little finger that they kept twisting themselves even when that person wasn't there.

Inez snorted. "Honey, the day when I work for an acronym is the day I roll on over into a grave."

In our ears, Rachel asked, "Does 'Agency X' count as an acronym? Because you used to wo–"

"Shut up," Inez told Rachel.

"*No!*" said Rose, who, of course, couldn't hear Rachel. She looked like she was about to take Joseph's suggestion and start hollering for help.

What a damn mess.

I said about the only thing I could think of that might shut her down: "We were sent by your mom. Rebecca. Remember her?"

That didn't have the effect I'd hoped. Rose just looked angrier. Her chin trembled. "She's part of it."

Joseph, though, straightened. "Do you really mean that?" he asked us.

Inez asked, "What'd you think we'd bust in here for? To complain about the volume?"

Joseph shook his head, as if taking Inez's answer at face value. "I thought it was a mistake. Or you were looking for somewhere to hide. We're not worth it."

These kids had been *inside* for too long. The warped narrative logic of Pearson's compound had seeped all the way in, probably too subtly for them to notice. They saw two possibilities: either the world was conspiring against them, or they were so far beneath the world's notice that they were gum underfoot, worth just enough notice to be scraped off.

At the end of the corridor outside, something *clicked*. A key in a lock. Hinges creaked. Someone was coming.

I slid the cell door almost closed, stopping it a hair before the lock could click into place and trap us all in here. (I mean, sure, Inez could smash the door open – but that would make a lot of noise.)

To be honest, I was itching for a fight. Whoever was coming down that hallway was volunteering themselves as a target. *Someone* was going to have to pay for what was happening here. But there was a good chance that whoever was coming was just as much Pearson's victim as these kids.

"OK," I said, quietly, "You want to tell me anything you know about how to get out of here?"

Rose said, "We can't leave."

Not *we don't want to leave*. "Tell me that again in thirty minutes, when we're all out of here."

Rose said, "We were only supposed to be in here for four days. The evaluation officers will be back for us any minute. You have to go. It's bad enough that the TV is broken."

Inez paled. Didn't see that often. "Wait just one corn-shucking minute. Four days?"

"Been here for five now," Joseph said, miserably.

"With that TV going all the time?" Inez asked.

"It could've been worse," Joseph said.

"Five days," Inez repeated. "No wonder y'all went crazy."

I elbowed Inez in the stomach a little harder than I meant to. I couldn't have hurt her, but she still flinched. She looked at me.

"Don't make fun of them." I said it quietly enough that I hoped the twins didn't hear me, especially if their ears were still ringing after so long with that television.

Inez opened her mouth to protest, but then caught the look in my eyes. She didn't know everything about my past, but she knew enough. Between the off way I'd been acting all night, and the barely suppressed anger in the curl of my lips now – hopefully she was starting to piece it together. I didn't want to have to explain it.

Even explaining it to a close friend, I didn't think I could bear it.

Inez held up her hands, palms flat, and stepped gracefully back. I breathed out.

"OK," I said, turning to Joseph. "Let's hear it. Why do you think you deserved it?"

"I'm the reason we're here," he said. "It was *my* infraction."

Rose folded her arms, faced the wall. I looked to her, and then back to Joseph.

"Father sent Rose here too," Joseph said. "He said so that she could be a 'good influence' on me."

When Rose said nothing, Inez said, "Pearson makes you call him 'Father?'"

Joseph blinked. "Well, yeah. Or Dad." As if it were the most obvious thing in the world. It had been a long time since he'd spoken to anyone outside the compound.

As he explained it, Joseph had caught Pearson's attention a while ago, and not for good reasons. He'd followed his sister Rose into the movement. At first, it had been to keep an eye on her. And then as a genuine believer. But his enthusiasm had been flagging ever since the exposé, when Pearson had retreated to the compound and insisted that more and more of his people stay shut in with him. To my complete lack of surprise, life at the compound had been more tolerable when Pearson had spent most of his time at the state capital in Springfield.

"I started making plans to go," Joseph said. His eyes were rooted on the floor. "I know it was wrong, thinking about it. But I couldn't help it."

Inez screwed up her face, but, out of deference to me, she didn't say anything.

"Father has a way of... of getting inside your head," Joseph said. "He called me in for an interview, just him and me, alone in his office. When I came here, started believing, I used to dream of that kind of opportunity, you know? Spending time with him. He tries to make time for everybody after his sermons, but there are so many of us. Five minutes with him used to be magical. He has this talent, you know? For understanding people. Figuring out what they came looking for. I must have said something, done something. He knew I was thinking about going."

Some people *were* just that charismatic. With Pearson, though, I figured there had to be a trick. Informants placed among the congregation, watching people like Joseph carefully.

"He asked me if I was going to talk to the media if I

ever went," Joseph said. He still couldn't meet our eyes. "I couldn't promise him no. I was just daydreaming about going home, back to the way things used to be. That's all I was focused on."

It had to be more than that if Joseph had told Pearson to his face that he was considering talking to the media. But five days of torture, self-recrimination, and Rose had broken him down to the point where that was all he wanted to say.

"What made you want to go?" I pressed.

He shifted. Maybe if his sister hadn't been here, he would have said more. "Life here can be... hard. Father can be very demanding. I guess I'm a lot weaker than I realized. I don't think I could've gotten past the guards anyway."

Again, spoken in a completely even tone of voice. As if it was *normal* to have armed guards blocking your freedom of movement.

"And I couldn't have gone alone." His eyes flicked to Rose. "Father said Rose should come down here too. Keep an eye on me."

Translated: Pearson had decided to punish Rose too, as a tactic to instill extra guilt in Joseph. A reminder that, if Joseph left, Rose would still be here for Pearson to take his frustrations out on. If Pearson needed an excuse, he would punish Rose for not "doing as much as she could" to persuade Joseph to stay – but if his control over the rest of his followers was tight enough, he wouldn't even need an excuse. He would just toss her in here again.

Pearson usually separated families as a means to better control them. But he was a creative man, and it all came down to emotional blackmail. He'd seen, accurately, that by harming Rose, he could better control Joseph.

In the corner, Rose's shoulders were shaking.

Joseph nodded to Rose. "This is her first time in Learning Quarters," he said. He couldn't quite meet my eyes. "It's my third."

"I shouldn't be here," Rose said. "I didn't do anything wrong."

Incredible pain flickered across Joseph's expression. Pearson's strategy was working. For Rose's sake, Joseph had almost extinguished the last spark of rebellion in him. Nevertheless, he said, "Father has hundreds and hundreds of hours of sermons to play for us."

"He's recording *that* much of himself?" Inez asked.

"He loves to get in front of a camera, or a crowd... anything, really."

"It helps him spread his message," Rose said.

I remembered Pearson's insistence on fitting as many people in the church as he could, and the knocked-down interior walls. The way he'd laser-focused on the men in the back getting up and leaving. It was a pathological need. Getting attention and controlling his audience. His "spiritual revolution," everything happening on this compound, were excuses manufactured to meet those needs. It was the only lens through which this whole place made sense.

"You'd better leave quick," Rose said, her voice tight. "Our evaluation officer is going to be here any minute. We're going to have enough to explain without you here."

"Rose," Joseph said. "Our evaluation officer hasn't been here yet."

"Is that normal?" I asked.

He shook his head. "Last two times I was down here, my

evaluation officer came by several times every day. I haven't seen ours yet at all."

Not a good sign. Things seemed to be gradually slipping, falling apart, all over the compound. I remembered how tired everyone in the church had looked. How few supplies Inez and I had stumbled across in the basement.

"You don't have to put up with this anymore," Inez said. "We're gonna getcha out of here."

Rose stopped shaking, as if she'd seized up.

"I know you still want to go," I told Joseph. "You don't have to say so." I doubted he would in front of Rose. But if he didn't deny it, that would be a victory.

"You can't," Rose said, in a voice much smaller than I'd heard her use before.

"You want to try us?" Inez crossed her arms. "You're coming along too."

Rose turned. Her eyes were redder than they had been a minute ago. Five days of this had pushed her to her emotional brink. "That's not possible."

"Are you gonna tell us that you don't *want* to go?" Inez asked.

She sealed her lips tight. Wouldn't answer.

Inez was starting to get how to deal with them. How to get them to speak through their conditioning. I was proud of her.

"If you don't want to, just say it," Inez said.

"I–" Rose started to say.

A shrill, electronic tone from above interrupted her. I winced, held my hand up to my ears. The noise was coming from yet *another* set of speakers above us, echoed in the corridor outside and the cells all around.

The tone faded, replaced by Dallas Bader Pearson's deafening voice: "My friends, my family – I have a very solemn duty to execute tonight." His voice audibly broke. He must have been doing this live. "A duty that seemed inevitable but that I was still hoping to delay."

"Heck's sake," Inez said, when I could hear her again. "Doesn't he ever get tired of talking? Hoped he'd gotten it all out of his system."

Joseph and Rose looked more alarmed than I'd expected. It wasn't just the volume or the jump-scare that had startled them. Joseph paled. He said, "I thought he called everyone to a sermon just an hour ago. We heard the bells in here."

"What do you mean, *just* an hour ago?" Inez asked.

Rose said, "Father's sermons usually last three or four hours. Especially in times of emergency, like it's been since he came back to the compound."

"Something must be wrong," Joseph said.

Pearson's deafening voice cut off anything else Joseph might have said. It was likely amplified in here to boost his announcements over the volume of the televisions – though I wouldn't have put it past him to subject everyone in the compound to this. "It has been brought to my attention," he said, gravely, "that the disruptions... the distractions in the city were more than temptations that the material... the material world was sowing to lure the vulnerable among us away from the movement. I suspected it when I first heard it, but I didn't want to alarm anybody by repeating it, but it's true." His voice hardened. "It was cover. Disguising an infiltration into our home."

"Uh oh," Rachel's voice said in my headset.

Pearson went on: "I have in my hands incontrovertible evidence that we have… proof that we have… we have been infiltrated tonight. A coordinated attempt by outside forces to send spies and saboteurs into our home. A prelude to some kind of… to test us, to prepare us for what I've warned you all will happen. And I have no doubt that whoever infiltrated us is still here."

Inez slapped her forehead. One of us must have left something behind. Bootprints by the fence, or on a roof. Or maybe Inez had left the fence too visibly damaged. I cursed, but resisted the urge to start a blame game. The fact was, it was inevitable that we were going to get caught sometime. If not coming in, then going out.[67]

Cameras I could beat. Security systems I could beat. If you'd shown me something to hack, I could have hacked it. But hundreds of paranoid people crammed into a handful of buildings, each of whom could pick Inez and me out as strangers, couldn't be beat. Not forever. It was a testament to our skill that we had gotten as far as we had.

We'd seen signs of trouble earlier: those two men that had interrupted the sermon to pull out another audience member – the ones whose departures had so visibly upset Pearson. They must have been security officers.

Pearson said, "For your own safety, everyone not on a security team who was not able to attend the sermon needs to get to the church now. Those of you who are sick, those of you who are elderly, who are taking care of the young ones – we need all of you here, tonight, as soon as possible. Help

---

[67] Part of me was still expecting to have to drag Joseph and Rose out of here.

your neighbors. Do everything you can to get here. Protection teams, sweep the buildings and make sure everyone gets to the church. Security teams, to the gates. Heavy ordnance. Go, go, go – like we drilled."

He must have kept all of his audience in the church, even after leaving to make his announcement. They were probably still crammed in there now.

"This is not a drill. This is… this is…. is a…" Pearson was audibly falling apart, losing his words. "This is exactly what we were all afraid of. Maybe worse."

Rose was saying something, but I couldn't hear it over the ringing in my ears. Inez waited a moment, gingerly took her hands off her ears, but chose exactly the wrong second. Pearson wasn't done.

There was an uncomfortable finality in Pearson's voice when he said, "See you soon, and God bless."

"Ow," Inez said.

"Yeah," Joseph said, loud enough for us to hear.

Joseph looked much more worried than he had when Inez and I had broken into his cell. I asked him, "Exactly what kind of heavy ordnance was he talking about?"

Rose and Joseph looked to each other, their tensions forgotten. There was still a barrier between us and them. Even Joseph had been so conditioned that he didn't want to give away any of the compound's secrets, even now.

"Rifles," Joseph said, when Rose didn't speak. "Lots of rifles. Some grenades. Old military hardware. Father put a lot of money into it."

"For our protection," Rose said.

I'd like to say I was shocked. That the news sent a frisson

of fear down my back. All I felt was tired. I'd already figured things had gotten this bad.

Inez asked, "Does what's going on now seem like protection to you?"

"You don't understand," Rose said. "They tried to assassinate him once. We all saw it."

Inez muttered, "Shame it didn't take." Lucky for her, our ears were ringing enough that only I could hear her. It wouldn't have surprised me to learn that Pearson had staged an assassination attempt on himself.

"Hate to break it to you kids," I said, "but the outside world is hardly aware of you. I doubt the FBI or the CIA or S.H.I.E.L.D. or anybody but your families has thought twice about what's going on here." They should have.

"No," Joseph said. "In our drills, he…" He looked to Rose, as if for permission to continue. Rose must have been genuinely worried, because she didn't deny him it. "He had everyone come to the church for a sermon, and started one, but acted the whole time like we were under siege. The CIA, or any other one of his enemies, or whoever, was about to break into the compound."

Inez and I exchanged a glance. "He wants you all always scared out of your wits," Inez said.

"It seemed like it could happen," Rose said.

Joseph was trying to make himself say something. He had to fight to spit it out. "He had the security teams act like they were really going to shoot us if we tried to leave the church. And then had us act like the CIA was going to burn down the church with all of us inside it. He said it would be the end of our movement, but the start of our revolution."

The cell might as well have dropped straight into a pit as far as my stomach was concerned. I couldn't speak for a moment. Inez picked up my slack. "That's a mighty damn ghoulish thing to practice for, isn't it?" she asked.

Pearson knew the CIA wasn't after him. His type was delusional, but only to a point.

If anyone was going to start that church on fire, it wasn't going to be anyone outside the compound. And I think Rose knew that.

"With so many enemies around us, it would have been irresponsible not to," Rose said. Even she didn't look convinced. She bit her bottom lip, looked to Joseph.

"You thought it would never come to that," I said, when I could speak again.

"I don't know," Rose said. "I believed it when it was happening. I mean, it seemed like something that *could* happen. But I thought we were better than that... that we could win..."

Just like the moment when Rose had accused me of working for the CIA, she and her brother had trained themselves to behave as though something was true even when they knew it wasn't. Pearson had done this to them – to all of his followers. Deliberately and methodically. It started with small things, little self-taught lies. *Father hadn't really made that prediction that hadn't come true. Father needs to lie to new members to bring them into the family.* And escalated from there. It was more than a way of life; it was a way of thinking.

"And just how often have you done these drills?" Inez asked.

"It used to be every other month... Since he came back from Springfield, it's been at least once a week. Sometimes more."

Inez looked as horrified as I felt. She said, "With all those people already inside the church, and armed guards outside…"

"This isn't really happening, is it?" Joseph asked.

I wavered. I felt like I was about to step off the edge of a cliff. "Will your 'evaluation officer' be coming down here to move you to the church too?" I asked.

"I don't know," Joseph said. "She hardly remembered to deliver our meals so far."

I took a step off the edge. Toward the door. "Then you're getting out of here."

"*No!*" Rose backed against the wall. Her hands dug into it, like she would have tried to physically cling on.

"Darlin', you can't seriously think this is the place for you to be right now," Inez said.

"I'm needed here," Rose said.

"Yeah?" I asked. "Is that why Pearson threw you in the basement?"

Inez glanced at me. I *was* coming in a little hard, especially after how I'd told her not to make fun of them. But I had a sense of where to push. I said, "Deep down, you *know* this isn't right. You know you have to come with us. Come on."

She yanked away from me and slid back farther into the corner. Her eyes were cold, but her lip trembled.

Well, I hadn't really expected her to give. Not on the first shove, anyway.

"Is Pearson still in that church?" I asked. "Where's he broadcasting from?"

Rose kept her lips sealed. She was shutting down. Get an "evaluation officer" or, hell, anyone else from Pearson's church in here, and she'd go right back to fighting us just to prove her loyalty.

"Father has an office," Joseph stammered. "It's not in the church, but right next door. Top level of what used to be school admin. Former president's office."

"Thank you. Then we're getting you two out of here right now."

"I'm not leaving her," Joseph said.

Inez set her hand on my shoulder. "Peaches," she said. "We don't have the time."

She was right. It would be hard enough to get Joseph past security, especially with security armed, alerted, and paranoid. And with Rose, there was no chance. She'd fight all the way.

"I'll stay here with them," Inez said. "You do what you know you want to do."

Best friends always have a sense for what you're about to do, even before you do. She'd seen where my feet were carrying me. To stop this.

"Alone?" I asked.

"You know that, with the compound kicked up like a hornet's nest, one person is gonna be able to move faster than two."

I didn't know what I would have done without her. "I'll stay in touch," I said, tapping my mic.

She touched her earbud. "Do."

And then I was out the door.

TWENTY-THREE

In the corridor outside the Munoz's cell, there was no sign of the "evaluation officer" or whoever we'd heard earlier. They must have heeded Pearson's summons. All the other cell doors were still locked. Pearson's recorded voice spilled through most of them. The evaluation officers had either forgotten their wards were down here, or they just didn't care.

Good. It meant Inez and the twins would be safe for a little while longer.

"Rachel, I need to know exactly which building, floor, and room the former president of this school had his office in," I said.

"On it." Rachel's voice was clipped and focused. She had heard the entire conversation, and knew the stakes.

The maintenance area we'd come through was still empty. A glowing exit sign marked my path. I slowed down just enough to keep from slamming through the doors.

Outside was a cacophony of noise. I crept up the recessed stairwell and peered over the edge, but I might as well have bolted pell-mell over the railing for all the attention anyone would have paid me. There were more people about, hustling under sidewalk lamps, than I had ever seen in the compound before. Old folks – confused and complaining or crying – hustled along by caretakers still in socks or bare feet. Men and women held screaming toddlers who'd just woken up. Farther ahead, that kid I'd seen earlier, Austin, was being pushed along by the same guard who'd escorted him away.

All of them were headed toward the open church doors. Somehow, Pearson's people must have found more space in there. Yellow light spilled from the entranceway, across the campus' snow-covered lawn.

So long as I headed in the same direction as everyone else, I probably could have just run out, unnoticed – at least until I reached the church. The church entrance was flanked by four armed, agitated-looking security guards. They took a look at everyone before waving them inside. Something I hadn't noticed until I'd seen them in the light: they all wore headsets and mics like mine. One of the four guards was speaking into his.

There were no other guards in the center of the compound. It wasn't until I raised my hand to block the lights that I was able to make out more guards: patches of shadow and silhouettes running against the compound's fence. They were locking down the compound. Making sure no one got in – and no one got out.

I could have taken the four guards by the church entrance, easy. Even if they were more trained, more experienced, and better equipped than I knew these ones were. I'd taken out worse. They weren't the problem – the hundreds of people on the other side of those doors were. I couldn't do anything more than terrorize them. I couldn't convince them to run, or to save themselves. Let alone get them away from Pearson for good. Even those like Joseph, who had their doubts, would never listen to me if I just busted in. And I was willing to wager there were a lot more people like Rose than like Joseph in there.

Hidden speakers screeched. They must have been mounted on the sides of the buildings somewhere, because Pearson's voice echoed across the open space at the center of the old school campus. Once again, I instinctively held my hands to my ears. People halted where they were. "Let's go – move, move, move. The longer you're out there, the more danger you're in. Move your children, move your grandparents, your great-grandparents – get to safety, get to the church. I can still see you out there. Don't stop because I'm speaking – go!"

I could hear the fury in his voice, even in the echoes that rolled off the horizon. His words were almost certainly carrying beyond the street, into the neighboring businesses, waking people beyond. This must have been the first time he had used his speaker system at quite this volume. If he did this regularly, the noise complaints alone would have shut him down. Never mind threats like this.

Then I realized: he *wanted* the police to come.

He needed to make this as public as possible. He wanted police beating down his gates – his people firing on them, the police firing back, as much spectacle as possible. A statement to the world. All its attention, on him.

At least I knew Pearson was still in his office, making the broadcast.

"Go to the first building west of the church," Rachel's voice said. "The one with five columns supporting the facade. School admin offices were on the top floor. Looks like your best access is third floor windows, either east or west side of the building. Either one will be the same distance to the center offices."

"Thanks," I breathed.

I sized up the yard, took quick note of where everybody was and what directions they were going in. Especially the security guards. I vaulted over the top of the stairwell and ran for it. So long as I stayed away from the lights, the night-blind guards by the church entrance should miss me. I would certainly draw some notice from those farther away, but with luck they would think that I was just another of Pearson's followers.[68] I got my grappling hook pistol ready.

I got maybe five steps before things went wrong.

A young woman, maybe twenty or so years old and wearing the overalls of Pearson's security team, stepped out from behind the next corner. She was carrying a sizable cardboard box, staggering under its weight. She spotted me immediately. The mark on my eye, and the weapons and tools on my belt and in my hands, made me impossible to mistake for anyone else.

Her eyes went wide. Her mouth opened to call for help.

Instinct seized me. I already had my grappling hook pistol in my hand. I raised it. Fired.

The recoil hammered my wrist. The blunt, curved hook head smashed into the woman's stomach. Her breath *whoofed* out of her. Her box toppled. She took several swaying steps

---

[68] You can tell when a plan's going to go awry when I start counting on my luck to work in just the way I need it to.

back in the direction she had come. I closed the distance between us and pushed her behind the corner, into the shadow of the alley between buildings. We crashed to the ground together. She landed on her back, driving what air she had left out of her lungs.

I held her to the ground with my elbow to her throat, ready to press down if she started making noise. With my free hand I was already dragging the grappling hook back toward me, planning to use the unspooled cable as bindings.

Somewhere in the back of my mind, I'd heard the box she'd dropped make a sloshing sound when it had struck the sidewalk. Now I could smell it. Gasoline. Turpentine. Lighter fluid. And other odors I couldn't identify. Looking behind me, I saw the red top and curved nozzle of a gasoline canister poking out of the open top of the box.

The smell wasn't coming from them, though. It was coming from the girl. Her clothes were suffused with it. She wasn't just carrying this stuff. She'd been getting it ready.

Getting ready to help murder all the people in that church. I looked back at the girl, rage building behind my temples. In her eyes, even as she struggled for breath, I saw that same rage reflected back at me.

A young idiot. The kind that made the best fanatics. Only Pearson's most devoted foot soldiers would have been entrusted with the duty she'd been given.

Sometimes my luck operated in ways I couldn't foresee. It didn't always lead me where I wanted to go, but sometimes it showed me the things I needed to see.

She was armed. A Glock 22 was holstered at her belt. A simple, reliable semi-automatic. She was new at this "security" game. She hadn't reached for it at all when she'd seen me. A better-trained guard would have instinctively grabbed for it in the same breath as she'd started to call for help. But she wasn't packing to protect the compound. She had it to threaten, or to shoot, anyone inside the church who realized what was going on and tried to get out.

I didn't give her time to try again to call for help. I pulled the Glock out of her holster and cracked her across the head with its butt.

By the time she'd shaken off the stun of the blow, she'd find herself trussed with my grappling cable, and the torn fabric of her sleeve knotted in her mouth. The building beside us had ground-floor windows partly recessed into the ground. I lifted her into the well and left her. That ought to keep her until whatever was done was done.

She wouldn't be the only one Pearson had assigned to start the fires. A lot of people here were just like her.

"You all right, dear?" Rachel's voice asked.

I wasn't. I didn't answer.

I was already searching for another way up into Pearson's office. My grappling cable was gone. For a hot second, I was afraid I'd have to make a ground-floor entrance, waste time fighting through however many people were between me and him. Then I saw the scraggly elm near the west side of the building. And the ivy-covered trellis mounted against the brickwork. I knew what I would have to do.

I started running.

TWENTY-FOUR

Trusting in my luck feels like jumping across a drawbridge as it's opening. Even if I think I'm going to make it, I still hold my breath. My luck isn't reliable. It's always working, but it can't be controlled, and it certainly can't be ordered around.

Once, on a bounty chase, I'd thought I'd found a shortcut in a pursuit. I'd taken a wild jump from a rooftop to another below that I couldn't quite see, counting on my luck to get me to a safe landing. I'd missed by a good twenty feet, but landed safely in a taut pavilion tarpaulin.[69] Another time, I'd escaped a bounty hunter after *me* by leaping from a runaway semi-truck,[70] and immediately smashed into the wall of an alleyway. As it turned out, that had saved me, because the bounty hunter had run straight down the alley expecting me to have gone on escaping. He hadn't been looking for me – breathless and in an embarrassing amount of agony –

---

[69] I lost the bounty. My luck doesn't care about my checkbook – or whether I look like an idiot in front of hundreds of people at an outdoor barbecue festival.

[70] Long story.

doubled over behind a dumpster.

The tree didn't look safe to climb. In the dark, I couldn't tell how old it was, or even if it was alive. In an Illinois winter, all trees look unhealthy – their veiny, wormlike branches like thin tendrils against the sky. I leaped, hardly seeing it, using my momentum to impel me up the trunk. My arms closed around the first branch. Hardly breaking my momentum, I levered my way up onto the next, and then the next. My luck held. Nothing gave way.

When I had almost reached the level of the third-floor windows, I darted away from the trunk, trotting as far down a branch as I dared. The branch creaked, cracked, and when I leapt, finally snapped underneath my toes. But I was already in midair.

I slammed into the wall above the third-floor window. If I hadn't already been holding my breath, the impact would have knocked it out of me. Luck saw my fingers into handholds on the trellis grate. Then the trellis too started to bend back, give way. I had two seconds, maybe. I swung my legs and kicked them into the window.

Good thing it was an old building, with a single-pane window. My momentum pitched me through the glass just as the trellis gave way – and I landed breathless on the polished floor of the corridor inside, shards tinkling and dancing all around me.

I scrambled to my feet, fighting for air. I'd scraped my arm and my shoulder good and bloody, but my luck kept the shards from finding their way to any of my arteries.[71]

---

[71] Crashing through windows is much more dangerous than movies would have you believe… but my luck means my life gets downright cinematic.

The hallway was three times as wide as it should have been for the number of offices it contained. The floor was polished hardwood and the office doors carved from heavy, dark mahogany. Those must have cost thousands of dollars. The school this place used to be had been strapped for cash, but they'd sure wanted visitors to know who was in charge. Pearson's people cleaned enough to keep the floors shiny, though several ceiling tiles were stained with unrepaired water damage.

Only one out of every three of the overhead fluorescent lights was on. The others had been switched off for the night. I needed a moment to suck in a breath, get my bearings, count office doors. The door at the center of the hall was about thirty feet away. Rachel had said that one should have been Pearson's. By the time the last of the glass shards stopped skipping across the floor, I was moving again.

I'd only just started when the door next to Pearson's opened.

Two men stepped out. One was younger, about mid-twenties. The other was middle-aged. Both had jet-black hair, and both wore security overalls. The older man wore a red sash – an extremely tacky way to indicate a higher rank.

Pearson's most devoted, most complicit followers would be the only ones still up here after that announcement. They were already looking in my direction, drawn by the sound of shattering glass.

No chance to hide. Not that I wanted to.

Both men had sidearms. The nearest man, the oldest, was the quickest to draw his.

I sidestepped. He jerked his arm to follow, but I had been feinting. He overcorrected.

I closed the rest of the distance and kicked the gun out of his white-knuckled hand.

It went spinning into the wall. The impact compressed the trigger.

In the darkened hallway, the muzzle flash was as blinding as the gunshot was deafening.

Sparks burst from the ceiling as the bullet ricocheted off a fire sprinkler, splitting it. The glowing remnants of both bullet and sprinkler head struck a smoke detector mounted in the corner of the ceiling – triggering it.

An alarm shrieked. Water sprayed from sprinklers ahead and behind – everywhere but directly overhead where, thanks to the broken sprinkler head, the water torrented down directly onto the younger man's hand. Just as he'd grabbed his own pistol. Half a second before he could have drawn a bead on me. His weapon slipped from his grasp.

All this happened before my foot hit the ground again.

Damn, it felt good to be lucky.

In the next second, I'd cracked the older man's jaw sideways. I felt his teeth slip loose under his cheek. Then I shoved him backward into his partner, and the two of them staggered back toward the doorway they'd emerged from.

The younger man managed to keep his partner's weight from toppling him, but only by the expedient of shoving the older man aside. The older man's head cracked against the door frame. He went down and didn't get back up.

The younger man roared and charged me. He was a meaty lad, easily one and a half times my size. I'd like to think I'm a great fighter – one of the best – but some things are just simple physics. I couldn't resist his charge. I didn't have the time to sidestep. He caught me with his shoulder. We plunged through the spray from the broken sprinkler.

My vision went swimmy. Water soaked through my hair instantly. Together, we crashed through the next door over.

Pearson's office.

The mahogany door clapped against the wall as we crashed through. I landed hard, with the security guard atop me. He'd been expecting to pin me. I arched my back, bracing my legs against the carpet. He was heavy enough that I would have had a hard time lifting him normally, but he still had his forward momentum.

With acrobatic prowess that impressed even me, I rolled, levered him over my head with my knees, and flipped him over me. He slammed onto his back. In one smooth motion, I rolled onto him, planted my knee on his chest, and smashed my fist into his forehead.

With one blow, he was out cold.

My muscles in my shoulder were burning after that punch. I'd be paying for all this tomorrow, in spades. I didn't care. I was pissed.

I was still in range of the door. I kicked it closed.

Pearson was still seated, frozen, behind a too-heavy, too-elegant desk. An enormous picture window covered the wall behind him. The distant Chicago skyline was a sparkling white-and-yellow diamond mirage on a black velvet curtain. This place was so isolated, I'd almost forgotten there was an outside world.

He had been looking out over his compound. His chair was still half-turned toward the window, where he'd probably been anxiously, pathologically, fixated on watching his people cram into the church. Pearson looked bigger here than he had from the rafters of the church. His hair was immaculate, undisturbed by the sweat on his forehead. He gaped at me, paralyzed.

I was soaked through. My hair clung to my forehead in ropey, dripping strands. I must have looked terrifying – my face frozen in a snarling demon's mask.

Good.

The lights here were out, other than a single overhead fluorescent tube. Interesting choice. Pearson, with his constantly red eyes, must not have been able to stand bright lights. No complaints from me. That made it less likely that anyone below looking in would see what was about to happen.

I still had my Beretta 92FS. I drew it.

A wet patch was creeping from the door. The water from the sprinklers outside. Beyond the door I heard panicked shouts, even above the shriek of the fire alarm. The people closest to Pearson must have known about the plan to burn down the church. Maybe they thought something had gone wrong – or that Pearson had decided to torch this building too.

Two voices passed just outside the door. Neither of them came in. They were running for the stairwells. If anyone else on this floor had heard the gunshots and shattered glass, it must have blended into the cacophony of the fire alarm.

"Call for them and die," I said.

Somehow, my headset had stayed attached to me. "Several police cars approaching," Rachel said. She sounded calm but, having known her as long as I have, I knew that was a lie. My eyes snapped up to the window. Almost lost among the sequin pattern of the street lights, several flashing red and blues shone below, getting closer. Just as Pearson had been hoping.

An old-fashioned intercom set, complete with wired handheld, had been drilled into the desk. Given the money he'd put into the rest of his AV equipment, I was a little astonished to see such a clunky-looking, old-fashioned system. He must have liked the feel of the handheld, of pacing around his office with it. Twining the cord around his fingers as he issued dictates.

Pearson's jaw was working. I heard a rasping, like he was trying to catch his breath. I stepped around the desk, leveling my aim right between his eyes.

Time to see how many of his delusions he actually believed – if he was really convinced that all the forces of the outside world were coming to get him, or if he was just using that as an excuse to make his grand statement to the world.

"You're going to pick up your intercom, very slowly," I told him. "You're going to call your followers and tell them to start leaving the church, nice and orderly. Tell them this was all a drill. The emergency is over. And to put the fire-starting equipment away. Do you understand me?"

I wasn't sure he did. "You… You did… I don't…" His voice trembled almost as much as his jaw.

The pale city lights showed me pill bottles on his desk. Some of them had their caps on. Most didn't. A silver flask lay in an open desk drawer. Whatever cocktail of drugs he was taking, he certainly shouldn't have been mixing them all.

I peered closer at him. His eyes had looked red enough from a distance, in the church rafters. Either they looked a lot worse up close, or his condition had deteriorated in the past hour. I'd seen this before. People who thought they needed superhuman energy all day, but weren't superpowered themselves. They were convinced they had to be moving and talking all day, so they started taking amphetamines to keep themselves on their feet.

How many years had he been doing this? None of the newspaper articles I'd read mentioned red eyes, or drug use. But in a lot of those older pictures he'd been wearing sunglasses.

"Do it," I said, "or you're not leaving this room alive."

"You're not… You're part of the… Who are you? The CIA? The Russians? Mob?"

I didn't have the patience to fit this into one of his paranoid fantasies. I stepped forward, touched the barrel of my pistol to the ridge of his forehead. "You'll never know," I said.

His hands were shaking, much more than they would have been if he were just scared. These were full-blown tremors. I'd only seen shakes like this in people many, many years older than him. He fumbled for the intercom handheld. Almost immediately, he dropped it. He looked to me, as if for permission to retrieve it, and then bent to get it.

I shoved him back into his chair and pushed him toward the window. I wasn't going to take the chance that he had some kind of weapon or hidden alarm switch under the desk. I grabbed the handheld by the cord and dropped it in his lap. In all this, my aim had not wavered.

He tried to pick up the handheld, and failed. And again. His hands would just not close around it.

With my free hand, I snapped the handheld off his lap, held

it in front of him, thumb ready on the activation button.

"You're not real," he said. "I made you up."

"Do it," I told him.

His red eyes met mine. There was still terror there, but something else now, too. A kind of resignation. Like he couldn't wait for this to be over.

"No," he said.

With more strength than I would have guessed his trembling hand possessed, he reached up and clasped his hand around mine. Forced my thumb into the activation button before I was ready.

"Fire teams," he rasped, to the whole compound. "Execute."

TWENTY-FIVE
THE EVERGLADES, SIX YEARS AGO

Hours after I came back to myself following Lazarus's mind-blast, I finally had enough self-composure to take stock of my prison.

My cell was painfully reminiscent of the one in which I'd grown up – at least, as it had been during my last days there, after the lab coats had stripped out everything. As then, I had one bed, a thin and cruddy mattress, light panels high in the ceiling, a sink, a toilet... and one security camera. The camera was old, and not wireless. It cabled into the ceiling.

Beatrice wasn't even trying to seem like she was different from the old Project Armageddon staff. She had no problem with their methods. She wanted control of the outcome.

A ventilation grate rattled in the corner opposite the security camera. It was no good to escape through, of course – it was only six inches high, and a little wider. My old cell had had a grate much like it, but I'd lived there for so long that I'd stopped seeing it.

That one hadn't rattled.

I stared at it, and then at my bed. The bed frame was bolted to the floor. The mattress had no blankets, no pillows.[72] Yellowish sweat stains had soaked into its surface. From another child like Lazarus, perhaps? Or a prisoner, like me? Whoever had left these marks, they'd probably ended up in the incinerator.

By flipping the mattress sideways on the bed frame and straining to fold it over itself three times, I made a stepping stool just tall enough that I could reach the grate.

Cool, dry air plastered my hair to my sweaty forehead. The grate was bolted onto the wall, but loosely. There were only two bolts. They poked out at awkward angles. Someone had bought parts that didn't fit the wall and tried to force them in. One of the bolts fell loose when I tugged on it, right into my palm. The other bolt took some straining, but eventually it snapped loose from the rust that had sealed it there.

The ventilation cover pulled easily out. Just a grate and a metal frame. But the frame was heavy and the corners were reasonably sharp. I jumped to the floor.

When I was a kid, I always wanted to do this next part, but I'd never had the courage.

I lined up my aim on the security camera and whipped the ventilation cover at it.

The camera's lens shattered. Fragments of glass and cracked plastic casing rained onto the floor. Satisfying. That helped take the edge off some of the adrenaline still coursing through me.

I turned my attention back to the duct. The lights in here

---

[72] I think the day the lab coats took those away from me was the day I realized they intended to kill me like they had all the others.

were too bright, and my eyes weren't adjusted to the dark. Still, by shielding my brow and concentrating, I could see slender shafts of light farther down the corridor, and evenly spaced. Other cells.

The thought of Lazarus drove a cold spike of involuntary panic down my back. I wasn't used to feeling like this. Whatever the kid had done to me had wormed deep into my subconscious, where I couldn't control it.

Still, he was just a kid. I had to try this.

"Hey," I hissed down the duct. Then, louder, "Hey."

Either the kid was ignoring me, or he couldn't hear me. I wasn't willing to shout. There'd be no point if anyone outside the cell could hear this, too.

Maybe the grate in his cell was muffling my voice. If it had been secured just as poorly as mine – and the mismatched parts made that likely – then it wouldn't take much to knock it loose. Knock the one bolt out and the whole grate would swing loose. The problem was reaching it. His cell's grate was many times farther than I could reach, and I could hardly squeeze my arm into the grate anyway.

I hopped off the folded mattress and weighed my options. I only counted one.

I told you it's always a bad sign when I have to count on my luck to do exactly what I want. But sometimes I have no choice.

I tossed one of the bolts from palm to palm, getting a feel for its weight. Then, hard as I could, I hurled it into the open duct.

The bolt ricocheted and *pinged* down the duct as hard as if I'd fired a bullet into it. One of the *pings* was replaced by a hard *clunk* – the bolt striking something solid.

When I clambered back onto the mattress and peered down the duct, the light had changed. The ventilation grate had fallen loose, just like mine. More light streamed into the duct.

"*Hey,*" I said, more insistently.

This time I got an answer. "Leave me alone."

"Can't do that," I said. "Not after everything that's happened. Sorry."

Silence.

"I grew up in a place just like this, you know," I said. "I used to dream about getting out… until things got really bad, and I just didn't have the energy any more. Which stage are you in?"

If silence could have a character, this one was sullen.

"You didn't used to be alone here, did you?"

His voice sounded tinny as it echoed through the duct: "You're going to get us into trouble."

"A little too late for me to worry about that," I said. "Little too late for you, too. There were other kids here, weren't there? What happened to them?"

There was a small sound – not quite words or a voice, more like a choke.

"How long ago were they all taken?" I asked.

"Please," he said, not hiding his desperation. "Stop."

"Do you want to leave this place?"

No answer. My opportunity to get anything out of this was slipping away from me.

"I have to assume that's a yes. I've seen what you can do. If you want to leave, why don't you?"

Nothing.

I doubted I was going to get anything more tonight. And, to be honest, a big part of me – the part still recovering from shock – was afraid to push him any further.

For a while, I stared at the door. If anyone was going to punish me for destroying the camera, they would be here soon. No one came. They knew I was just rattling around in my cage.

My nerves were shot. My body felt like it had been churned through a meat grinder. My pulse was still pounding in my ears.

I pressed my hands into the mattress, testing it. Some broken springs. I didn't think I had done that. This place had a long history, and I was just catching glimpses of it. I wondered how many years other kids had been held here, and if they and Lazarus had ever talked through the ducts.

I had nothing better to do but mull over those questions as I tried, and failed, to catch some sleep.

TWENTY-SIX

There was no way to tell time down here. Eventually, my cell door rolled open.

I was on my feet instantly. Beatrice, in a crisply pressed set of fatigues (still with the nametag and shoulder sleeve insignia torn out), was waiting for me – along with two armed Project Armageddon guards and, distantly behind them, Lazarus.

My blood froze at the sight of Lazarus. Reflex reaction. Like placing my hand on a hot stove and yanking it away. My unconscious self had learned to fear him.

Bristling, I tried to stifle as much of my reaction as I could. But I couldn't help the twitch, or stiffening.

Beatrice smiled.

"Come along, dear," she said.

I couldn't fight. Not with Lazarus so close. I stepped out. With a prod of his shoulderslung rifle, one of the guards directed me down the hall. I think he was one of the men I'd clobbered last time. That explained the hard jabs to the small of my back.

Lazarus, I noted, trailed well behind. Well out of reach of me.

They led me through the vault door, into the facility proper. From there, down a winding sequence of hallways, all deserted of people, empty even of paintings. Worth noting. However Beatrice had really gotten control, she had inherited a facility far larger than she had people to populate it. Maybe the people who'd worked this section had refused to follow her. Maybe they had ended up as ash and bones in that incinerator.

I idly wondered if it had happened to any of the lab coats I'd used to know. I would not shed any tears.

Our destination was behind a pair of double doors, sized for gurneys. Beyond was a mix of a physician's examination room and a laboratory. The room was ringed with counters, desks, chairs, and computers. Diagrams of human skeletal, nervous, and muscular systems were tacked to the beige walls, along with those of a few other organs – a dissection view of an eyeball, a human brain, a heart, a spine. Quick references, meant to be used on the fly. And, at the center of everything, was a surgical table with restraining straps hanging off its side.

I halted. The guard's rifle dug into my back, but I didn't care. Even with Lazarus behind me, there was no way I was going to get on that–

"Fortune makes a fool," Beatrice said.

I was getting better at resisting my post-hypnotic trigger, but not so much that it didn't stun me. It felt like my spine had formed little needles, poking into me. I couldn't keep myself upright.

But it did not have the impact on me that it had had when Lazarus said it. There was something in the kid's voice. When he wanted, he could turn the words into an electric prod jammed straight into my nervous system. Beatrice wasn't anywhere near as intense.

By the time I recovered my will to move, the guards had slammed me onto the table. One cinched the restraints tight around my wrists and ankles, and the other tugged something tight over my upper arm. It was a blood pressure cuff.

I tried to swallow my panic, but either this place, or what Lazarus had done, had brought out the worst in me. I must have looked much more terrified than I'd wanted.

Lazarus bit his lip. His hands were shaking. He didn't want to see this. Beatrice, my doting mother, just raised her eyebrow.

"Her post-hypnotic trigger is a relic," she told Lazarus. "I'm sorry to have to use it. The old Project Armageddon staff knew, by the time she was five years old, that none of her class were the perfect weapon that they'd hoped for, but they still wanted to get some use out of them. Trained agents and spies, mutants with abilities that they'd help hone. The post-hypnotic phrase was a method of control of last resort, a way to shut them down on the battlefield if they ever went rogue."

Lazarus sat still. He was accustomed to listening to her go on. I doubt he understood half of what she'd said.

"You've used trigger phrases before, like you had to, and you did a very good job," she said. "But you can already see that she's getting better at resisting it. It's a handicap, Lazarus. It's like a crutch. You can control her without it. Do you understand?" He nodded. "You can do it without relying on the trigger phrases."

"I'm right here, you know," I muttered.

She turned to me, without missing a beat in the conversation. "The old Project Armageddon staff were monsters. All of them. I'm sure you know that. They didn't think that you were people. They thought of mutants as livestock. And, later, diseased livestock. They would have eventually gotten rid of you, too."

The two armed guards had remained in the room. Beatrice nodded in their direction. Now one of them wheeled some kind of heavy device over to the head of the examination table. From my perspective, I couldn't see much of it. Some kind of steel hoop, split in half, connected to a larger machine behind it. The hoop slid over my skull, just above my temples, without touching me. Some kind of scanner.

"You were the closest the old Project Armageddon got to the 'perfect weapon' before Lazarus. I knew right away that there was something special about me, about my genes." I braced myself for a speech about how special and unique and important she was, like I'd heard from a hundred narcissists before her. But she was content enough with just the *insinuation* that she was special, beyond human, Christlike.[73] "I told them wso, but they still only used my genes to clone one of their next batch of subjects. And it was my child who finally fulfilled their project."

Villains and their exposition, I swear. Best not to interrupt. The trick with this woman was that she didn't seem to realize she *was* a villain. She thought she and I were just having a conversation.

She returned to Lazarus and set her hands on his shoulders.

---

[73] A lot of cult leaders used false humility as a tool. Dallas Bader Pearson did the same.

A caring, supportive mother. "I know this is difficult for you. Remember those meditation exercises we went over? This would be a good time to start them. Get warmed up."

He nodded again, folded his legs onto the seat of his chair, and closed his eyes. His expression was completely flat. In spite of his age, I had never seen anything childish in him.

She grabbed a chair of her own and rolled it over to the side of my table.

"Comfortable?" she asked.

If she had been in range, I would have bitten her. "What happened to the kids who used to be in all the cells around Lazarus's? You killed them?"

"I told you – the Project Armageddon staff were monsters. That was why I took over."

There had been an awful lot of gurneys in the corridor leading up to the incinerator. I doubt they'd all been left there for months or years. She was playing fast and loose with the timeline. But I couldn't press her on it. I didn't have all the facts, and pushing would have just given her another opportunity to spin lies.[74]

She said, "It would be much simpler if you were to relax. I know it's difficult. But it will be easier on you."

I forced my voice to stay even. "What do you think you're doing to me?"

"This may sound kind of funny, but it would interfere with the results to tell you."

"That does sound *kind of* funny. And you only *kind of* sound like you've lost it."

---

[74] Never try to argue with Beatrice's type. They have a million ways to waste your time, to tie logic and reason up in knots, and they've practiced all of them.

"You and I and your brother can change the world, Neena."

"That's not helping your case."

As if to make a show of being self-effacing, she smiled. One of the guards, seeing it, chuckled too. But there was no humor in Beatrice's eyes. "I was just hired to be an office manager, you know. But someone in the recruiting pool must have known I carried the X-gene. I certainly didn't. They only sprung it on me after they had me trapped in an underground facility, and I'd cut off all my ties to the surface. Too late to go home."

"I know you're lying."

She raised her eyebrow. "There's no reason for me to lie."

Narcissists always exaggerated the challenges they'd faced. "You may not have been in charge when you came here, but you had a lot more power than that. More than an office manager."

She rolled her chair over to the side of my table. "What makes you so sure about that?"

"Rudolpho Boschelli."

Her scowl set in instantly. "I never should have trusted him with you. And if I'd had as much power as you said I did, I never would have needed to."

She'd had plenty of followers. Enough to get me safely smuggled out of the Project Armageddon facility. I didn't think Father Boschelli had lied to me, but what he'd told me had been vague enough that I would probably never know the truth.

The only thing I was sure of was that Beatrice was lying. And that she was a pathological liar, too – she lied about things that didn't matter. There was no reason for her to have told me that she was just an office manager, except to pointlessly try to impress me with the scope of the challenges she'd faced. I wondered how many times she'd told that lie to her followers here, even people who knew better. And how many of these people had decided that their own memories were wrong.

"It must've really bothered you that he left, didn't it?" I asked. "You kept trying to draw him back in. Making him offers he couldn't refuse." Keeping him involved with the project by sending him me. She'd known he couldn't have tossed me out into a Chicago winter.

"Not many people get involved with the project and choose to quit. I owed it to him to do everything I could to bring him back into the fold." Her scowl deepened. I'd struck a nerve. "Rudolpho was an immense disappointment. He had so many opportunities to come back and refused them. And then he raised you. Made *you* what you are."

I could not help a bitter laugh. "He'd be astonished to hear that last part."

All told, I'd lived with Father Boschelli, in the Church of the Sacred Heart, for less than a year.

"He never even told you about me," she said.

Gingerly, as if stretching, I tested the strength of my restraints. "He told me," I said. I understood now. He hadn't said anything more because he'd wanted to protect me from what he'd seen here. He knew that, at some point, I would have gone looking for her, and gotten drawn into her web. Especially at that age, I would have had no defenses against her.

"I had thought," Beatrice said, "that once I had settled things here, I could send someone out to find you. Bring you back. But you disappeared into the world. And when we found you later, I didn't care for what you'd become."

"You cared enough to check up on me."

"You're my daughter."

"I don't believe that, either."

That, at least, caught her attention. Her gaze snapped to me, more sharply than it had the last time I'd called her out.

It made me wonder if she *wasn't* telling the truth, after all. She certainly cared whether I believed this part of her story.

"You're my mother, Lazarus is my brother... sounds like delusions. Fantasy. Trying to wrap a neat little narrative around things." I didn't know what I believed. I was mostly saying it to provoke her. Anything to keep her from doing whatever she was about to.

Beatrice set her hand on the examination table. The closest she could come to caressing my head without actually risking coming into my range.

"I really wish you hadn't come here," she said. "We'll do the best that we can by you."

"Thanks... *Mom*."

She opened her mouth to answer and then stopped. As if a timer in her head had gone off, she turned to Lazarus. "Are you ready?" she asked.

He opened his eyes and nodded.

"You're going to have Lazarus root around in my head again," I said. Saying it turned the dread into something more concrete. Something I could fight.

"The first time was an emergency, dear, and very artless. Lazarus is capable of much more."

Against all my instincts screaming to do anything else, I

looked to Lazarus. He and I locked eyes. For a half second, he looked as terrified as I felt. One deep breath later, and he was back to his practiced stoicism.

"He can do so much more to help you," Beatrice said.

Lazarus opened his mouth.

This time, I heard a sound – a low, inhuman hum, like a diesel engine buried deep in the earth. A snap-spark of electricity jolted through me. Made me jerk against my restraints. It was like somebody had discharged a static shock into the base of my spine.

I waited for it to get worse. It didn't. The humming persisted, and the deep low-down growl of the vibration worked its way into my bones. But that initial shock was as bad as it got.

The guard standing above me said, "Pulse spiking. Blood pressure rising." The others didn't seem to be hearing the same thing I was – or, if they were, they weren't bothered by it.

"Her brain?" Beatrice asked.

"Some blood vessels dilating."

"That's all?"

My joints felt like they were grinding together. There was no way that kid's throat could produce the sound I was hearing. It had to be inside my head. Telepathic resonance. Telepathic shock. The lab coats would have had different terms for it. Definitely some component of it was linked to sound. The rumble stopped when the kid closed his mouth, inhaled through his nose. Resumed when he opened his mouth.

I tried to meet his gaze again. He looked right at me. I have no idea what I must have looked like to him.

If the kid had *really* wanted me to leave him alone last night, he could have made me. Even a low-power rumble like this, and I would have shut the hell up fast.

My throat seized up when I tried to speak. Eventually, the rumble built up into a kind of pain. Like sitting through aircraft turbulence for too long. I could tolerate the first few minutes, but eventually the sheer sensory shock of it started to be too much. The table felt like it was rattling, but I'm sure the shaking came from me.

On and on it went like that, into what seemed like hours.

Finally, Beatrice shook her head and waved her hand in front of Lazarus. He stopped at once.

She stepped around the back of his chair, set her hands on his shoulders. Just for a moment – a gentle, encouraging mother.

"Look at her," she said. "Your sister's depending on you to do better than this."

He nodded. No complaints, no excuses, just agreement.

I stretched my jaw, made sure I could still speak. "You're still trying to get your 'perfect weapon' to work."

She shook her head. The only answer she was willing to give.

I had more of my wits about me than I'd had after the last time Lazarus had screwed with me. "Don't tell me," I said. "Letting me know will 'interfere with the results.' So let me guess. You're trying to get him to change me *permanently*, aren't you? Turn me into someone I'm not. Someone more malleable." A "perfect weapon" was a gun that, fired once, never needed to be fired again.

I asked Lazarus, "Is that what you want to do to me?"

Very minutely, so much that I almost didn't notice but for

a shift of muscles under her wrist, Beatrice tightened her grip on Lazarus's shoulders.

If Lazarus had even heard the question, he gave no sign of it.

"With a little work and development, your brother can change the world," Beatrice said.

"You're delusional." I nodded up to the man standing over me. "You two meatheads know that, right?"

It was like I hadn't even spoken. They did nothing. And Beatrice said, "They've seen enough of the outside world to know that something has to change. It's full of people like what you've become. You don't see past your moment. You don't plan for your future at all. Not next year. Not next decade. Never. You just try to swallow up as much as you can right now."

I shrugged, as far as my restraints would allow me.

"Don't you pay attention to the world, Neena? See how many heroes and monsters and villains are battling it out for the fate of humanity every week? How many times was the world 'saved' this year alone?[75] How many times in the next decade is the Earth almost going to be lost, or civilization doomed? In the next century? The next ten thousand years? Do you really think humanity can survive into deep time, looking like it is? We've always been on the cusp of destroying ourselves, or being destroyed."

She glanced up to make sure that the two guards were following her. For all her calm voice and clinical attitude, she was a creature of deep and psychotic emotional need.

---

[75] Saved the world myself a couple times. And, after this was done, I would go on to save it a few more. Remind me to tell you about the vampire mermen and the Creation Constellation sometime.

"I know what the future looks like," I said. One of my oldest friends, Cable, had told me a little about it. It hadn't been nice. Cable had come from the future. He had fought in wars beyond what I was capable of understanding. He was the one who'd gotten me into mercenary work, and in more ways than just showing me the ropes. The glimpses he'd given me of his future had cemented my thoughts about spending all my energy living in the present. Always eat the marshmallow when it's offered. Never count on the second to arrive.

Beatrice wasn't wrong about the future. Ours didn't look bright.

"We need to make ourselves better," Beatrice said. "We need something that will *make* us better, because I doubt we're capable of doing it on our own. I hate the outside world, Neena. I hate what we've done with the chances we've been given. We've come up with ten thousand ways to destroy ourselves."

"Give or take," I muttered. It wouldn't surprise me to learn this had been part of Project Armageddon's ideology from the beginning. Beatrice was more tied into it than she admitted.

"How many thousands of nuclear warheads do the nations of the world have poised to fire off at each other on an instant's notice? And, if we don't do ourselves in, how do you think we're going to face the threats that we know are out *there?* The alien warlords, the planetdevourers, the multiverse-ending catastrophes? We can't scrape through by the skin of our pinkie fingers every time. Some part of this rotten, hateful species has to give. That's why I'm doing what I'm doing. People need me."

"You mean they need your 'perfect weapon.'"

I'm not sure she caught the barb. Or she chose to let it go. "I should have given up years ago. I should have left this place, left this world, a long time ago."

I'd been waiting for it to come all the way back around to her. It almost felt reassuring to hear, to know that my read on her had been right all along. But most of me was still too busy feeling awful.

"But I didn't," she said. "And here we are. I'm not sorry, Neena."

With that, she nodded to Lazarus. Enough resting time, apparently. Lazarus opened his mouth again. The noise ground my bones together, made my teeth feel electrified. Even though I was sure the sensation wasn't physical, I couldn't convince my body of that. It *felt* real.

Lazarus could have done worse. I was sure of that. He *had* done worse to me before. But he was holding off this time. I watched him. He couldn't quite meet my eye.

For a while, I was afraid they were forcing some deeper, more insidious change onto me. Something I wouldn't even perceive. Like I would wake up tomorrow with half my personality extirpated, a happy little zombie. But, when the last session ended, Beatrice was scowling.

"You've got to do better than this next time," she told Lazarus. Her voice was tight.

He just nodded. Used to agreeing with her.

Beatrice nodded to the guard above me. He wheeled back his scanning device and undid my restraints. I considered punching his throat in. But something, a reflexive fear, made me glance to Lazarus first, and I caught the look in his eye.

Very briefly, he shook his head. A plea, or a warning. I didn't know.

TWENTY-SEVEN

The trip back to my cell was short. Lazarus stayed behind us, as he had during the trip here. I tried to look back, meet Lazarus's gaze, but he stared through me. He was a thousand miles away.

The guard behind me never got tired of prodding me with his rifle. If only he knew how lucky he was to still have a throat.

I only got into my cell when he jabbed my back hard enough to make me gasp. I turned. Beatrice stood framed by the doorway, her arms folded. She studied me like she might have a petri dish. Her eyes were pitiless.

Just like Project Armageddon's lab coats used to look at me.

Shortly before the door slammed, she turned to Lazarus. When she did, those eyes softened.

One of those was an act. I was the failure. He was the success, the culmination of Project Armageddon's work. *That* was the only difference. I heard the reverberating slam of another cell door just a minute later. Lazarus's cell.

I felt a hundred years old. Lazarus may not have lobotomized me yet, but whatever he'd done had taken a physical toll. I wanted to collapse onto the mattress.

I had to keep going. I never had any choice about that. Freelancers like me never do.

I double-checked the camera in the corner. Still smashed. They hadn't bothered to replace it. Maybe they'd counted on me not coming back to the cell as myself. No new hidden cameras under the mattress or behind the fixtures, either, as far as I could tell.

After giving Lazarus a few minutes to collect himself, I folded the mattress again and boosted myself up to the open ventilation duct.

"You want to tell me what all that was about?" I asked.

No answer. Rather than pressing, I gave Lazarus some time alone with the question.

It worked. Three minutes after I asked, he said, "Mom wants me to change people."

"I know that. *Can* you change people?" As soon as I asked, I regretted it. No, I knew he could. I still couldn't think about what he'd done to me in that hallway without all my muscles clenching. He again didn't answer, and this time not even after I'd given him several minutes of silence.

"Do you *want* to change people?" I asked.

"Mom can make the world a better place if I can help her."

"That wasn't what I asked."

"Mom wants the best for everybody."

"And you?"

"I…" he started, and paused. "I want to help her."

The kid had been programmed. He was answering in a different language than the one I was asking questions in. I wasn't sure he was capable of saying what *he* wanted. He didn't have the vocabulary. What he wanted had never been a going concern before.

"What if I don't want to be helped?" I asked.

Nothing back. Not even when I gave him a few minutes of silence. The kid was growing up fast – he was already to the morose teenager phase.

My stomach panged. My body was starting to come back online after today's torture session, and it was hungry. "How do you get room service around here?"

This time the response was immediate. "Most of the food here is pretty bad."

"Yeah? How do you know that? You've been somewhere other than here, to have something to compare it to?"

"I have things the adults eat sometimes."

"One of them feeding you on the sly, or something?"

A pause. "Can you keep a secret?"

"Lazarus – I've kept so many secrets that nobody would believe me if I ever told them all." I knew things about Deadpool that no one else ever would. Things I'd take to my grave.[76]

Lazarus started singing.

I flinched when I heard it. I couldn't help it. His voice was low, and it sounded so much like what I'd heard in the examination room that everything inside me clenched, and I instinctively pushed away from the grate.

But this time was different. He wasn't very good. I mean, he *was* a child. And he sang with a child's voice, albeit a little lower than most children would have sung. It was a repetitive

---

[76] No, you can't know them either.

chant, the kind I'd associate with a prayer. He was like a little monk.

I held off from asking him what he was doing. After a minute, I heard the *thunk* of a distant cell lock.

The sound of his song diminished, changed pitch, but did not stop. He was moving, being taken away, but still singing.

"Lazarus?" I asked.

His voice vanished.

A second later, my own cell's lock *thunked*. I leapt off the mattress. I landed on my feet, my hands ready in a practiced battle stance. My meathead guard, the same one who'd stood over me all day, opened the door. He was unarmed. He was out of striking range, or I would have advanced.

But he stepped back. Behind him, still singing, was Lazarus.

My hands froze where they were, but my jaw went slack.

The singing must have been what he'd been doing *to me* all day. His powers were targeted. He could choose who he affected. This low, childish dirge was how it had sounded to everyone else. No wonder Beatrice and the meatheads hadn't been perturbed. Now the guard's head must have been filled with the same white static that mine had been.

Gradually, his voice trailing off, Lazarus stopped singing. I braced for the guard to snap out of it, but he never did. He remained looking straight ahead, as casual as I'd ever seen anybody.

Lazarus said, "They usually deliver a meal in about an hour, but I found something better. Do you wanna eat?"

Recovering as much of my wits as I could, I nodded. I didn't trust myself to speak.

He led the way down the corridor. I stayed just behind.

Part of me rebelled at being this close to him – whatever he'd done to me earlier had left an instinctive fear I had to clamp down on – but I was getting better at controlling that. For his part, he seemed to trust me implicitly. Didn't glance back at me even once. I could have staved his head in,[77] and he knew that. He also knew I wouldn't. Or that he could stop me if I tried.

Or maybe he was just a child, and he didn't think about that kind of stuff. He just trusted.

I peeked into some of the doors we passed. Supply closets. Bunks for the on-duty watch so they wouldn't have to exit the locked vault (and with a big painting of Beatrice mounted on the wall). And one little infirmary, complete with a child-sized examination table and glass cabinets stocked full of drugs. Made sense. These people had sunk quite an investment into Lazarus. They would want the means to help him close at hand.

The security cameras whirred back and forth in their corners. As we approached the end of the corridor, I asked, "What about the cameras? Aren't you being watched?"

In answer, he stopped by one of the doors and nudged it open. The room on the other side was dim, hardly larger than a closet. A bank of computer and television monitors covered one whole wall. They showed empty corridors, empty rooms. A few people sleeping in well-furnished rooms. Security camera coverage for, at the very least, this whole section of the Project Armageddon facility.

A red-haired woman in her mid-thirties, wearing the same

---

[77] Not that I would have. Never to children.

uniform as the other guards, sat at the cameras' control console. She wore the same uniform as the other guards. And the same vacant expression.

"My song reaches her too," Lazarus said. "They only have to hear a little."

I didn't hear any microphones. Lazarus's voice, coming from all the way in his cell and down this corridor, would have been barely audible. The reach of his power must have been enormous.

We left her alone and headed to the next room over. It was only a little larger, but the lights were better. It was clearly some kind of staff break room. It had a table with dinged-up folding chairs, covered in crumbs. A clean countertop held a sink and microwave. Cupboards lined the walls. A trashcan overflowed with plastic wrappers and soda cans. Another guard, a young man with a tattoo of a crucifix on the back of his neck, stood in the corner. He didn't seem to perceive either of us.

Lazarus went right over to the cabinet under the counter. Someone had left a half-full plastic container of red rope licorice under there, and two boxes of unfrosted toaster pastries. For a kid who'd probably never been allowed to have this stuff on his own, it must have been a treasure trove.

He grabbed one of each and moved on. In the next drawer over, one of his guards had stashed a box of raisin bran. Without waiting or saying anything, he opened the box and started picking out the sugar-covered raisins. Even with that terror still clenched in my gut, I laughed, imagining one of the soldiers here pouring out a bowl and then losing the rest of their day trying to find out who had pranked them.

Lazarus turned to me, plainly concerned that I was laughing at *him*. I shook my head.

He was too short to reach the upper doors. I popped them open and found the usual detritus of a workplace break room: sugar, old bags of tea, plastic plates and silverware, a grab bag of assorted awful candy,[78] some graham crackers and marshmallows,[79] and a rumpled bag of potato chips with nothing but crumbs in the bottom.

I plucked the bag of candy and the marshmallows out of the cabinet, set them on the table. Lazarus's eyes went wide. He left the cereal, followed to the table, and pulled himself onto a chair.

I contemplated the marshmallows. An awful idea struck me. I pulled one of the marshmallows out of the bag.

"Want one?" I asked.

He eyed it, and then back at me.

"Go on," I said. I set it on the table. "But I'll give you another one in five minutes if you don't eat it until th–"

His eyes never leaving mine, he picked up the marshmallow. So fast that I couldn't have grabbed it away from him, he plopped it in his mouth, and looked at me defiantly.

I grinned. "Good boy." I pushed the rest of the bag over to him, and the candy. We really were siblings. Not just genetically speaking.

We ate in companionable silence. I had enough of the toaster pastries (untoasted – if you're going to have them, it's the best way) to make me a little sick. But the hunger pangs ended.

---

[78] Don't ever come at me with taffy.

[79] No chocolate for microwave s'mores. The privation.

Lazarus, naturally, ate nothing but candy and marshmallows. I envied the iron stomachs of the young.[80]

I still couldn't help a reflexive little trill of fear in my gut whenever I looked at him, but it was getting smaller all the time. Whatever he had done to my nervous system didn't seem permanent. Still, it was awkward eating with the vacant-eyed soldier still in the room, standing in the corner. I nodded toward him.

I said, "When you did that to me the first time, it hurt me. Does it hurt them?"

Lazarus shifted, and he looked uncertain. And then deeply uncomfortable. "I didn't mean to hurt anyone."

"It does. Doesn't it?"

"I- I think it did the first times I did it. I didn't know." He looked more and more upset.

"It's all right. You can tell me. I'm not going to be angry."

"Do you promise?"

"I promise."

Guilt. That was what was on his face. *Guilt*. And not just, I realized, because he was breaking Beatrice's rules. "When I do that enough to people… it stops hurting them after a while."

"They get used to it?"

"I didn't know it hurt at all until after I'd already sneaked out a few times. They'd already gotten used to it. I told them not to remember what I'd done, and they didn't, but… I had already changed them. I didn't mean to."

I thought I understood, from what little he had the

---

80 I'm *not* old. But next to Lazarus I felt it.

vocabulary to explain, what he meant. He had started singing his song to the guards around his cell to sneak out. He didn't realize he'd been hurting them. Somehow, later, he figured it out. But by then it was too late for these guards. The parts of their brains that resisted control had already burnt out.

"You don't like 'changing' people, do you?" I asked.

He shook his head. Then he said, "Mom wants me to."

"You've been holding back."

"Mom says I can make the world a better place."

I said it so he didn't have to. "When I was on that table, you could have 'changed' me again. Like you did during that fight in the hall. But you didn't."

"I don't want to hurt people."

"Thank you for that."

"I'm trying to be good," he said, and for the first time his voice sounded his age. Like he was about to cry.

The last part of me that was afraid of him crumbled away, scattered like dust in the wind.

I stood, lifted him out of his seat and onto the ground. He didn't protest. This isn't usually my way, but I kneeled to his level and set my hands on his shoulders.

When he didn't back away from that, I hugged him.

His back shook for a moment, and I felt him raise a hand to his eyes, but that was all. Tough little kid.

Circumstances like his, he must have been tempted to cry more often. I know when I had been growing up, I had cried. But the lab coats hadn't cared when I did. It hadn't helped. So I tried not to. I couldn't seem weak in front of the other kids – certainly not once the lab coats had started pitting us in more cutthroat competitions.

I wondered what Beatrice did when he cried – if she ignored him, or if she scolded him. The only thing I knew for sure was that she did not comfort him. Not if he fought so hard to hold it in now.

"We've got to get you out of here," I said.

Mistake. He seized up. "No. No, this is my home."

"They're just going to try to make you hurt more people here."

Lazarus pushed away from my arms. "This is where I live. It's home."

"Do you really think things are going to get better for you here?"

"Mom's here."

"Your mom isn't being very good to you right now," I said.

His eyes hardened. He wasn't prepared to say, maybe even think, anything ill of her right then.

"Lazarus," I said. "I know. She's my mom too. And she wasn't very good to me either."

"Mom wants the best for me."

"Do you think she wants the best for me?" I asked.

That gave him pause. "Aren't I her child too?" I pressed. "She told you I was."

"Yeah…"

"What makes you think you're going to get any better from her when you're my age?"

He didn't answer, just stared at the candy without really seeing it. I wasn't sure what I expected him to say. I wasn't going to break through to him in a night.

The sound of a door crashing open echoed down the far end of the corridor. I jumped to my feet. Lazarus did the same. I felt him push into my leg.

A set of briskly moving footsteps tromped toward us.

The man standing vacantly in the corner had a sidearm, a military-standard M9. I should've grabbed it earlier, but it hadn't seemed right. Not with the kid watching, and me trying to make a good impression and all. He'd been just about to open himself up. And he would've shut down if he knew what I was doing.

I edged closer to the guard, but stopped. Lazarus was in my way, pressing against my leg. I think he recognized the cadence of the footsteps. Knew what was about to happen. And I was suddenly out of time.

Beatrice stepped through the door. She was flanked by a scowling crewcut meathead with a drawn handgun. The instant he saw me, he leveled his weapon.

But Beatrice didn't seem to notice me. She looked straight to Lazarus. "How long have you been doing this?" she demanded.

Rather than let Lazarus answer, I interrupted. There was no way I was letting this noxious relationship continue while I was in arms' reach. "What do you do when he doesn't act like you want? Smack him? Shock him? You lied about being 'just an office manager.' How much were you involved in the way I was treated?"

Beatrice ignored me. Glaring at Lazarus, she pointed at the floor beside her. "Come here."

Lazarus responded instantly, as if programmed. He was gone before I could think to reach down and stop him. He halted where Beatrice had pointed, looking ahead. His expression was once again absolutely placid. Blank.

Controlled.

So long as he and Beatrice were in the same room, he was Beatrice's creature, and there was nothing I could do about it.

I stood, frozen, in the sights of the goon with the gun.

TWENTY-EIGHT

Beatrice told Lazarus, "It's my fault. I should have checked on you much more often. I tapped into your room's feed because I wanted to see how you were resting after exerting yourself today. Imagine my surprise when I find you forcing your protectors to open your door. And *hers*. Do you know how much danger you were in? What she could have done to you?"

"We hadn't been fed," he said. "I was hungry."

Much more childlike than he'd been two minutes ago. Survival technique. He was protecting himself.

"You've been hiding yourself," Beatrice said. "Concealing your abilities. You could have done a lot more."

"*No*," he said.

He sounded like he was going to say something else, but she planted her hand on the crown of his head, forced him to crane his neck to meet her eyes. "Lie to me again," she said.

If this went on, he was going to admit to anything. Show her the full scope of his powers. I wouldn't have blamed him. When you're that scared, that alone, and that small, you'll do anything.

I couldn't let it happen. I said, "It was my idea. I tricked him."

For the first time, Beatrice seemed to recognize me. She turned toward me, snarling. "Is there *anything* I could do to you to make you stop lying?"

"I've mostly told the truth since I got here. Have you?"

"All you've done since you got here is make things worse for me. And for Lazarus."

Without thinking, Beatrice took a step forward. The meathead to her side remained where he was, still aiming at me.

I was acting on the idea before I'd even realized that it had formed. I took a step backward, as if afraid of her sudden emotional intensity. My heel jammed against the bottom of the sink cupboard.

"I need to tell you one important thing," I said.

Beatrice wasn't combat-trained. She wasn't used to thinking like I was. She started forward. Her escort caught the danger a fraction of a second too late. She was putting herself in his way.

"You should have brought more than one guard," I said.

I ducked to my right, fast as I could. Toward the tattooed soldier still standing vacantly in the corner. Putting Beatrice between her escort and his drawn pistol.

In so small a space, the report of a gun came close to being the loudest thing I'd ever heard. In a confined space like this, you'd be lucky if a gunshot didn't rupture your eardrums. The bullet ricocheted off something behind me, and again off the metal door. I saw sparks.

Beatrice's escort jerked. His weapon hand waved. He'd been struck by, at the very least, fragments of the bullet. My luck looking out for me again. I hoped it was looking out for Lazarus too.

My hand closed around the handle of the vacant-eyed soldier's M9.

Everything happened in a flash of panic.

I raised the pistol, clicked the safety off, slid my finger into the trigger guard. But Beatrice was on me. She grabbed my shoulder, tried to shove me aside. The jolt squeezed my trigger finger.

The escort's head snapped back. A cloud of blood droplets painted the wall behind him. He fell.

Beatrice shoved me against the counter. I slammed into it and used the rebound to knock her back. She tried to swipe my gun away, but I raised my knee, stomped on her heel, and then kicked her away.

She stumbled backward. I drew a bead, right between her eyes.

Her lips slackened. She stared straight down the muzzle.
She knew I had her.

"No!" Lazarus cried. I could hardly hear him. His voice was tiny under the ringing.

All my muscles felt on edge. Something deep inside my bones had made a little knife, was picking away at me.

There was an odd cadence to it, and I realized he was trying to use his power on me. Maybe on both of us. Only it wasn't getting through. The ringing in my ears was too much.

Beatrice was trying to say something too. Trying to speak to me, maybe. Or call for help. She wasn't trying to hide her fear. If she got away, she was never going to let me get her in a position like this again.

I was only ever going to have one shot at this. One chance to pull the trigger, or decide not to.

"*Stop,*" Lazarus said.

This time, his voice went straight into the core of my chest. The word squeezed my lungs. Stopped my breath as I drew it.

But it was too late. My finger was already pulling the trigger.

The recoil was a jab of pain in the heel of my palm. It helped keep me focused, from slipping away into Lazarus's control. The renewed ringing in my ears took away the rest.

Beatrice crumpled. Went down.

My vision went white before she hit the floor. The room fuzzed out. I was pretty sure that Lazarus had stopped singing, but what little fragment had gotten into my head in the instant before I'd pulled the trigger was taking its toll now.

There was a tremendous amount of power in even the tiniest note of his song. It was small wonder that Project Armageddon considered him to be their perfect weapon. I thought what *I* could do was exceptional, but Lazarus's power was leagues beyond mine. Or anyone else's I knew. If Beatrice had succeeded in shaping him like she'd hoped, the rest of the world never would have stood a chance.

When I returned to myself, I was slumped against the side of the break room cabinets, just below the sink. One of the chairs had toppled atop me. I must have pulled it over when, flailing and under Lazarus's spell, I'd fallen.

Beatrice's escort had landed in a seated position by the door. He stared, slack-jawed and open-eyed, around the hole my bullet had punched through his head. And Beatrice lay face-up on the floor, her arms askew. Lazarus kneeled by her side, leaning over her, his hands on her shoulders.

My head was pounding. The little knife in my bones hadn't gone away. But I couldn't hear Lazarus singing.

He was sobbing instead.

The tattooed soldier in the corner of the room, the one whose sidearm I'd stolen, stared dumbly at nothing. If the gunfire so close to his eardrums had hurt him, he showed no sign of it whatsoever.

With effort, I pulled myself to my knees, and then my feet. All my joints hurt. My chest and stomach stung like I'd been punched in the gut. The kid's voice had that much of a physical effect on me.

He could have been doing that even now, if he wanted.

I set my hand on his back. He flinched. But he didn't stop crying.

From this angle, I could see over his head. Beatrice was definitely dead. She could not have survived what I'd done to her. And Lazarus had seen everything. More gore than any child his age should ever see.

"I'm sorry," I said. "I had to."

I could hardly hear myself over the ringing. But Lazarus must have. He turned to me. I caught the only sight that really stayed in my mind – the burning, searing, *passionate* hatred in his eyes. It was well beyond his years.

I'd earned every morsel of it. He was gone to me.

I told you, when we started this whole thing, that I couldn't remember her face. I wasn't joking. I still can't.

You'd think that after a lifetime spent wondering about my mother – and what felt like three lifetimes searching for her – the instant I saw her, everything about her would've been permanently seared in my memory like it had been burnt in with a laser engraver.

At the time, that's certainly what I thought. Like I said at the beginning of all this. *Funny.*

Nobody said *forever* couldn't also be short. You can fit a whole eternity into the space of a second.

And I was living one of those seconds now.

TWENTY-NINE
CHICAGO, NOW

There's a peculiar kind of thing you're supposed to do when you're a hero and you have a murderous villain at your mercy. You're supposed to spare them. Demonstrate that you're the better person. And maybe, if they take advantage of your generosity and try one more time to harm you and the people you love, you can get away with killing them. Just like in the movies.

I've had a hard time making that choice.

It cost me friends. I could have been close to Shang-Chi, you know. *Closer* than close. Like Black Widow, he'd been a super super-heroic idol of mine. We hadn't known each other long, but we'd already fought back-to-back, formed the kind of bond that can only come from holding each others' lives in our hands. Except then I'd made *that* decision in front of him. I'd held a beaten, bloodied woman at gunpoint. I'd already thrashed her good. She couldn't have done anything to me, not right then.

But she was dangerous. She was a mutant, too. She'd had

a power capable of nullifying my power, and other mutants'. And she hadn't surrendered. Even as I pressed the gun on the bridge of her nose, she'd promised to hunt me down again. Hunt down my friends. And told me that she would never, ever stop.

I'd shot her.

After that, Shang-Chi never had anything to do with me again. I hadn't made the *heroic* decision. I'd put myself, in Shang-Chi's eyes, on her level. And he'd walked away. Everything he could've been to me, everything we already meant to each other, vanished.

The same decision cost me my brother. I'll never be able to forget the look of hate in Lazarus's eyes after I'd shot Beatrice. No matter how much time passed, whenever I saw him again, it had never quite gone away. As he'd gotten older, it had come with something just as bad. *Disgust*. On the rare occasions when I showed myself to him, he was disgusted to see me.

I held Dallas Bader Pearson by his collar, with my Beretta pressed into his forehead. He still held his intercom in an outstretched hand. From my angle, I couldn't knock it away from him.

This was the moment in which all my lives kept crashing together. I kept making the same decision, over and over. I had always convinced myself, sometime afterward, that I had made a mistake.

Maybe they had been mistakes. Maybe that was why I'd always be a merc, and not the kind of person people call a hero.

Tough. I knew what I was.

No matter what anybody else called me.

Pearson tossed away his intercom's handheld. He looked to me, defiant. He'd told his followers what he wanted.

I pulled that trigger.

I shot him three times. Just to be sure. I kept my smoking gun raised and ready, just in case anyone had heard the gunshots and would come charging in to see what had happened.

No one did. The fire alarms were still screaming. I didn't think anyone was near enough to hear.

I've had to do worse before. Kill people who meant more to me, and at greater cost. And now, as all of those moments of my life smashed apart in a torrent of memory and post-traumatic flashback, I knew I wouldn't take any of those decisions back.

Maybe that would change later, once the adrenaline faded. It usually did. In that moment, I knew that I had done the right thing.

Dallas Bader Pearson would have stopped at nothing to continue to harm people, kill people, and bring more people under his power. Even in jail, he'd have had a million opportunities. He couldn't do that any more.

But I was still wading through the hell he'd unleashed. I didn't have time to dwell. *Fire teams*, he'd said. Little doubt about what that meant.

I turned to his office's picture window. Outwardly, not much had changed. Fewer people were on the compound's sidewalks. The Chicago PD must finally have realized something serious was going on, because now more red-and-blue lights shone in the distance. More flashing police lights had halted on the drive just outside the compound's locked gates. Pearson's guards would be there, ready to hold them off.

I could have run through the building, down several flights of stairs, past however many of Pearson's associates remained inside. There wasn't time. There were a thousand ways to get lost or sidetracked. The "fire teams" would be on their way to the church now, if they weren't already in place.

I could not see what was going on directly below. The reflection of the overhead light blocked everything.

My headset's mic had jarred loose. With my free hand, I pushed it back into place. "There's about to be a gunfight at the compound's gates," I said. "Fox. Widow. Are you in place to help?"

My ears were still ringing from the gunfire. My pistol was silenced,[81] but the gun the guard had fired right next to my head hadn't been. I could only hear through one of my headset's earpieces.

"Do we have clearance to shoot to kill?" Black Widow asked.

"No," I said. And then, after an instant's consideration, "Last resort only."

"I'm not sure what you expect us to do," Black Widow said.

"We were hired to save lives," I told her.

"Is that what we heard on your side of the mic a minute ago? You saving a life?"

I clenched my mic in my fist so she didn't hear my immediate reaction. When I let the mic go again, I said, "Yes."

Something in my voice must have kept her from answering. White Fox spoke next. "We'll do it."

---

[81] Although "silenced" doesn't mean *silent*. A silenced pistol still sounds like someone slamming a crowbar on a carpeted concrete floor.

They were creative and long-experienced. They outmatched their opponents in every possible way. I knew they were both capable of finding a way. If they expected to be on my team, they'd do what I asked.

I shoved Pearson's corpse aside. He slumped unceremoniously off his seat. I wrapped a hand under his chair's backrest.

I stepped back from the window, lifted the chair, and swung it. The crash of the glass shattering was not as loud as it seemed like it should have been, but my ears were still ringing.

Without the one fluorescent light's reflection in my way, I could see more of the yard. Security around the church doors had tripled. Twelve armed guards stood there now, keeping the people inside from spilling out. More silhouettes milled around the church's sides. Guarding back exits, maybe. Or Pearson's "fire teams."

There were more people outside around the other buildings. Including the dormitory in which I'd left Inez and the twins.

"Inez," I breathed. "Gonna need help."

She started to answer, "All right, I'm com–"

I was running short on time. I leapt from the window.

When I'm relying on my luck to see me through, pausing is death. My luck is usually looking out for me, but it doesn't have to be gentle. My heels struck a window ledge a floor below. Quick thinking kept me from breaking my feet. I bent with the blow and bounced off the building – and into a small tree I hadn't noticed, barely larger than a sapling. Its branches whipped across me, slicing my skin. Then I crashed into the trunk. The whole tree was skinny enough to sag from my weight, arresting the speed of my fall.

I dropped, battered and bleeding from a hundred scrapes – but landed on my feet. Pain spiked up my ankles. I didn't have time for pain. Rage and terror[82] poured through my veins, keeping the pain at bay.

The guards in front of the church's entrance were twenty feet away. They had seen my whole fall. They were so stunned that they hadn't lifted their weapons.

That gave me all the time I needed. In quick, measured strides, I was on them. Adrenaline made everything seem distant. The crack of my fist on the closest guard's jaw was a muted nothing.

One of the guards drew her sidearm. Another tried to step in front of me. A poor combination. I shoved the second back into the first, whose shot went wild. The same thing had happened in the hallway above. Before I got too much déjà vu, that first guard recovered her wits and slugged me good.

Even through the adrenaline, it hurt. She was sharp. Certainly sharper than the guard who'd stepped in front of her while she'd aimed a loaded weapon at me. Not sharp enough to retract her arm in time. I grabbed her shoulder, wrenched her toward me, and slammed my fist into the bridge of her nose. She flopped bonelessly to the ground.

More of the guards were drawing their weapons, but I was already in their midst, too close for pistols to be effective. One of them shoved me back. The force of the push reversed my momentum. I went with it. I used it to wheel around, kick

---

[82] Oh, yes. I get scared when I do things like that. At other times, I might try to tell you otherwise. Don't believe me.

the next guard squarely under his chin.

Between the adrenaline muting my pains and the ringing in my ears, my whole body felt at a remove. I was half here, half in the past. In the Everglades.

After I'd killed Beatrice, I hadn't been done fighting.

When I'd picked up Lazarus, I'd been afraid *he* would fight. Or, worse, use his powers. He certainly hated me enough. If he wanted to fight me, he would have just used his voice. I wouldn't have stood a chance. *He* was the perfect weapon. Not me.

But he didn't. He just kept crying.

Eventually, from lack of anyone else to turn to, he wrapped his arms around me and cried into my shoulder. But I knew this didn't mean I was forgiven. Or even that he understood.

We'd been a long ways underground and out in the middle of the Everglades – with nothing around us for miles. We'd had a long way to go, and a lot of people to get through. I'd hoisted Lazarus over my shoulder and taken a second pistol to see us along our way.

I had plenty of opportunities to grab guns off Pearson's followers. I knocked them out of their hands instead. I sidestepped a man charging me and drove a flat-heeled palm into the side of his head – by luck, right into his temple. He wobbled and fell. The next guard to charge me received a quick jab to his throat. He choked and backed off, gagging.

I would have been kidding myself if I had pretended that none of these people would have, at the least, lifelong debilitating injuries because of what I was doing. There was no safe violence. But they were, at the very least, alive.

I had not extended the same credit to Beatrice's followers. Maybe I'd gotten softer with age. As I tore through the dozen armed cultists guarding Pearson's church, I didn't *feel* soft.

As soon as I'd stepped back into the corridor carrying Lazarus, the far door opened. The same one I'd heard Beatrice come through. Another young guard was running towards me, drawn by the alarm. I'd shot him between his eyes.

The gun had gone off too close to me again. In the confines of this underground bunker, there was no way to protect myself from that. My hearing was all but blown.

It wasn't until I felt the vibrations in Lazarus's back, and looked down at him, that I realized he *was* trying to sing. Only the ringing in my ears was saving me from him.

In front of Pearson's church, my ears were still ringing too. I heard, at the lower registers of my hearing and my attention, cries of surprise and terror. An echo of children screaming, adults yelling, from deeper in the church. Some of the people inside had figured out what was going on. Rumors must have been going wild.

They'd all heard Pearson say *fire teams*. They'd rehearsed FBI or CIA or S.H.I.E.L.D. invasion often enough for them to have a glimmer of what he had planned. Pearson's guards had been keeping them bottled up. Now, some people by the doors were slipping out, sidling along the wall, and then running for it.

About half of the door guards were down. I saw the butt of a gun coming my way just in time to avoid it. It glanced off my shoulder – painfully – but continued into the forehead of a woman who'd been coming up behind me.

I swung around, tripped the guard who'd tried to pistol-whip me, and cracked his head into the concrete sidewalk. Even I winced at the sound that made.

The four remaining guards had seen enough. I'd come at them out of the dark so fast that they'd probably thought they were facing an army. They bolted.

I'd disarmed most of them, but not all. One of them turned, drew his pistol to fire while retreating. I swore. If they missed me, they would hit the church, and maybe someone inside. I did something I hadn't wanted to do: pulled my Beretta out of its holster.

I hadn't had the time to aim that carefully, but my luck saw me through. The bullet sliced through the fleeing guard's ankle. He cried out and toppled. His weapon flew into the dark.

More screams from behind me, from just inside the church's entrance. The people inside had heard my gunshot. I holstered my gun again and held up my arms, trying to show that I didn't mean them any harm – for what little good it would do.

The people at the very front plainly didn't want to come out, were trying to backpedal, but the press of people behind them weren't leaving them any option. They were being forced out, into the courtyard.

This was about to turn into a stampede, and I didn't know what I could do about it. That would kill nearly as many people as Pearson planned to.

The people inside had heard Pearson's order for the fire

teams. They'd rehearsed an invasion, a last stand, enough to have some idea what was going on. Panic in there must have been spreading like fire in a windstorm. There was no way I'd be able to calm the stampede once it started in earnest. I wouldn't have been surprised to discover that people were already being crushed against the walls, their breath squeezed out of them. It was a terrible way to die, being mechanically asphyxiated. There would be so many people pushing behind them, pressing into their backs or chests, that their lungs wouldn't have the space they needed to expand.

I cast my eyes about, searching for side or back entrances – any way to relieve the pressure. A pair of silhouettes crouched at the far corner of the church.

If I had to bet, that was one of the fire teams. They huddled over something suitcasesized. A quick glance along the opposite wall found the same thing: another pair of shadows, working hard on something close to the ground.

A staccato sequence of hollow *pops* broke through the ringing in my ears. Gunfire. At the compound's entrance, some of Pearson's people had taken positions behind shrubs, brick columns, or mounds of dirt, and were firing into police cars parked behind the gate. I saw officers diving, taking cover behind their cars' doors – and firing back.

Sirens screamed in the distance, racing this way.

There were more shadows moving around all of the other buildings, the same as I had seen at the church. Pairs of silhouettes either ran towards one of the buildings, or were already crouched and working. Fire teams.

There were too many directions to go in at once. Too many people to fight. Too many people to save. I took a step backward toward the church and turned. And halted.

A bright orange light flared and sparked along the church's side. Flames. The two silhouettes I'd seen there a second ago were running away from the package they'd left at the wall. Some kind of incendiary.

Even if I raced over there, somehow managed to put that one out, Pearson's other fire teams were setting more incendiaries along the other walls. And the other buildings.

I couldn't stop all of this. I didn't even know if I could stop *any* of it. I didn't know where to start.

THIRTY

Lazarus was trying to neutralize me. I only had a minute or so before my hearing returned. Then I'd be lost to his song, and we'd both be lost to this place. I tried to talk to him, to coax him into stopping, but I doubted he heard me. I couldn't hear me. I only knew I was talking from the feel of my muscles moving in my throat.

I carried him swiftly down the corridor, toward the little infirmary we'd passed earlier. He didn't kick, or squirm, or try to fight. He was used to being overpowered. I guessed that the adults here, our mother included, had manhandled him often.

I fumbled through the glass medicine cabinets. All were locked. I smashed my fist through them, one at a time (cutting my hand badly, but, in my panic and desperation, I hardly noticed), until I found what I was looking for. Tranquilizer. The soldiers' last resort to stop Lazarus if he went wild on them. They probably would have sent in someone wearing ear plugs to administer it. I hated to do this, but I hated being caught and killed even more.

And the soldiers would "just" kill me. They would have worse in store for Lazarus.

I'd already done one unforgivable thing today. My hands trembled as I plunged the syringe into the vial and drew the plunger up. Lazarus was propped on my shoulder, facing away. He couldn't see what I was doing. Lucky him. I jabbed the needle into his rear and pushed the plunger down.

I held him until he stopped trying to sing. Eventually, he went limp.

I'd had no choice. I couldn't have trusted him around me anymore. Even, especially, while I was trying to save us.

I had never felt so alone.

And I wouldn't feel that alone ever again.

The chaos of Pearson's compound dwindled away. A roar like a waterfall plastered my hair to my scalp. A freezing wind pelted me from above – a half second before a spotlight caught me.

In checking all my angles, I'd made an amateur mistake. I'd forgotten to look up.

I did now.

The wind wasn't from rotors. The sound wasn't a police copter. A Wakandan airship burned through the night sky, all shining running lights and billowing thrusters.

It was shockingly close. Too close. The airship didn't hang above the buildings. It clove *between* them. Another few dozen feet to its right and its starboard wing would have clipped the office building I'd just dived out of.

The airship was heaving toward the church. Its nose angled steeply downward.

The furious wind had come from its thrusters. While coasting on hover engines, Shoon'kwa's airship used compressed gas jets for fine maneuvering. The biting cold of the gale was from more than the Chicago winter. The pressurized exhaust flash-cooled as it expanded. Dangerous to breathe too much of it in. It was a nitrogen gas mixture, not overtly toxic – but it contained no oxygen.

Shoon'kwa was taking her airship as close to the church as she dared. Its nose nearly brushed the brickwork. But, at her angle of approach, her ventral bow thrusters were pointed directly at the spreading fire.

The fire billowed against the wind, mushroomed higher, licked across the church's walls, and then – all at once – guttered and died. Starved of oxygen.

"I finished those repairs faster than I'd anticipated," Shoon'kwa's voice said in my headset.

My heart pounded against my ribcage. It was very much a struggle to keep from showing how relieved I felt. But only for a moment. Anger swiftly overwhelmed relief. I said, "You've been listening to us this whole time."

"I happened to be in the neighborhood."

"One of these days, you and I are going to have a chat about what it means to be on a team. And keeping your team leader informed."

"I can turn around, if you would like." Her voice was icy.

"*No*," Rachel and Inez said at once.

"Mark it on your calendar, because it's going to happen," I said. I was serious. None of the problems that had forced us to keep the airship away had vanished. There were lots of organizations around, heroic and otherwise, who would be taking a special interest in all this now.

I had a hard time staying irritated at someone who'd just pulled my butt out of the fire, literally.

Shoon'kwa was a teenager. She wasn't used to working on a team. She'd been exiled from her home, been left with nothing and no one to trust. Hell, the first time we'd met, she'd hired me for a bounty hunt and I'd double-crossed her, and we'd ended up getting into a fist fight. She'd gotten used to withholding trust, acting independently.

Like the rest of us, she'd always felt alone. And, also like the rest of us, it would take her a long time to learn that she didn't have to. All of us had left home, or been kicked out, for one reason or another.

Another searchlight swept over me. I shielded my eyes. Her airship spawned dozens of them. The searchlights wheeled across the compound, guided by the airship's sensors and inboard AI, locking on any significant source of body heat and movement. Myself included. But also Pearson's people – the fire teams crouched by the church and other buildings, and the gunmen by the gates. There were more people out than I realized. Some of the gunmen started shooting, uselessly, at the airship.

"Get that damn light off me!" I told Shoon'kwa.

It took Shoon'kwa a few seconds to find me, override the AI keeping the spotlight pinned on me. I lowered my hand. Thanks to my quick thinking, I'd preserved my night vision.

The same couldn't have been said for the nearest of Pearson's fire teams. A harried, wild-eyed young man and woman were crouched by the church's far corner, still working furiously to unpack their incendiaries. They were fumbling, reaching for things that weren't there. They must have looked directly into Shoon'kwa's lights.

I spotted a stone against the church's wall, seized it, and threw. The stone cracked across the young man's head. He tumbled into his partner. She wavered, but managed to stay on her knees. Thanks to her night blindness, she never saw me. Never had a chance to duck the boot to her head.

They had not stopped working, even under the spotlights. Nor had the other fire teams. The gunmen at the gates had not stopped firing. Bullets *pinged* off the airship's hull, but most of the gunmen were still firing into the police cars arrayed outside. We still had our work cut out for us.

With Lazarus, I'd only had so many hands. I'd had no choice but to carry him over my shoulder. It left him more vulnerable, but it was the only way I could keep my gun in one hand and still be able to open doors with the other. Holding him and a gun at the same time did not feel responsible, but I had no idea what responsibility was any more. Should I have left him behind? Given him back to Beatrice's followers?

I lost track of where I was in those twisting underground tunnels. I tried to follow the path I'd taken to get from here to the incinerator, but everything looked different, and my head was spinning. Part of Lazarus's song must have gotten through to me. I wasn't only alone, but lost.

The smell of blood wormed its way into my nostrils. I couldn't tell whose. I'd spilled so much of it. Eventually, I found my way back to the incinerator room, and its caked-in stink of ash and filth and smoke. Maybe it was the after-effects of Lazarus's song making me sick, but the smell made me gag. I almost threw up in the corner.

Some things sear themselves into your memory hotter than anything else, even the things you couldn't imagine forgetting. Like a face that had, at one time, been the most important one in your life. I never wanted to remember that smell, but it stayed with me.

My palm was numb where the recoil from my pistol kept punching it. I didn't fire to kill, although I'm sure I killed along the way.

I'd hated to tranquilize Lazarus. If he hadn't been trying to control me, I wouldn't have. But I was glad he wasn't awake to keep watching this.

He would never understand. He would never recover from what he had seen me do.

The ear-splitting thunder of Shoon'kwa's thrusters, and the shock of her airship's searchlights, had temporarily stemmed the press of people at the church's entrance. The awe would only last so long. But we had a minute to work with that we hadn't had before.

I bent to check on the young man whose head I'd cracked with the rock. He stirred muzzily, but didn't seem to see me. He'd need a hospital stay, at the very least. So would a lot of the people crowded into that church, no doubt – overheating, exhaustion, malnutrition, abuse.

"I hope we've got someone besides more people with guns coming this way," I said.

"I've already placed the calls," Rachel said. "Ambulances on the way."

Rachel was exquisite, as always. In spite of all this, I smiled. I didn't know how she was convincing the city's emergency services to send as many medical first responders as we would need. If anyone could have finessed it, though, it was her.

Another of Pearson's fire teams was setting up incendiaries by a door that looked like a side exit. Three armed escorts stood with them, gaping at Shoon'kwa's airship. They were pinned under one of her searchlights, night-blind. They didn't notice me darting around the corner and charging until I'd already disarmed one of them and broken the next man's elbow.

The third guard, a pale woman who looked like she hadn't seen the sun in months, was faster on her feet. She kicked out my ankle and, while I stumbled, raised her weapon. My reflexes were only just fast enough to deflect her arm.

Her gunshot pierced the shoulder of one of the two people unpacking the incendiaries. I ripped the gun from her with one hand, whirled around, and smashed my elbow into the back of her head. Not enough to knock her out, but it must have scared the hell out of her. She bolted. So did the other guards, and the two members of the fire team were right behind them. The one who'd been shot in the shoulder staggered, but kept up with them. Shoon'kwa's spotlights chased after them, leaving me in darkness.

Another fire sparked below one of the dorm buildings. In that flash of light, I saw Inez plunge into the pair of fanatics who'd set it, fists swinging, her face twisted with rage. Relief flooded my veins, chilling the aches and pains of fighting.

Shoon'kwa's airship pivoted, and rose on a column of thruster jets. Carefully, she maneuvered her airship along the rooftops, toward the new fire.

More gunfire rattled off near the gates, interrupted by a pair of heavier thunderclaps. Flashbangs. They would have blinded me if I'd been looking. I counted seconds under my breath before checking it out.

The flashbangs had fallen right in the middle of the cultists who'd opened fire on the police cars. Still pinned under Shoon'kwa's lights, they'd fallen out of their cover, or just rolled on the ground. Some of them had even dropped their weapons.

A pale blur raced along the edges of the spotlight. White Fox. She moved faster than I could track – which was how I knew it was her.

As a kumiho, White Fox may have been superhumanly fast, but she was still as vulnerable to bullets as a normal human. She'd hurtled right into the line of fire. Or what should have been the line of fire. But none of the police officers outside the gate were firing back.

Black Widow crouched behind one of their armored car doors, her hands raised, palms flat. The officers must have recognized her as an Avenger. She'd taken charge of half a dozen strangers with practiced efficiency, and was coordinating a battle plan.

One of the dazed fanatics tried to raise his weapon. White Fox slammed his head into the dirt and kicked the gun from his hand. Another man, across the yard, tried to aim at her. She opened her mouth. I couldn't hear her voice from so far away, but I knew what she was doing, and it still sent a shiver across my back. A kumiho's mesmeric ability was small compared to, say, Lazarus's, but it was enough. The fanatic stopped. His eyes went wide, his jaw slack. The grip of his pistol slipped from his hand.

Outside, Black Widow pointed at one of the parked police cars and waved ahead. The car's driver gunned its engine, leapt forward, and smashed into the gate. The chain lock snapped as the car crashed through.

Black Widow charged through the gates, leapt over the police car's hood, and slid into the compound, a half-dozen police officers right behind her. They spread out among the fallen gate guards, rapidly disarming those who'd clung to their weapons.

No one other than me was near the church. All the people inside were my responsibility.

The side door that Pearson's guards had been watching, and that his fire team had been trying to set alight, had jarred open a crack. A slim column of light spilled out. I peered in and saw a throng of people – mottled hair, terrified faces. Some were visibly praying. I had never seen a crowd like this jammed in so tightly.

Shoon'kwa's lights pouring through the windows, and the roar of her thrusters, had halted the stampede. But their shock wouldn't last forever. And Shoon'kwa had taken her airship to some other part of the compound.

Nobody was pushing through this door yet. Either they hadn't noticed it or they'd been warned away from it. They'd find it soon. Now that the thunder of Shoon'kwa's thrusters was diminishing, and the crowd was starting to stir. Before long, they'd be crushing themselves to get to this exit or any other.

I couldn't let myself think. Thinking was hesitation.

Hesitation meant a stampede, and that would mean death. There were children in there Lazarus's age. And younger.

I took a deep breath, took a step back, and started running.

THIRTY-ONE

I slammed through the door. A middle-aged couple stood on the other side. The force of the door opening knocked them apart, and made just enough space for me to push through.

The crowd beyond them was a solid wall.

I had to trust my luck. I couldn't lose my momentum. One person stepped forward just in time for me to, with some quick contorting, slip past.

Past them, an elderly man was stricken with an abrupt coughing fit. A woman who must have been a relative or caretaker shifted closer to pat his back – opening another space.

Next, a tired-looking two year-old sat perched on an older man's broad shoulders. The kid saw me rushing toward them, shrieked, and grabbed at the man's hair. He shifted to turn toward me, opening a narrow gap just behind him.

And on and on like this – past a dozen more people moving at the right moment, and into spaces that shouldn't have been there. Ducking, dodging, weaving through gaps just large enough for me, and some a little smaller. I stumbled around an unaccompanied child, fighting for space among the crush of people. I didn't have the breath to mutter apologies. Someone's elbow landed in my face while I knocked past, but I hardly noticed.

Impossibly, I kept going. There was only one place I could go. The one clear space in the church was around Pearson's podium.

Even in circumstances like these, Pearson's people stayed away from *his* spaces, like they were afraid that he would come back.[83]

One woman up front was bent over a child, trying to lift him up. I tripped over someone's ankle. I careened into the woman's back, rolled over it, and stumbled gracelessly onto the raised floor by the podium. By luck alone, I stayed on my feet. I grabbed the podium's edges just at the right moment to halt – and to look like I'd meant to do that all along.

A few people close had noticed me, were pointing. But the mass of people were looking elsewhere. The crowd was surging, trying to press toward the main entrance.

To the few people looking at me, I must have been terrifying. Torn clothes. Wet hair. Battered, bruised, and bloodied by my fall from Pearson's office. I'd lost track of how many ways and places I'd started to hurt.

But I wasn't the kind of threat that Pearson's followers had been told to expect. He'd spun them tales of CIA and S.H.I.E.L.D. infiltration, assassins, and super-spies[84] and

---

[83] That was probably – even now, after they'd heard what they must have known was his order for their deaths – what many of them were hoping for.

[84] To be fair, Black Widow *was* outside, but she wasn't representing any group but mine. Probably.

massive conspiracies. From this angle, most of the audience couldn't even see my pistol. I hastily unholstered it, stashed it beneath the podium, just in case.

The bulk of the space under the podium was taken up by controls and equipment. Pearson had had a sophisticated professional AV console. So many of the people here looked malnourished and exhausted, and were dressed in torn and fraying old clothes, but the equipment behind the podium was pristine.

The controls were dense and impenetrable, but one label caught my eye. "Bell." I hit that button.

The tremendous *clang* from overhead briefly made me forget the ringing in my ears. The noise was amplified by speakers all around the church, and probably all around the compound. It screeched with feedback. I'd done something wrong. It didn't matter.

Pearson had trained them to respond to that sound. He'd had so many sermons every day. The press of people against the front doors halted. Several people in that direction cried out, yelling for people to get back. So many people near those doors must have been getting crushed, the breath squeezed out of them.

I fumbled for the microphone, found the switch that controlled it. I hoped I'd gotten here in time. I only needed to hold their attention for a few minutes. Long enough for a more orderly exit to start. And for the police officers outside to reach us.

I racked my mind, trying to think of what to do now. "You're safe," I stammered. "Nobody's going to hurt you or your families."

That did not convince them.

Some of them started to turn away. The nearest had gotten a better look at me, at my blood and scrapes, and had started to push back toward the doors. Those by the doors were still shoving back, fighting for breathing space. The crowd clashed in the center, like two waves smashing together. Before long, it would break down into a scrum.

When I finally found a door out of the Project Armageddon facility and stumbled out into a deeply humid night, I'd started talking to Lazarus. He couldn't hear me, but I felt it was important that I keep talking.

Maybe it was all for my sake. But I needed him to understand what I'd done, and what I was doing. I needed to pretend I wasn't alone.

Moonlight guided my path, and clouds obscured it more often than not. I stumbled along between the facility's buildings, blind, and half deaf.

Eventually, I had broken down. It had all caught up with me – the knives in my bones, the endless isolation and stress, the fact that I had just shot *my mother* in the face. By the time I found the empty truck sitting on a dirt trail, I'd just kept repeating the same words over and over. The only words I could think of that might have been comforting.

I buckled him into the passenger seat and started driving. After he'd woken, and could understand me, I'd tried to explain what I'd done, why I'd had to do it. I might as well have just tranqed him again for all the difference it would have made. He looked at me like I'd looked at every adult when I was his age, if not worse.

He hated me. And he always would. He was closed to me.

I couldn't explain myself to Pearson's people either. I couldn't tell them that Pearson was dead, or that his closest associates were trying to murder them. They'd refuse to understand. They weren't in a space where they were capable of it.

It didn't matter if they understood. I hadn't done it so that they would *understand*. I'd done it to save them. Whether they'd wanted to be saved or not. I was here – and I would do it.

So I told them the only thing that, driving in that truck along the dirt trail, I'd been able to tell Lazarus. The same words, again and again. The only ones I'd thought he'd really want to hear.

"It's over."

They looked so tired. It was the first thing I'd said that got them to listen to me.

I had to keep going from there, but those words had been the ones they wanted to hear, the ones that kept their attention. Pearson had kept them on their feet for weeks. Interrupting their sleep. Feeding them poorly. Keeping them crammed together, isolated, under his thumb. Constantly terrified of the world. They couldn't have borne it forever. More than anything else, they wanted it to be done with.

They would hate me when they found out what I'd done. If they didn't hate me already. Didn't matter.

Funny thing: I'd spent so much of my life thinking of myself as a merc and not a hero, but some deep down, dirty part of me had still craved the kind of recognition I'd imagined heroes got. I hadn't been aware of that part of myself until well after I'd found Lazarus. But it had always been there.

One of the things that made heroes *heroes* was how much they were willing to sacrifice for their causes.

If Lazarus hated me because of what I'd done – that was just one more sacrifice I would have to make.

I wouldn't have to make it alone. Shoon'kwa's lights again shone through the stained glass windows, turning the people near them all kinds of new colors.

When I was young, living in the Church of the Sacred Heart and trying to forget where I'd come from, I thought the past never changed. That's not true. You don't need a time machine to change the past.

Memory isn't a window into the past. It's not even a lens, bent and distorted around the edges. It's a prism. It changes *every* time you pick it up and look at it again. The light bends and twists, splits and refracts and blends with the light you're shining in on it.

I knew more about what I had done. About why I'd done it. About who I was.

And knew I could live with all of it.

I held the congregation's attention until Black Widow and her police officers arrived, and could start safely shepherding them outside.

THIRTY-TWO
CHICAGO,
ANY TIME AND EVERY TIME...

The day I decided to run away from the Church of the Sacred Heart was a dark gray March morning, full of sleeting rain and hail.

That was the first day I'd admitted it to myself that I would be going. I had known, buried somewhere deep inside me, that I would be leaving someday. I hadn't wanted to face it any more than I'd wanted to face my history. When I looked out the dorm window and saw the weather, I knew I had the perfect opportunity. It wasn't going to get better than this for weeks, if not for months.

No one would have voluntarily gone outside in weather like this. The people shuffling back and forth along the sidewalk, bundled inside their coats or under umbrellas, were too focused on their own feet to pay attention to me. When the missing child report went out a couple hours from now, there would be few witnesses to remember me.

It was a Saturday morning. Most of the other girls were still sleeping. If it had been raining like this on a weekday, that would have been an even better opportunity – I no longer went to school with the other kids.

I had a few possessions. But I traveled light. I'd been trained to not get attached to anything.

The things I took with me were all of practical, immediate value. My hooded winter jacket. Changes of clothes. Pads of paper, pencils. Water bottle. Insulated cooler bag, with as much food as I could smuggle out of the kitchen. And a backpack to carry it all in.

I didn't kid myself. If I hadn't been who I was – what I was – my odds wouldn't have been good.[85] Technically, my odds *still* weren't good. But I had worked out that luck was on my side.

I wasn't so foolish as to think I had a plan. I knew a few places where I could find shelter – empty apartments, old squats – and some places to shoplift food. Nothing that would last. But I knew I had a power no one else did. And, when I was out there, I could stop hiding it. And maybe I could find some other mutants on the fringes. I wasn't prepared to admit that I was looking for company.

In my internal monologue, I would only tell myself that I would be fine on my own. Deep underneath, I knew better.

Or maybe that's just the way I remember it. My life in the present interfering with my memories of the past.

The winter jacket helped me hide what I was carrying, so

---

[85] If I am learning to play at being a hero, I should issue a PSA. *Don't* run away from home. Unless you're in danger there. Or unless your parents are about to join a cult. Or unless – actually, you know what? Never mind. You do you.

it just looked like I was trying to protect my textbooks and schoolwork from the rain. Good thing, too. I ran into Father Boschelli in the orphanage's foyer, hanging up his coat. My blood froze. I had to force myself to act normal, and remember that I didn't look suspicious.

"And where are you off to in weather like this?" he asked.

"Library. Got some reading to do." After my third fight at school, I'd been suspended pending an expulsion hearing. I didn't expect it to go well. Kids from the Church of the Sacred Heart got very little credit at that school, and I'd done everything in my power to burn mine. Father Boschelli had done his best to keep me up to date on schoolwork, getting textbooks and course plans from Chicago's public schools[86] – but, every day, I saw his faith in me slip bit by bit.

"I've been in touch with school admin. I thought you'd like to know you almost broke Jason's arm in two places. He has a fracture in his forearm, too."

Jason's family was rich. Which meant, of course, that they had threatened to sue the impoverished Church of the Sacred Heart into the ground rather than pay a fraction of the cost of his cast and ER visit.

"How many times can I say I'm sorry?" I asked.

"Only once, if you mean it."

Right to the quick. Which only made me more sullen.

"Do you need somebody to walk you there?" Father Boschelli asked.

I shook my head.

He gestured to the closet opposite the coat rack. "Umbrella?"

---

[86] This was not his first time aboard the expulsion train.

I had to force my voice to sound normal. "No, I'm good."

If he'd had any inkling of what I was about to do, it would have been irresponsible of him to let me walk past. I don't believe he knew. But, as he hesitated to step out of my way and then gave me a sad smile, I had to believe he knew *something* was different.

"All right, Neena," he said. "I trust you."

I slipped by him. I couldn't make myself look at him again.

He was trying to keep me in his world by showing he still had some faith in me.

The freezing cold pierced my jacket the moment I stepped outside. I drew my hood tight. I could withstand this, I told myself. I knew what I was in for.

I figured I'd learned enough about the world outside the lab coats' facility that I could survive without the church now. I knew places I could squat, but hiding out in those would have been foolish. All the missing child reports would be concentrated in Chicago. I had to get away from the city. Bus, train – whatever options opened up to me. The weather down south would be more amenable to someone without reliable shelter. Or so I figured.[87]

I studied the skyline. The faster I got to Union Station, the better. I figured I could slip aboard an Amtrak train and be out of the city by the afternoon. I didn't have a ticket, didn't have ID, but I trusted my luck enough now to get me past these obstacles.[88]

My mind was far away from the buildings around me. I

---

[87] I was, if you hadn't noticed, an idiot.

[88] As it turned out, *that* trust was well placed.

didn't pay any more attention to them than on any other day, but it was how they looked – under a gray veil of icy mist – that stuck in my mind for years.

The bus that took Rose and Joseph home took the same street. Inez and I sat behind them, escorting them on this final leg of their trip. They had asked us along. They'd needed courage to step onto their mother's doorstep after all the bridges they'd burned. I told them that those bridges were so far from unburned that, whatever they'd done, their mother hadn't even mentioned it to me.

They didn't look convinced. I didn't ask. And then, when I glanced out the window, the shock of recognition was enough to make Inez look at me with concern.

I'd walked this street every school day to get to our bus stop. A cyclone of gentrification had swept through, destroyed the bodegas and corner restaurants and upstairs nook apartments, and left only chain cafés and expensive clothing stores behind. But I still recognized half of the buildings. The signs. The bus stop shelters.

The Church of the Sacred Heart was down another street, around a corner, almost visible from here.

It was a sunny winter day. Icy cirrus clouds haloed the sun. That made it feel even more alien. The day that I'd left the church, with its pelting hail and soaking horizontal rains, had been the image that had seared into my memory.

That, and the evening I'd said goodbye to Lazarus.

At the Project Armageddon facility, I'd injected Lazarus with enough tranquilizer to down an adult for two days, but he woke up before we got out of Florida. He was a mutant, after all. No reason his voice had to be his only power. Sometimes super endurance came along with the package. Just ask Inez.

He refused to talk to me no matter how gently I tried. Not for days and days on the road. It drove a dagger into my gut. But he did not try to sing to me, either.

He could have destroyed me. Taken over my mind. Easily. But he wasn't that kind of kid.

He *was* listening. He followed all of my instructions to the letter. He had never been in the outside world before – had only been *taken* outside and seen the sky once a week or so. If he was at all in awe, he was careful not to show me.

He watched the world roll by with dead eyes. When we stopped at a restaurant or fast food joint, he wouldn't say what he wanted. He just ate whatever I ordered. He didn't try to escape from any of the hotels we stopped at. He didn't so much as ask for a bathroom stop.

I had recognized Lazarus as my brother, or at the very least a kindred spirit, because he hadn't known how to be a child. Neither had I. It had taken me a long time to even figure out what childishness *was*. And then, when I'd come to the Church of the Sacred Heart, all the other kids tried so hard to be adults too.

It took a long time for my spirits to lighten to the point where I learned how to play. When I could approach something as simple as a game without making it deadly serious.[89] I couldn't have done that at the Church of the Sacred Heart. And that was a big part of the reason why I'd had to leave.

But it wasn't the only one.

---

89 One of the reasons I'm like I am as an adult. Making up for lost time.

Lazarus and I couldn't keep this up. Even if my presence wasn't poison to Lazarus, my lifestyle wasn't suited to raising a child.

Rose and Joseph were adults, but I had a hard time knowing what to say around them, too. So mostly I didn't say anything. The bus left the gentrified neighborhood, Church of the Sacred Heart and all, well behind. We all disembarked seven stops later.

Inez stuck by my side. She seemed to have gotten the idea that I needed escorting as much as the twins. Ever since I'd gasped while looking out that window, she'd been treating me a little oddly.

She had no reason to be concerned. I was fine. I swear.

Rose and Joseph walked ahead in a daze. They knew exactly where they were going. They'd grown up on these streets. They probably didn't think they'd ever be back here.

Once or twice, Rose tried to point something out on one of the buildings, or a street. Something that had changed, maybe. Her voice was small, and Joseph wasn't listening anyway.

Rebecca Munoz lived in a little rental unit jammed together on a street full of clashing colors. The sides of the streets were packed bumper-to-bumper with parked cars. Rose and Joseph weaved their way through them. After a certain point, Joseph started leading. Rose lagged. Inez and I were behind her, though, and she wasn't willing to run away while we were watching. She squared her shoulders and kept after Joseph.

Rebecca was sitting on their doorstep. Waiting for them.

Inez and I had called ahead. We hadn't told the twins that part.

Honestly, I hadn't been sure they'd have the willpower to

ring the doorbell. One less thing for them to worry about.

Joseph's footsteps trailed to a halt. Rose surprised me. She kept going, and passed him. She headed right toward her mother. That startled Joseph into following.

When Rebecca had first told me about the twins' problems, and again when I'd met them in that cell in Pearson's compound, I'd wondered if one of them had egged the other on. But that had never quite fit. Now I realized the truth was much simpler: they *carried* each other on.

When one of them had gotten into trouble, they'd both gotten into it. And now they were both going to get out of it.

Rebecca stood when she saw them. She held her hands cupped over her mouth.

She had never told me what the twins had done to her before they'd left. It must have been something bad, judging from their reactions now. I'd told the twins, back in that cell, that whatever they'd done didn't matter anymore. I saw now that I was right.

Rose stopped a good ten feet away, and tried to keep herself at that distance while she said hello. Rebecca wouldn't let her. Faster than Rose could react, Rebecca swept off the doorstep and wrapped her arm around Rose's shoulders. With her other hand, she drew Joseph into it, too.

Inez and I didn't intrude past that point. Wouldn't have been right. It wasn't what we had been hired for. We couldn't have helped, anyway.

It felt good to just see this much.

But it didn't feel like it was over. Inez and I waited another fifteen minutes for a bus to come back around, and by the time we boarded, the feeling still hadn't gone away.

Too many stirred-up old broken memories. I kept trying to run from them, push myself back into the present. But they always came with me.

When I closed my eyes again, I was in Project Armageddon's stolen car, with Lazarus.

He'd tried to sing to me right after I'd killed Beatrice, but that had been the last time he'd used his power. He'd learned the hard way what effect his voice had on people. After discovering what his voice had done to the guards outside his cell, he had tried to avoid using it again in all but the direst circumstances. No matter how hard Beatrice had pressed him, he hadn't used it on me. Not until I became a threat.

He wasn't a weapon. He had all the abilities Project Armageddon had wanted in a mutant. But not the character to use them. He was more empathetic than anyone his age should have been. Maybe empathy was a component of his power – something I doubted any incarnation of Project Armageddon could have understood.

Maybe Beatrice and her cult could have turned him into a weapon someday. People like Beatrice specialized in warping people.

I budgeted plenty of time for Chicago traffic. I needed it. The Chicago Skyway was a wall of brake lights two miles from the tollbooth. Lazarus looked at the skyline as if hardly seeing it. Same way he'd looked at Atlanta and Indianapolis when we'd passed through. Somewhere inside, he had to be impressed. But he wasn't going to let that part show around me.

The driving got hairier as we got deeper into the city. But the streets grew more familiar. The gentrification then hadn't been quite so bad as it would be when Inez, Rose, Joseph, and I had gone by. Nothing was clean. The brick walls were stained by decades of diesel fumes. It was like a comfortable old blanket.

I scavenged a parking space a block from the Church of the Sacred Heart. Lazarus stepped outside when I opened the door. He looked at me, plainly wanting to ask a question but hating me too much to actually voice it.

I didn't answer it for him.

Father Boschelli was in the church. I knew he would be. I'd been checking up on him for a few years. I also had a Google alert set on his name, and it pulled up stories about his charity work from time to time.

He was a creature of routine, and that hadn't changed in all the years I'd been away. Every Wednesday, it was his turn to take the overnight shift guarding the orphanage's dormitories.

I caught him in the foyer, just about to lock up for the evening. Keys in one hand, stained coffee mug in the other. His eyes must have been getting worse. He only noticed me when my shadow fell across him.

I wasn't wearing any kind of disguise, but I'd timed my travels carefully. We'd arrived in early evening. The church had a west-facing door. The sun behind me was blinding. I, on the other hand, had a good view of him.

He'd kept himself up well. He'd aged into his late fifties like he'd taken every part of himself and turned it up. Gained a little bit of weight. His hair was all gray, but, if anything, it had gotten thicker. His mustache was bushier.

"I have a lost child here who needs some care," I said.

"I'm afraid you're at the wrong address," he answered. "This isn't the Chicago police department."

"You *do* still take care of children without families, don't you?"

"We're not a dumping ground for families looking to avoid their responsibilities." Despite the edge in his words, his voice was kind, if tired. He let out a long sigh. "It's not a simple process for us to take guardianship of a child. The state is involved. There's a great deal of necessary steps in the process, paperwork–"

"That's not going to matter this time."

He frowned sharply, shielded his eyes with his hand. "What makes you think that?"

"I know you've been able to bypass these things in the past."

I couldn't see his eyes under the shade of his palm. His mouth opened, but he didn't say anything. Not for a long time.

"Perhaps I have," he said, eventually.

I wasn't in the mood for a long reunion. I didn't think I could have borne it. Difficult enough to keep my expression flat.

I've made decisions that kill me to think about. But I couldn't say I'd been wrong to make them. Making those decisions had been one struggle. Accepting them another. Story of my life.

Father Boschelli said, "I am obligated to ask – is he your child?"

"No," Lazarus and I said, at the same time. It was the first time Lazarus had said anything since leaving Florida. I looked at him.

Father Boschelli looked to Lazarus. "What is your name?"

Lazarus didn't answer. Almost imperceptibly, he shifted

back. And then realized that it was *me* he'd stepped toward, and stopped.

"His last name is Thurman," I said. And his first name could be whatever he wanted it to be now. Lazarus or anything else.

I started walking. Didn't look back. Lazarus wouldn't have wanted me to look back.

That would just be another thing for him to hate me for later. That, in its own way, would be better. It would give him a chance for a clean break. If I were irredeemable in his eyes, he wouldn't have my memory as something to look back on and haunt him. Hate was a precious simplicity in a complicated world. Right now, the last thing he needed – the last thing that would be good for him – was to have mixed feelings about me.

I couldn't keep my step from faltering, though.

THIRTY-THREE
CHICAGO, NOW

Inez, Rachel, and I had a tradition after a successful job. Spend a night on the town. No matter where we were, unless it was a complete hellscape or the middle of nowhere – but even then, there was probably a town or a city nearby and something worthwhile to do.

There were some caveats. The older I got, the more I had to get some post-mission rest. After taking Rose and Joseph back, I slept for twelve straight hours, and still felt tired afterward.

The pain of my cuts in the shower woke me right back up, though. After that, ready to party. Stiffness and muscle aches be damned.

Rebecca Munoz hadn't had all the money she'd needed to cover our bill. No surprise. And, the last time I'd seen her, she'd had bigger things on her mind. I wasn't going to press her on it.

So, yes, there were caveats, but I tried never to make any exceptions. It was important to live our lives. Remind ourselves why we got in this business. No sense in saving for a rainy day if every day was a storm.

But, this time, I had a stop to make first.

We had to get up to the rooftops the hard way. It was never good manners to take any kind of airship, Wakandan or not, this close to a city. Shoon'kwa and I still needed to have our talk about that. The buildings around the Church of the Sacred Heart seemed to get taller every time I visited. On the upside, that meant that the view they offered got a little better, and a little less obtrusive, too.

But the winter wind sure seemed worse. The buildings upwind of us made a perfect wind tunnel. Black Window hugged her arms to herself. "You take us to all the best places."

"You all didn't have to follow me here." I was actually a little irked that they had.

"And miss the chance to see where so much of our money goes?" Black Widow asked.

Whenever I made a good payday, something that would keep my friends and me on our feet for quite a while, I always set a part of it aside. Any merc in the business has a number of ways to anonymize a check. I cut one and sent it directly to the Church of the Sacred Heart. Every mission. Always.

Father Boschelli didn't need to know it was me. If he'd known, that might have jeopardized the help I'd sent. I'd gotten involved in some pretty questionable things in my past. And us mutants were always a political hot potato. Even if Father Boschelli's superiors accepted money from me now, that might change in the weeks, months, and years ahead.

Today, that didn't bother me as much as it usually did.

There was still lots of clean-up work to do in and around

Dallas Bader Pearson's compound. His people were terrified and scattered. Some were injured. No one, other than Pearson, had died. The Chicago PD had even opened a desultory investigation to search for his killer. But that was small in comparison to the now-massive investigations into his church's financial crimes, abuses, kidnappings, tortures, and killings. Three bodies had been discovered so far, cemented into iron drums, buried under the compound. I was sure they wouldn't be the only ones.

Cults didn't die easy. There would be splinter groups. Recriminations. Lawsuits. Trials. Some of Pearson's followers would idolize him in death. A lot of them must have put two and two together, realized that the bloodied-and-wild-looking woman who'd kept them calm during the police raid must have had something to do with his killing. They wouldn't forgive me any more than Lazarus had.

The police weren't going to spend much time looking for me. Few of the stories about the raid on Pearson's compound even mentioned a Wakandan airship. Black Widow's Avengers connections went a long way.

But it would be best for everyone if our involvement ended here. I had done what needed doing. More people hated me for it than not. Only a few people knew the truth, understood the choices I'd made.

It would have to be enough.

Inez had brought her tray of peanut-butter-chocolate bars to share. The vegan café's staff had looked at her slack-jawed when she'd come back, wading through the police cars and their wailing sirens, to collect them. White Fox chewed thoughtfully. Shoon'kwa and Black Widow had turned them down. Their loss. The bars were good.

"Just let us know when you're done having your fun," Black Widow said. She didn't bother to hide her impatience.

"Not all of us get to be the stars of our own movie all the time," I told her. "Let me have this one."

White Fox looked at Inez. "You *must* be cold now. Right?" she asked.

Inez snorted and didn't answer. Just like any of the times I hassled her about the same.

I had made Inez sleep in that apartment last night. Told her to find the problems with it. She'd come back looking fresh and ready, and dressing just as light as ever. Sleeveless up to her shoulders, and jean shorts that rode higher than looked comfortable.

But, when I looked out of the corner of my eye, I saw goosebumps prickle along her skin.

Victory. It was gonna be fun to see how long she could keep up the act.

She was committed now. Maybe the next job could take us to the Arctic. *Sometime* she'd slip up and start shivering.

Rachel, as always, dressed up to the occasion. Bright, heavy, violet jacket. Fur-lined boots. And a scarf to match, whipping in the wind. "As much as I appreciate dramatic posing on rooftops, I hope you're not going to keep us up here for long."

"You *really* didn't have to come up here," I repeated.

"Dear," she said. "Would you really rather be alone?"

When I'd started up the staircase, I'd thought so. Now I was glad as much for the distractions and for the company. Distractions are underrated.

"I'll never get used to this," Shoon'kwa muttered. She

folded her arms. She went on nights out with the rest of us, but she was the only one who never showed any sign of enjoying it. She never refused them either. She was, for lack of a better term, our designated driver. Too young to drink. And, knowing her, she would have turned down the offer.

But she still cared enough to want to spend time with us. She was getting more and more adapted to this lifestyle.

"Never get used to what, darling?" Inez asked. "The weather? Or us?"

"This," Shoon'kwa said, and nothing else.

As the neighborhood around the Church of the Sacred Heart had grown up and gotten harder for small folks to live in, the church had stayed exactly where it was. And looked exactly the same, at least on the outside. I hadn't seen the inside since I'd left, but I knew, thanks to some of the articles I'd dug up about the church, that things had changed there, too. Expanded classrooms. Better sanitation. Better food. More adult volunteers and even paid staff. Wider access to Chicago's schools. And every kid that came through the Church of the Sacred Heart, whether they found adoption or a foster family or not, had college tuition paid for and a stipend to keep them on their feet through their twenties.

It wasn't all down to me. Plenty of the orphanage's other alumni, who'd beaten their own odds, sent money back too. But I helped. By a lot. I was gonna make sure that, no matter what Lazarus wanted to do with his life, he had the option to do it.

Some day, he might even figure out that I'd contributed. But I wasn't going to be the one to tell him.

Below, a line of schoolkids filed out of the church's main

doors. Nice and orderly. A far cry from when I'd been there, but the church had more adult staff available now. Two of them stood beside the doors, ushering the kids onto the sidewalk, toward their bus stop. Kids in freshly laundered, neatly ironed clothes.

And, at the end of the line, Lazarus.

He'd chosen a different name now. Zachary. Still nice and Biblical, and kept many of the same sounds. Lazarus was a little too unwieldy for the modern world, raised too many questions.

His pitch-black hair made him easy to spot from above. He still kept it cut in the same style he had back at Project Armageddon.

I kept an eye on him not just because I loved him. But also because he still had his song, his powers. He remained Project Armageddon's ultimate weapon. It would have been irresponsible of me not to check up on him, and to make sure someone hadn't found out who and what he was.

My read on his character remained the same. I didn't think he would abuse his powers. He was a good kid, and I was sure he would always try to be a good kid. But I couldn't trust my judgment absolutely. There were a lot of innocents around him. He'd grown up a lot, and he still had a lot of growing up to do.

He'd grown fast. The last time I'd seen him, he'd hardly been as tall as my stomach. Now, side-by-side, he would have come up a little below my shoulder.

He was at the end of the line of kids. He stopped. Hesitated. Seemed uncertain for a moment.

Looked directly up at me.

I didn't step back, or try to hide myself. Just looked back.

Then he turned deliberately away from me, and kept walking. Nice and calm. And plainly dismissive.

The others on the rooftop stayed silent. I hadn't told all of them the full story about Lazarus, or even about where I'd come from. Only Inez and Rachel. Even they only knew bits and pieces.

Rachel set a hand on my shoulder. "Have you seen enough, dear?"

I remembered every second in that break room, with Lazarus and Beatrice, as freshly as if it had happened just an hour ago. On the night I killed Dallas Bader Pearson, nothing had changed for me. Yet now, looking down at Lazarus, my story felt like it had a different ending.

"Yeah," I said. Plenty of other days, I'd been on a rooftop just like this one, seen the same thing. On any of those other times, I'm not sure I could have said that. I certainly couldn't have meant it. "For now."

I turned around. Faced my people.

"Let's go make our day."

ACKNOWLEDGMENTS

This book would not have gotten past the conceptual stage, let alone seen the light of bookstore shelves, without the trust, care, and hard work of the Aconyte Books team. In particular: Lottie Llewelyn-Wells, the brilliant editor of this novel and many of Aconyte's other Marvel novels; Marc Gascoigne, who I've been lucky enough to work with before and to whose faith in me I owe this opportunity; Nick Tyler, whose hard work is foundational to everything; and Anjuli Smith, Aconyte's virtuoso marketing and publicity coordinator. They and everyone else at Aconyte have done outstanding work in the face of an ongoing pandemic, and any flaws remaining are mine, not theirs.

Of course, Domino could not exist without the craft and skill of her creators and the many people who have written for and drawn her over the years, who are too numerous to list in full here. But special mention goes to Gail Simone, whose vision of the character and her team in Domino's 2018 comic series (and the 2019 follow-up, *Hotshots*) formed the foundation of how she appeared in *Strays*. Domino's backstory was further fleshed out in Joe Pruett's 2003 Domino miniseries. Though those series are technically not in the same continuity as the Aconyte novel-verse, this Domino would not be the same without them, and I paid them as much homage as I was able.

My fabulous partner, Dr Teresa Milbrodt, provided invaluable feedback (and you should buy her books, too!)

ABOUT THE AUTHOR

TRISTAN PALMGREN is the author of the critically acclaimed genre-warping blend of historical fiction and space opera novel *Quietus*, and its sequel *Terminus*. They live with their partner in Columbia, Missouri.

tristanpalmgren.com
twitter.com/tristanpalmgren

MARVEL

ASTOUNDING TALES OF MARVEL'S ICONIC SUPER HEROES IN EXCITING NEW PROSE NOVELS

LEGENDS OF ASGARD
THE HEAD OF MIMIR
by Richard Lee Byers

The young Heimdall must undertake a mighty quest to save Odin – and all of Asgard – in the first heroic fantasy novel set in Marvel's incredible Legends of Asgard.

ACONYTEBOOKS.COM

MARVEL

Xavier's Institute
LIBERTY & JUSTICE FOR ALL by Carrie Harris

Two exceptional students face their ultimate test when they answer a call for help, in the first thrilling Xavier's Institute novel, focused on the daring exploits of Marvel's mutant heroes.

Marvel Untold
THE HARROWING OF DOOM by David Annandale

Our thrilling new line bringing new tales of Marvel's Super Heroes and villains begins with the infamous Doctor Doom risking all to steal his heart's desire from the very depths of Hell.

Legends of Asgard
THE SWORD OF SURTUR by C L Werner

The God of War must explore a terrifying realm of eternal fire to reclaim his glory, in this epic fantasy novel of one of Odin's greatest heroes.

@ACONYTEBOOKS

CALLING ALL FANS OF WORLD-EXPANDING FICTION!

For exclusive insights and all the news

join our free mailing list at

ACONYTEBOOKS.COM/NEWSLETTER

Be the first to know *everything*.

Follow on Twitter, Facebook and Instagram

@ACONYTEBOOKS